whiskey BURNED

JESSALYN JAMESON

ALSO BY JESSALYN JAMESON

The Flawed Heroes Series:
Chlorine & Chaos

The Completely Rocked Series:
Atlas
Cade

From The Girl Power Collection:
Some Like It Hops

Anthologies:
The Storybook Pub – A Contemporary Romance Collection

Cover design by Cover Lovin' Designs, updated 2020
Edited by Tamara Mataya

ISBN-13: 978-1535506885
ISBN-10: 1535506881

WHISKEY BURNED

For my favorite leading man:
I love life with you.

Updated 2020 Foreword from the Author:

Please be advised that although I do *always* promise my readers happily ever after, sometimes it takes the characters a while to reach that point. Frankly, this series is chaotic.

The *characters* are chaotic.

The *romance* is chaotic.

Each time they *break-up, make-up, wash, rinse, repeat*, it's—you guessed it—chaotic.

If you choose to continue reading about Tamryn and Jake, then fill your glass and hold on tight. It's going to be a bumpy ride.

XO,
Jessalyn

WHISKEY BURNED

Chapter One

Stepping out of the cool, dark bar and into the brightness of mid-afternoon, Jake's shirt clung to his torso almost instantly. Wiping the sweat from his brow, he shook his hair out of his eyes, squinting into the sun to admire the sign his old man hung above the bar thirty-some-odd years ago. The paint had chipped in too many places to count, and the brass "B" hung upside down, swinging back and forth with the breeze. Jake wasn't too proud to admit the thing was tattered.

But, neon? He eyed the new sign, wary of taking the final step and hanging the "upgrade".

Wary of moving forward without his old man.

A cloud passed over the sun, as though Mr. Johnson looked down from above. Jake lifted his gaze to the sky with a sigh. "Sorry, Pop, but I've been told we need to change with the times." He spat at the dirt, swiping his rolled-up shirt sleeve across his mouth. Lifting the hefty sign, he stepped up onto the ladder. "And if I break my neck doing this, I'll know it's you, ya ornery old coot."

Silence answered him as usual, but he knew his father watched from above, a smile on his weathered face and a shot of whiskey in his hand. Always house whiskey, never the good stuff.

"Jake? Are you out here?" TB's voice carried to him up on the roof.

"Up here, kiddo."

"I wish you'd stop calling me that."

She'd mumbled under her breath, but Jake heard the words. He always heard them, which was mostly why he still called her kiddo. He'd taken over as the annoying older brother when—

"Randy's drunk again."

Jake looked down to meet her blue eyes, taking a few long seconds to soak in the sense of calm they brought him. "Tell me something I don't know, TB."

"Something you don't know?" She crossed her arms and glared up at him. "Well, for starters, my name is *Tamryn*."

Jake raised an eyebrow. "Your name is TB, kiddo."

"My name is not *tuberculosis*. And I'm not your kiddo, old man."

"Your name is TB, Tiny Baker. There's really no sense in fighting it." Jake smirked; messing with her was his favorite part of the day.

"Tamryn."

"TB."

"Tamryn," she growled, eyes narrowing further.

"TB." He twirled the hammer in his hands as he stared down at her.

"Tamryn."

"Tamryn." Jake grinned.

"TB." She slammed her mouth shut.

Jake laughed. "Gotcha."

"Damn it all."

"Aw, don't be sore, TB."

She brought her hands to her hips, feigning annoyance. "You're an ass. Your friend is an ass. I'm surrounded by asses."

"It's a good thing we're cute asses, then, ain't it?"

She cocked a brow. "That's debatable."

Jake winked. "What? I didn't hear you. Can you speak up?"

TB dropped her hands to her sides, fists clenched. "I *said*, that's debatable!"

He motioned toward her head. "I think your ponytail might be a bit snug today. You're wound so tight."

Her lip twitched.

Jake held her gaze, waiting for her to crack a smile. When she didn't, he shrugged. "I'll handle Randy. Gimme five."

"Fine." TB stomped back inside, but Jake knew she wore that trademark Baker smile on her face, the one that shined like a hundred-watt bulb and never ceased to remind him of the best friend he'd lost to a war he didn't believe in.

"She's a real pain in the ass sometimes, Colby."

Jake finished hanging the new sign, God-awful as it was, careful to cradle the old version in his arms as he stepped down the ladder. He knew exactly where he'd hang it inside in homage to his old man, right above Pop's favorite table, broken "B" and all.

Crossing the covered wooden porch, he stepped into the dark cocoon of The Bar, Jacob Johnson *senior*'s tribute to a bygone era of cowboys and gunslingers, of saloons, and the wild, Wild West. Inhaling a lungful of old leather and cigar smoke, the only scent he'd ever call home, Jake strolled over to the half-moon corner booth, stepped onto the worn wooden bench and positioned the weathered old sign beside Colby's Purple Heart and dog tags. His friend's boots rested on a shelf immediately to the right, still caked in the reddish dirt from war-torn Afghanistan.

Jake couldn't even distinguish the musty scent of them anymore; the boots had blended in with the familiar odors of the bar, just another antique among many. Jake sighed. How he'd lost the two most important men in his life in as many years, he didn't know. How he'd survived the crushing blows of those deaths was an even bigger mystery.

Jake retrieved a worn-out purple bra strewn across Colby's boots, then whipped it up onto the exposed wooden beams with the other forsaken undergarments that dotted the ceiling.

Satisfied with this latest addition to his makeshift memorial, Jake inhaled a deep breath, patted the sign, brushed his fingertips over the dog tags, then turned to find Reed and TB watching him. He immediately met TB's gaze, searching her eyes for any signs of sorrow.

"Stop worrying about me, Jake. The old sign looks nice there. Your dad and Colby would love it." TB smiled, held his gaze for a long few seconds, then pointed. "That, however, does not look nice."

Jake followed the direction she pointed, his gaze landing on Randy passed out in a booth near the bar.

"I've got him." Reed stepped away from TB toward Randy. "He can sleep it off on my couch before the evening crowd."

"He's staying at your place again?" TB asked.

Reed laughed. "What do you think?"

Jake jumped down from the booth. "I'll help you load him up in the truck, but I'll drive him over to your place. Someone has to tend my bar." He made his way across the bar, pausing to pat TB's tush. "Do I pay you to stand around, kiddo?"

13

She scoffed. "Oh, do you *pay* me?"

Jake winked, then tugged on her blonde ponytail. "College fund." He turned and began to step away.

"What if I don't want to go to college?"

Jake tilted his head, frowning, then spun back to face her. "This isn't up for discussion. As long as you work for me and live in my home, you'll keep your tips and I'll keep my promise. I'm helping you save for school, TB, regardless of how long it takes us. End of story."

TB's shoulders fell. "You sound like a parent. I wish you'd stop treating me like a child."

"There's nothing childish about planning for a future." He crossed his arms; they'd been through this a million times in the nearly two years since Colby died, and the outcome was always the same. Wasn't she tired of talking about it?

Tamryn's eyes narrowed as she brought her gaze back to his. "You forgot to tell me I'll thank you for this someday."

"You're right." He grinned. "You'll thank me someday." He tipped his head to her and strode off to help Reed retrieve Randy from the booth.

"The college shit again?" Reed whispered as Jake approached.

"Every week." Jake shook his head, sliding his arms under Randy's.

"You think maybe you should ask her what she wants?"

Jake's brow furrowed. This had been their agreement all along, the one thing Colby asked of the two of them in his last letter. Jake would be damned if he didn't honor his best friend's final request. Girls never made sense, and Colby's kid sister was no exception.

Tamryn sighed as soon as Jake's truck engine rumbled to life, rolling her shoulders and bending her neck back and forth to try to release some tension. Working for Jake was brutal.

"Stressed out, Tamryn?"

Smiling at Reed as he reentered the bar, she crossed the dance floor and slid up onto a bar stool. "Something like that."

"You know he's only looking out for your best interests, right?"

Tamryn sighed. "Yeah. Right."

"He's hard on you for Colby."

Tamryn nodded.

"And you know he's an idiot not to realize how you feel about him."

She looked up at him, cheeks warming as she met his gaze.

"Colby should have put *that* in his letter."

"What?" she asked.

"Something like, *'My sister is the best thing that ever happened to you, dipshit'*." He smiled, hazel eyes twinkling.

Tamryn couldn't fight the grin that pulled at her lips. "Thank you, Reed."

He held her gaze, running his hand through his short, dirty-blond hair. "I know what you need." He disappeared through the double doors, returning a few minutes later with an unopened bulk bottle of cherries. He twisted the lid off, removed the seal, and slid the massive jar in front of her.

She peered down at the bright red maraschinos, eyes wide. Her mouth watered, but she frowned, pushing the air out of her lips in a raspberry. "No wonder he thinks I'm such a child."

Reed snorted. "Having an obsession with formaldehyde doesn't make you a child, Tamryn."

She reached in and grabbed a long stem, then popped the fruity goodness into her mouth. "Mmm." She focused on the rows of liquor that lined the wall behind Reed. "Which bottle is up next?"

Reed shook his head, reaching for the top shelf. "Explain to me again why you're determined to like this stuff?"

Tamryn watched as he poured the amber liquid into a shot glass, then pushed it toward her. Reed knew perfectly well why she'd been working her way through sampling every bottle of whiskey they stocked. She brought the glass to her nose and inhaled, the pungent scent forcing her to grimace.

Reed shook his head, then filled another shot glass with more cherries and set it in front of her. "Your chaser."

Tamryn smiled and gave a curt nod, then raised her shot glass. "Cheers to…" She paused. "I don't know what."

"To the new sign," Reed offered.

"To the new sign." Tamryn looked over her shoulder at the old sign hanging on the wall beside Colby's boots. *Cheers, Col.* "Bottoms up." She tipped her head back and fought through the shot of whiskey, shuddering as the golden liquid slid down her throat like fire. She blew out a breath of hot air, then looked at Reed.

"Are you a whiskey girl now?"

"Not yet."

Reed chuckled as he opened a beer. "Let's stick to what we know."

"Sounds like a plan." Tamryn took a long swig of ice cold beer, calming the burn in her throat. "Until tomorrow, of course."

Chapter Two

The thin stack of money atop her tray didn't bode well for tonight's take-home, which only fueled Tamryn's anger toward her situation, stoking the flame of her anger toward her brother, forcing her to think of him and miss him that much more.

Which, logical or not, made her pissed off at Jake.

Anger was easier.

The bar doors flew open and Jake strolled inside. *Speak of the devil.* His t-shirt was tucked into the back of his track pants, exposing his bare chest, shiny with perspiration.

Yeah, anger was easy. It was this other stuff that drove Tamryn crazy.

The way he strolled into his bar with so much confidence she could almost taste it in the air. The way his pants hung so low on his hips she wondered how they even held on as he approached.

She clenched her jaw, inhaling deeply though her nose. Looking up at the ceiling, she imagined beyond the building to the sky where she believed her brother watched out for her from above...probably laughing. Colby had always known of her feelings for his best friend—the source of relentless teasing, of course—and she figured this was his way of torturing her for the rest of her life the way a good brother is supposed to. "Couldn't you have picked someone ugly to babysit me?" she whispered.

"Breathe, Baker. You're about to start sweatin' like a whore in church."

"Reed!" Her cheeks flushed as she met Reed's knowing gaze.

He winked as he passed her on his way to the stage.

Tamryn shook her head and took a breath, then focused on Jake, swallowing hard as he stepped toward her, his abs taut and glistening with tiny beads of sweat. Like every other night, his post-run ritual involved stopping in the bar for a beer before he found his way to his house at the back of the building for a shower. Tamryn didn't know if he did this to torture her specifically, and she doubted that was the case, but...purposeful or not, this was the part of each day Tamryn most loved and loathed.

Jake stopped just a foot away from her, much too close, and his scent filled her nose. Manly, rugged, natural. Like...earth, freshly tilled, or—

Damn it all to hell, she'd forgotten to breathe through her mouth. Warmth pooled deep in her belly, her body longing for him as fervently as her heart.

"How's the crowd tonight, kiddo?"

Tamryn licked her lips, then swallowed, opening her mouth just enough to breathe, but not so much that she looked like a total knob. "Fine." She cleared her throat. "I mean, they're not tipping, but—"

Jake leaned down, bending slightly to bring his bright blue eyes level with hers. "Well, that won't do, will it?" He smiled, exposing the dimple in his right cheek. "I hear your boss keeps all of your paychecks."

She scoffed, then forgot herself again and inhaled through her nose, his intoxicating scent curling up into her senses and spreading warmth deep down into her belly. Her mouth watered, and her gaze fell to his lips. If she could just kiss him once—*twice?*—maybe she could shake the desire from her system. Maybe the reality wouldn't measure up to the fantasy and she could move on.

Jake's lip twitched, and Tamryn quickly brought her gaze back to meet his, heart thumping.

He tilted his head, searching her eyes.

Crap! What love-struck expression had fallen over her features this time? Tamryn quickly straightened, then turned on her heels. "Put some clothes on, old man. Nobody wants to see that."

Jake laughed behind her, the sound followed by a loud thump as he jumped onto the small stage. "Hey, hey, everyone! Thanks for stopping by tonight...especially you, Larry. I know how you cheat on us sometimes and sneak over to Bill's place instead."

The few patrons chuckled as Jake called Larry out, and Tamryn made her way to the well. "Two Bud drafts, please, Gen."

Gennie smiled dreamily, her eyes glazing over. "That man sure does wear shirtless well, don't he?"

Tamryn clenched her jaw as she glared at the night bartender who was much too distracted to notice, then looked down at her tabs, trying to focus on unclenching her jaw and not on the redhead who shared Jake's bed far more often than Tamryn cared to admit. "Yeah, I guess so. Those Buds?"

"Sure thing, hon."

And Gen had never been anything but nice to Tamryn, so hating her felt...wrong. Especially since Gen had no idea Tamryn was in love with Jake.

It was her own damn fault for hiding it.

"Have I got a treat for you tonight, folks!" Jake's loud voice boomed through the bar.

Tamryn smiled, knowing what came next. She turned to the stage, meeting Jake's gaze, then leaned back, her elbows resting on the old wooden bar. She'd wait for the invitation.

"What are you waiting for, kiddo?" He extended his hand, and waved her over. "Git yer little ass up here!"

"Knock'em dead, hon," Gennie called.

Tamryn strolled to the stage, her shoulders straight and her chin up. Singing with Jake every Friday night was the only time she felt his equal, the only time she could imagine he actually saw her.

On stage beside him was her favorite place to be.

Reed grabbed the guitar and joined them on stage, his agile fingers strumming the opening chords to Jake's favorite Johnny Lee song.

Settling in beside Jake, allowing herself this one moment to bask in him. She took a deep breath through her nose, inhaling her favorite scent in the world, then winked at him. "Put your shirt on, Hefner."

He leaned away from the mic, covering it with his hand, then whispered, "Am I too distracting, kiddo?"

Tamryn snorted and rolled her eyes. "Please."

If he only knew.

Chapter Three

The evening ended on a high note. No fights had broken out, no drunk chicks fawned all over Jake, and some road-trippers staying at the shack of a motel down the road stopped in and tipped Tamryn a twenty on a ten dollar tab. They'd also purchased every last one of the blackberry lemon verbena muffins she'd made this morning, which pleased her to no end. She fingered through her tips, counting the stack of bills—wait, never mind. That twenty only rounded out the shift with a whopping thirty-six dollars in her pocket.

"How'd you do tonight?" Jake slid into the booth across from her, his back against the wall and his long legs hanging out over the edge. He'd changed into his characteristic jeans, t-shirt and boots, and smelled of freshly cut grass—an aftershave he'd worn as long as she could remember. An odd choice, yes, but so perfectly him.

Tamryn was thankful she didn't live in a suburb somewhere green like Missouri or Colorado, so she didn't have to be reminded of him every waking second of every single day. She imagined walking outside on any given morning to find every neighbor mowing their grass.

No, Jake consumed her thoughts enough as it was, thank you very much.

He waved his hand in her face, wafting his scent over to her like an invitation. "Hello? Anyone home?"

Pouting for effect, she looked up through her eyelashes and met his gaze. "I only made thirty-six bucks."

"What? *Only*? Heck, TB, that's thirty-six more than you had this morning!" He slapped the table and laughed.

What an ass. She'd never convince him to give her the paychecks she made if he wouldn't take her seriously or empathize with her plight. She shook her head. If only she could leave this place, set out on her own and get a job somewhere else…

But that would mean leaving Jake, and, worst, leaving the memories of Colby. Jake and this place, this town, were all she had left of her brother, and his final request that she stay with Jake was one she'd honor, regardless of the frustration she often felt.

Jake cleared his throat and Tamryn looked up into his perfect face. Who was she kidding? The eye candy alone was reason enough to stay.

"Oh, hey, that reminds me. Can you make another batch of muffins tonight?"

Tamryn smiled; he'd asked the magic question. "Of course. What kind?" She lived for two things: baking, and Jake Johnson.

Jake considered the question, then grinned widely.

She shook her head on a laugh. "Seriously? Again?"

Forcing a pout, Jake batted his eyelashes. "You know they're my favorite."

"Fine." Tamryn shook her head.

"You're my favorite baker, Baker." He ruffled her hair, then jumped up and walked toward the bar, chuckling.

Speaking of baking…now was as good a time as any to tell him about her dreams for the empty storefront he owned next door. She inhaled a deep breath, gathered her courage, and spoke before she could stop herself. "Hey, Jake?"

He turned around. "Yup?" Holding her gaze, Jake waited.

With his bright gaze on her, bravado slipped away. She swallowed hard. "Uh—"

"Jake, honey, you ready?" Gennie called from the bar.

Jake tilted his head and held his hand up in the air. "One second. TB?"

Chest tightening, she struggled to find words. The familiar and absurd notion that she should beg him not to leave with Gennie, again, eclipsed all thoughts in her head, nearly making her forget why she wanted to talk to him in the first place. Any ounce of courage she had was suffocated beneath images of Jake and Gennie ripping each other's clothes off—

"TB?" he asked again, frowning.

Tamryn swallowed hard and cleared her throat. Gen and Jake, and whatever they did behind closed doors, had nothing to do with Tamryn's dreams for the old storefront beside The Bar. "Um, I want to offer singing lessons. Next door." Only half the truth, but at least she hadn't slipped up and begged him not to go with Gennie tonight. And, this way, if he agreed, she could use singing lessons as a front while she worked on converting the space. Doing so was risky, but maybe, just maybe, her initiative would pay off in the end.

Maybe, just maybe, if she brought her goals to fruition, he'd finally see a woman when he looked at her, not a little girl.

Jake strode back to the booth, his face crinkled. "In the empty shop?"

"Yeah. Can I? I mean, do you mind? I know it's not mine to use, and it's yours, and its empty, and maybe you have other plans for it. Are you going to rent it out? Maybe you're planning to sell it. I don't know." She waved her hand in the air and sucked in a breath. "But I could pay rent or something, maybe work extra shifts or help out on inventory days, or…" She closed her mouth to put an end to the word vomit.

Jake's lips twitched on a smile, then he looked up to the left, considering. Coming to a conclusion, he shrugged. "I don't see why not. Let me know when you want to start, and I'll clean the place up for you."

"No, it's okay. I can do it!" She sounded like a too-eager beaver, but she was excited and she finally had a chance to prove to him she could handle things on her own. Once he could see how easily she cleaned up next door, she'd let him in on her long term plans and pray he agreed to them. Excitement bloomed in her chest, tickling with warmth he could probably see in the red flush of her skin. "I just need the keys." She smiled sweetly, hoping he'd hand them over without question.

"Jake, baby, I'm starving. Let the girl count her tips in peace."

Jake glanced back at Gennie, who stood halfway inside the backdoor. She waved him over.

"One sec, Gen." He met Tamryn's gaze once more, narrowing his eyes. "I feel like you're up to something."

"What? No, of course not." *Rein it in, Baker.*

Jake tilted his head, clearly not buying it. "Suit yourself. But if you need me, don't try to be all stubborn about it." He pulled out a set of keys that would make any janitor green with envy and handed over a tarnished old key ring with one single key, holding it just out of reach. "Deal?"

"Deal." She wrapped her fist around the key, one step closer to her goal.

He released the key then quickly wrapped his hand around hers.

Tamryn's heart stopped as she tried to quickly memorize every detail of the way his hand, so warm, so firm, felt wrapped around hers. What would those hands feel like roaming her body?

"Don't be late tonight. You have muffins to bake me." He winked.

"Yes, *dad.*"

Jake chuckled, his blue eyes crinkling, then gave her hand a quick squeeze before letting go and strolling over to Gennie. Tamryn sighed as quietly as possible, bringing the hand with the key to her lap, the skin still vibrating where he'd touched her.

Gennie waved goodbye to Tamryn, then slid her arm around Jake's waist and a vise around Tamryn's aching heart.

Don't be late tonight, he'd said. If only he knew why she stayed away after work—especially the nights he took Gen with him. If only he knew that she never actually went anywhere, just hung around The Bar with Reed or Randy, or whoever would stay with her after hours so she wouldn't have to hear Gennie giggling down the hall. In Jake's room. In Jake's bed. In Jake's arms.

Where Tamryn so desperately wanted to be.

She considered the muffins she'd promised Jake, and though these late night, early morning hours were her favorite time of day for baking, when all the rest of the world was asleep and Tamryn could be alone with her thoughts, there was just no way she could thrive in the kitchen with Gennie and Jake doing it down the hall.

Once the two of them disappeared out the back of the building, Tamryn joined Reed at the bar.

He met her gaze, eyebrows raised in question. "Singing lessons, huh?"

Tamryn looked away. "Yep."

"Mhm." He nodded, then slid a cold wheat beer toward her, tossed an orange wedge in the air, spun around once and caught it, then placed the fruit on the top of her beer bottle.

Tamryn smirked. "That's not going to fit."

"That's what she said." Reed grinned, crossing his arms over his chest and waggling his eyebrows.

"Gross, Reed. Can I have a glass, please?"

"Look at you, all classy and shit."

"You know it."

"So," Reed began, dragging the word out. "Do you want to come back to my place, maybe use my kitchen?"

Tamryn smiled. "Thanks, but…I'm sure they'll be done in a little while. I'll bake then."

His smile wavered, and he glanced toward the back of the building, Jake's house just beyond.

She followed his gaze. "I wish you'd just tell Gennie how you feel."

Reed whipped his head back around to face her. "Well, isn't that the pot calling the kettle black?"

"That's not fair. It's different with Jake and me. He…" She tugged on her bottom lip, dropping her gaze to the floor. "He thinks I'm his little sister."

"Yeah, well, for all I know, Gennie thinks of me as a brother." He sighed, then tossed back a shot of tequila. "Or doesn't think of me at all."

Tamryn looked up as Reed refilled his shot glass. "I have an idea."

He slammed his shot back, then met her gaze. "Is it dangerous?"

"Sometimes."

Reed grinned. "This time?"

"Maybe."

"Could we get into trouble?"

"Maybe?"

He raised an eyebrow.

"Okay, yes."

"I'm in."

"Aren't you the least bit curious?"

Reed grinned. "Nah, I trust you."

"Famous last words." Tamryn jumped off the barstool and grabbed a set of keys from the wall. "Come on."

They slid through the back door quietly, then locked up The Bar. Tamryn grabbed Reed's hand and pulled him toward the old barn.

Reed gave a low whistle. "You wouldn't."

Tamryn looked back at him and winked, then set to work unlocking the padlock on the massive barn doors. "I would."

"He's going to kill us."

Tamryn brought her finger to her lips and shushed him. "He doesn't even have to know." She hauled the giant doors open and flicked on a light, while Reed stood there helpless, clearly questioning his blatant trust for Tamryn. She laughed, then nudged him forward. "I mean, if you're too chicken…"

Reed turned around, a wicked smile on his face. "Now, Tamryn Baker, when have you ever known me to be chicken?"

Tamryn giggled, then skipped toward the Panhead, delicately tracing the handlebars with her fingertips. "He loves this thing, you know."

"He's going to kill us."

"You mentioned that. What are you waiting for? Help me push it outside." Reed still hesitated, so Tamryn smiled. "Remember what he did to your Bertha? You owe him a little payback." It was a shitty thing to say, but she knew the memory would bring him to the dark side.

Reed shook his head, but his eyes danced. "Low blow, Baker." He stepped up to the bike anyway, shaking his head. "I must be out of my mind."

"The best people are."

A quarter of a mile out of earshot later, sweating from exertion and the rush of adrenaline, Tamryn slid onto Jake's baby behind Reed, straddling the bike and wrapping her arms around Reed's waist. She buzzed with anticipation, excitement making her smile a permanent fixture on her face. She'd ridden a motorcycle before, but never behind Jake and never on his most prized possession. Not for a lack of trying, though; she'd begged him a million times. And even though this wasn't the perfect scenario she'd been waiting for, because this was Reed between her legs and not Jake, she was no less excited about this secret ride.

"He'll murder me if anything happens to you." Reed's words were muffled by the bandana he'd wrapped over his face.

"Please. He'll murder you if anything happens to his *bike*." She squeezed Reed, then whooped. "Let's go!"

Reed shook his head, but Tamryn leaned forward, pressing herself against his back and tightening her grip on his waist. She rested her head against him and held on tight as the engine rumbled to life beneath her. A steady growl vibrated between her legs, and all at once her body lit up with adrenaline. Reed guided the bike forward, picking up speed as they cruised down the deserted highway.

Chapter Four

Gennie slid her hands up and over Jake's shoulders, her feather-soft touch growing more firm with each motion, massaging his abs, his chest, his shoulders, then repeating the motion. He pulled her earlobe into his mouth, eliciting a soft moan from her lips.

"Jake, honey, you're killing me."

Always in such a rush, this one. She didn't want foreplay, didn't need intimacy. She wanted Jake and she wanted him right now.

Normally, such haste wasn't an issue, but tonight felt somehow…less than.

Less than what, Jake didn't know, but something nagged at him, and he couldn't quite focus on the task at hand.

Something he'd forgotten to do, or something he needed…

A motorcycle roared to life in the distance, drawing Jake's mind to his baby in the barn. He hadn't taken her out for a spin in a while. Maybe he should finally take TB for that ride she always bugged him about. She'd have to braid her hair, seeing as how long it had grown over the past few years, and—

"Jake, honey, where are you tonight?" Gennie's hands travelled south, her fingers tugging roughly at his jeans as she nibbled at his jawline. She ran her mouth down his neck, biting and suckling—something that usually drove Jake wild.

Tonight, though...he struggled against the urge to wipe Gennie's saliva from his skin. What the hell was wrong with him?

Gennie worked his button fly quickly. First one button, then the next, and within seconds she'd freed him. She ran her palm over his shaft, then paused. "Something on your mind, darlin'?"

Jake groaned, grabbed her by the waist, and pushed her backward until her legs hit the bed. "Turn around."

Gennie's green eyes lit up like a sparkler and she licked her lips, stumbling in her rush to obey. She shimmied out of her jeans and leaned forward, stretching out across the bed, her ass arced straight up in the air. She practically vibrated with want.

Jake ran his hands up her pale back, pressing into her. She wiggled a bit, and he sprang to life, his dick throbbing against her supple cheeks.

"Jake, *please.*"

He leaned forward, kissing his way up her spine. Why would TB want to clean out the cobweb and dust-covered empty building by herself? Why didn't she want his help?

Jake couldn't decide if he was angry or hurt that she'd dismissed him so easily.

He kissed Gennie's freckled shoulder, gazing at the wall, his eyes blurring out of focus. Lord knew the last time that empty space had been cleaned. For all Jake knew, a family of rattlers could have moved in and set up shop. No, he couldn't let TB tackle such a hefty task alone. Colby wouldn't have done that.

Damn. That's what ate at him. Guilt. He'd been a poor excuse for a fill-in brother. He should go tell TB that he was going to help her clean out the space whether she liked it or not.

"Jake? Hello?" Gennie looked back over her shoulder.

Jake blinked, realizing he stood frozen against Gennie, his dick softening with every passing second. He quickly licked his lips and pressed against her center, squeezing his eyes shut to focus, and hardening when she stood on her tiptoes then lowered back down, sliding her slit against his shaft, coating him with wetness. She nestled her supple cheeks against his dick, then repeated the up and down motion until she was practically writhing against him, impatient for him to fill her.

Jake pressed the tip of his dick against Gennie's opening, teasing her until his dick grew hard enough, quickly slid on a condom, then thrust inside with one long stroke. Closing his eyes, he moaned when Gennie pushed back, clenching his cock from within. She reached back and grabbed the meat of her ass, massaging the pale flesh. Gennie Hayes was a woman who knew exactly how to fuck.

What would TB be like in bed?

Jake almost choked on the thought. *What the fuck?* He focused on the woman in front of him as he pounded harder, each thrust of his dick intended to push the thought of TB from his mind.

You do not think of TB while fucking Gennie.

Jake shook his head. *Ah hell.* You do not think of TB when fucking *anyone.*

Yet here he was, thrusting into Gennie with Colby's kid sister on his mind.

Legs still vibrating from the ride, Tamryn tiptoed back behind The Bar to the front of the home she shared with Jake. Careful not to miss the doorknob, she slid her key into the lock and slowly turned until the door unlocked and she could push it open. She looked back at the parking lot side of the bar and waved to Reed, then slipped inside the house.

Creeping down the hallway, she froze as Gennie's soft moans filled the silence.

Tamryn squeezed her eyes shut, then inhaled a deep breath and continued to her room, pushing the door into place quietly so as not to alert them of her presence. Moving around in the darkness of her room, she kicked her shoes off, then stripped down to her bra and panties.

Something—or someone—thumped against the wall.

Tamryn groaned. *Fucking Jake.*

Flipping off the couple in the next room, she slid in between the covers and closed her eyes, but the attempt was futile. No matter how hard she tried to go to sleep, her mind relentlessly bombarded her with images of what went on just one room over.

Gennie riding Jake.

Jake riding Gennie.

Whatever it was, she'd imagined it time and time again. A personal copy of *Jake Does Gennie* on constant loop in her brain.

Hell. On. Earth.

Tamryn sighed. The sweet oblivion of sleep would never come. She might as well bake. At least the kitchen was a bit further away from the master bedroom, since Gennie was clearly in it for all night this time.

Mumbling under her breath, Tamryn stood, grabbed her robe, then quietly opened her door. Poking her head into the darkened hallway, she listened for any signs of movement. Noises from down the hall had ceased; they were probably done for the night and off to sleep. Satisfied that she was alone, Tamryn slipped her apron from the hook near the doorway and tiptoed from her room, eyes downcast, focusing on the path before her.

A board creaked a few feet away. Tamryn froze, a breath caught in her throat and only one arm in her robe.

"Can't sleep?"

Tamryn smiled in the darkness; his voice was her favorite sound in the world. She lifted her head and gasped.

Jake filled the small hallway, naked from head to toe.

All oxygen disappeared from the tight space. The apron fell from her hands, and the robe slipped off her arm, falling to the floor.

Desire slammed into her body, pooling with a heat so intense she thought she'd fall over if she dared to move. She swallowed, blinking as her eyes focused in on the man standing before her.

Shadows didn't hide the hard edges of his muscles; they *framed* those lines, magnifying each dip and curve of his physique. His pecs were strongly defined, but his abs, good God, his abs. Two rigid lines formed an arrow south to part of this man she never thought she'd see. Her eyes widened and the breath she drew was ragged, this forbidden image of the man she loved searing itself into her brain.

Tamryn licked her lips, butterflies quivering in her belly, warmth pooling deep, her legs weakening further. She ached for him in more ways than one, and more fiercely than ever before. He was so close, too close, close enough to touch. Tamryn's fingers twitched.

If she just reached out her hand, she was close enough to—

Jake cleared his throat, and she raised her gaze, meeting his eyes. Eyebrows bunched together, as stunned by this moment as she was, he watched her with an intensity she'd never seen from him before. The hunger in his gaze was so palpable her knees weakened. She'd only ever dreamed of being on the receiving end of that gaze.

Tamryn's mouth dropped open on a soft gasp, then the heavy rise and fall of Jake's chest pulled her attention downward again. Focusing only briefly on the smooth skin of his chest, she dropped her gaze further and her pulse sped as his cock twitched, hardening before her very eyes.

She took a step forward before she could think better of it.

"TB," he whispered, the name so soft on his tongue she barely heard it.

Pulse racing—had she been too bold?—she flicked her gaze back to his face, but his focus was on her chest, his lips slightly parted. She looked down at her bra, the soft blush-colored lace leaving nothing to the imagination, her nipples taut against the sheer fabric.

She inhaled a breath, held it, and looked up at him once more.

Jake searched her gaze, then ran his tongue over his bottom lip, nearly dropping her to her knees with that languid motion.

All she had to do was take one more step forward. One tiny step. And then she could climb this man like a tree. She licked her lips, her pulse thundering in her ears.

What did she have to lose?

Just one step, that's all it would take. Tamryn dropped her gaze; he was fully erect now, his shaft thick, ready. Her fingers twitched as need filled her. Breath heavy and heart pounding, she lifted her hand—

A door creaked open down the hall and Tamryn flung her gaze back to Jake's eyes, dropping her hand to her side.

He shook his head, his brows furrowed.

"Jake, honey, did you get lost on your way to the kitchen?"

Tamryn raced back into her room, shutting the door behind her. Gennie.

Gennie. Gennie. Gennie.

What was Tamryn going to do, fuck him in the hallway when Gennie had just had her turn minutes before? She closed her eyes and slid down the door, releasing a stream of frustrated tears down her cheeks.

When Jake's door closed down the hall, Tamryn slammed her head back against the door with a soft *thud*, wishing the action would slam some sense into her lust-filled brain. "What the hell was that?"

She swiped at the tears, then stared at her empty bedroom, heat still pulsating through her veins, and the ache of need between her legs almost unbearable. How could she be so heartbroken and so damn horny all at once?

She needed to talk to her best friend. She grabbed her cell and started to dial Luce's number, then looked at the time. It was the butt crack of dawn, and no time to call a friend in the middle of exam week at Columbia. "Ugh," Tamryn groaned, pushing up off the floor. "I need a drink."

Jake was off limits. At least for the time being.

But were things about to change? She'd seen something in his eyes, felt it in the air between them. He'd gotten *hard*. If Gennie hadn't been there, Tamryn had been one second away from wrapping her fingers around—

"Dammit." She shook her head, frustration heating her chest as she tiptoed from the room. One step into the hallway and she froze, ice splashing over her like a fucking waterfall.

The unmistakable sound of wood hitting wall thundered out from Jake's room, his door still wide open. Every time he pounded into Gennie, the headboard crashed against the wall.

A whimper escaped Tamryn's lips, so she slammed her hand to her mouth. He'd been looking at her that way in the hall, hungry eyes and desire heating the space between them to near boiling, then wasted no time jumping back into Gennie. He hadn't been attracted to her— she'd just interrupted them.

What a fool she was!

Tamryn ducked to grab her robe from the hallway floor, then didn't slow down until she was safe inside The Bar, skidding to a stop just beyond the kitchen doors and letting out a roar of frustration.

Reed stood behind the bar, prepping the citrus fruit for tomorrow. He looked up in surprise, then his gaze fell to her torso, eyes wide when he finally met her gaze.

The muffled swish of the doors as they swung back and forth seemed magnified in the heavy silence.

He set the knife down, then crossed his arms over his chest. "You're practically naked."

Tamryn tugged her robe closed, tying the belt around her waist. Shaking her head, she shrugged. "I thought you left?"

He waved toward her clothes—or lack thereof. "Obviously."

"I'm sorry, I"—she struggled to push Jake's nakedness out of her mind, while also searching for words to explain what just happened, why she was here—"It's almost four in the morning."

Reed frowned. "Figured I'd prep then crash on your couch."

"I thought you left after our ride."

Reed nodded slowly. "So you've said. What's wrong?"

"I had to get out of there."

He frowned, then pushed the cutting board aside, reaching instead for a bottle of Patrón and a shot glass. "Feeling guilty about our little joyride?"

"What?" Tamryn shook her head. "Not at all." She glanced past the swinging doors to the hallway that led out back.

"Oh. That bad, huh?"

Her eyes widened. "*That* bad." Tamryn slid onto a barstool. "You know, yeah. It was that bad. Make me one of those. I don't think beer is enough to cleanse *this* night from my brain."

Reed raised his eyebrows, pausing mid-pour. "Don't you have some muffins to make tonight?"

She shrugged.

"And, wasn't it just you who noted what ungodly hour of the morning it is?'

Another shrug. "I bake better when I'm drunk?" She smiled.

"I'm supposed to accept that as a response?"

Tamryn laughed. "Well, you can either pour it for me or make me pour it myself, but either way, that tequila will be in my belly, and only one option doesn't make you look like an asshole."

Reed's eyebrows flew up his forehead. "Easy there, killer."

Tamryn motioned for him to hurry up and pour. "And let's be honest, drunk *is* when I come up with my best recipes."

Reed hooted as he finished the pour and passed the glass to Tamryn. "Like 'Whiskey Maple Surprise'?"

"Yeah, well, that one wasn't supposed to take off." Tamryn blushed. "I mean, I kind of made it as a joke."

He cocked an eyebrow. "You put whiskey and bacon in a muffin. Of course he loved it." Shaking his head, Reed poured himself a matching shot of tequila, then lifted it into the air. "Here's to loving those two"—he dipped his head toward Jake's house—"for whatever that's worth."

Tamryn snorted and raised her glass in salute. "Amen to that."

"Early mornin' shit tankin'?"

"Did you just invent a thing?"

Reed winked. "When it comes to drinking, Randy's not the only guy with experience."

Tamryn brought her glass to Reed's with a *clink*. "To shit tankin'."

Jake gripped Gennie's hips, slamming into her as if doing so would erase the way he'd just looked at Colby's little sister. With each thrust, he tried to memorize the tightness of Gennie's pussy, the bounce of her breasts, the way her mouth formed that perfect 'o', but all he could see was TB, burned into his brain, her pert nipples pressing against their lace prison, begging him to run his thumbs over them, then his teeth, then—

Ah, fuck.

He grunted as Gennie pushed her ass back harder against his wild thrusts, taking everything he could give, even as wildly as he fucked her.

With each cry of pleasure she made, he pounded harder into her, chased by the image of TB and all the things he wanted to do to her—almost *did* to her—right there in that dark hallway. Unable to escape his horrific thoughts, he sank deeper into Gennie.

He'd fuck away thoughts of fucking TB if it took all night and half of tomorrow. Dangerous, disrespectful thoughts about the girl he was supposed to be protecting, not lusting after. Gennie was good. Gennie was safe. Gennie was someone he could be with. No strings, no past or future.

Anger and confusion pulsed through him as his dick twitched with release, flooding Gennie as guilt gripped his chest, his heart.

How dare he look at TB that way?

He roared, clenching his eyes closed with one final thrust, but it was TB's face behind his eyelids, TB's body curving beneath his.

"I know, baby," Gennie panted, flush against the bed. "That was amazing. You're really something tonight."

Yeah, he was something.

A right fine piece of *shit*.

Chapter Five

Tamryn didn't remember when they'd moved their 'pity party for two' to the empty space attached to the bar, but here they were, Reed splayed out on an old plaid blanket they'd found, and Tamryn rambling a million miles a minute about her plan. She'd never told anyone her ideas, least of all Jake's best friend, but, apparently, tequila made this girl's filter come off.

Speaking of which.

She plopped down on her knees beside Reed and held out her empty glass. At some point, she'd begun using a pint as a shot glass. Reed filled it to about a third of the way, sloshing a bit over the side as he poured. No wonder she was trashed.

He put the bottle to his lips and took a long pull of the amber fire. No wonder *he* was trashed.

"We're going to pay for this tomorrow," Tamryn said, a hiccup breaking tomorrow into too many syllables.

"Today. And I have to open." Reed shrugged, raising the tequila bottle to clink it against her glass. "I like your plan." Reed scanned the interior. "I can picture it."

Tamryn sat down and stretched her legs out alongside Reed's, smiling widely and looking around the room. "You can, right? I mean,

I know *I* can, but you can too now, so I know it's a good plan. Because we both can see it, so it's a good plan." She took a sip of her tequila and grimaced as the liquid burned her throat. "It's a good plan, right? I mean, I think it's a good plan, but..." She gazed out into the open space, eyes glazing over. She smacked her lips together. "We need limes. This is supposed to get better as you drink it but that's not happening."

Tamryn tried to stand, but wobbled, and Reed reached out to steady her. Just as blitzed as she was, he pulled her down instead of helping her up, and she landed in a heap on top of him, tequila drenching both of their chests.

Eyes wide, Tamryn looked at the mess she made, then snorted, breaking into a fit of laughter and rolling off of Reed.

He sat up, looked down at his short-sleeved plaid shirt, then glared at Tamryn, lips twitching on a grin. "Look what you did, you little jerk!"

"Did you just quote *Home Alone*?" Tamryn pressed her lips together, fighting back the laughter.

Reed tossed his head back on a laugh as he unbuttoned his shirt and pulled it off, then ran his hands over his still-wet chest. "I smell like a bar."

Tamryn snorted. "Me too." She untied her belt, then unwrapped and discarded her robe to the floor. She froze, realizing her mistake. Looking back up at Reed, her cheeks flushed with heat.

All amusement had left Reed's face, those greenish-brown eyes seeing so much more than just her exposed body beneath too-thin lace, peering deeper into her soul than she'd like.

"You're beautiful."

She shook her head and looked away, reaching for her robe.

"Look at me." Reed reached over, placing his finger and thumb on her chin and lifting her face up.

Reluctantly, she looked up into his hazely eyes.

"He's a fool."

Tamryn smiled. "So is Gennie." She dropped her gaze, focusing away from the intensity in Reed's eyes to his pecs, and the way they stood out against his chest in the soft glow of the lantern's amber light. She tilted her head. Tormented by a desperate thirst for Jake that would never be quenched, an ache that remained even after she'd tried to obliterate it with alcohol, and fueled by far too much tequila, she reached up and ran her fingers over Reed's chest, then trailed them down the ridges of his abdomen.

Reed's skin trembled beneath her fingers and he sucked in a breath. He pushed up onto his knees, ready to leave, but didn't make that final step and rise to his feet.

Tamryn looked up, but his eyes were squeezed shut. "Look at me," she breathed, repeating his words back to him.

He opened his eyes and looked down at her. "We can't do this, Tamryn."

"Can't never did nothin'." She placed her other hand on his stomach, tentative, soft.

Reed grimaced, the muscles of his torso tightening from her touch.

She leaned forward and slid her lips against the skin just above his jeans.

His sharp inhale was audible.

"Why can they do it but we can't?" She regretted the words almost instantly, the way they made her sound so malicious. She didn't want to have sex with Reed to spite Jake. And Reed shouldn't have sex with her to spite Gennie. Both of them were blind, but that didn't make them bad people.

Still reeling from her encounter with Jake in the hallway, Tamryn's loins throbbed with lust so heavy it hurt. She ran her fingertips along the waist of Reed's jeans. Did she even really want to have sex with him? Was this just the tequila? The loneliness? The hunger she couldn't shake?

She pushed up onto her own knees, then sat back on her heels and looked at Reed, really looked at him, not as the guy she'd known her whole life, but as a man kneeling before her half-naked. His body was sun-kissed from all the hours spent working his daddy's field. His muscles were strong, defined. She slid her hands up around his back, pressing against his shoulders when they tensed beneath her touch. She pushed up further onto her knees, bringing her gaze more level with his, and studied his face. Strong jaw, straight, slightly-pointed nose, laugh lines around his eyes. A light dusting of freckles across his nose, and a week's worth of blond beard stubble. She fluttered her fingertips across his cheek.

Reed closed his eyes again, shutting her out. "We can't."

"We can." Tamryn's words made the decision for her while her brain still fought to catch up. She kissed his jaw, and he sucked in a breath. Leaning back to rest on her heels, she waited. *Your move.*

Reed didn't budge. "I don't have drunken one-night stands."

This was a half-lie. He didn't have drunken one-night stands *any longer*; you'd have to be living under a rock not to know he'd lost Gennie back in high school because of a drunken mistake.

Tamryn didn't voice the words, just shook her head. "Me neither."

He opened his eyes and met her gaze, then licked his lips. "Tamryn...I don't have feelings for you...not like this."

"Good. Me neither." She reached behind her and unhooked her bra, then let it slide to the floor.

Reed remained focused on her eyes, but his chest rose and fell with quicker succession.

She reached out and slid her fingers around his hand, studying his face for a response, but all that changed was the quickness of his breath. Slowly, she brought his hand to her chest.

"Tamryn," he whispered, gently shaking his head. "This is just the tequila."

"It is." She pressed his palm into her breast and massaged her hand over his until his fingers moved on their own. He cupped her, gently, delicately, holding on even after she let go. "It's just tequila, just a man and a woman about to have sex, no strings attached." The words, though slurred, made sense. What was wrong with a little 'friends with benefits' sex? *Seemed to work pretty well for Jake.* She cringed, then shook the thought away. No Jake.

He shook his head, then slid his arm around her waist and pulled her to him, crushing his mouth over hers. She opened up to him as he plunged his tongue inside, kissing her fervently, clearly as desperate as she was to feel, to love, to *be* loved. He slid his other hand into her hair and held her to his mouth, tasting her with a hunger she knew mimicked her own.

Their feelings for Jake and Gennie aside—no, *driven* by those feelings—Tamryn kissed Reed like he was the air she needed to breathe. Right now, she'd let him be just that.

He held her close, and she inched her knees closer, pressing against him, reveling in the feel of his erection against her. She'd had sex before, but it felt like ages ago; she'd been waiting for Jake so long. Hoping.

What a fool.

She pushed her hands against Reed's chest, pushing him back just an inch or two so she could unzip his jeans, careful as she slid the zipper over his erection. Reed didn't believe in underwear—anyone who knew him knew it—but this fact had never intrigued her quite the way it did now amid her alcohol induced lust.

Her eyes widened as his cock sprang free of his pants, and she swallowed hard.

She looked back up at Reed, who frowned.

"Are you sure you want to do this?" He searched her gaze.

Tamryn bit her lip, nodding, then resumed tugging at his jeans.

"Okay, then slow down." He placed his hand over hers, stopping her fingers. "If we're going to do this, we're going to do it right." He slid his hand down into her panties slowly, holding her gaze as he guided the lacy material aside and ran his fingertips softly over her wetness. "Are you sure about this? We can stop at any time." He slid one finger against her center, pressing into the opening, just enough to make her body scream with need.

Tamryn gasped, then opened her legs wider, one knee slipping past the edge of the blanket. She'd worry about splinters later. "I'm sure," she growled, pressing onto his hand.

Reed leaned forward, running his tongue over her bottom lip as he slid his finger all the way inside her. She moved against his hand, craning her neck to kiss him, and he slid another finger inside. He pulled back, watching her face as he worked his fingers.

A garbled sound from deep in her throat pushed past her lips as he pressed against her inner wall, practically lifting her higher with just his two fingers. She rose, wanting to follow his hand anywhere it guided. Reed smiled, then dropped his gaze to her mouth. Pushing harder with his hand in deliberate, firm motions, he watched her face, then gripped the back of her neck and held her firmly in place as his hand moved faster and deeper.

He slid a third finger inside, spreading his hand and stretching her further. Pleasure and pain radiated from their connection, but warmth soon replaced pain as her body coated his hand, readying itself for his cock, and as Reed massaged her, she writhed—

He withdrew his hand and Tamryn crashed back down to earth, mouth opening on a question that was answered before she even spoke the plea out loud.

"Stand."

On trembling legs, she obeyed, chest heaving on her near-orgasm.

Reed reached up, slid his hands up her thighs and in between the fabric and her hips, then slid his hands back down, pulling her panties with him as he went. Once she stepped out of them, he gripped her hips, stopping her from kneeling back down.

With a wicked glint in his eyes, he looked up at her, then rubbed his thumb over her folds, spreading the silky wetness. Slowly, he slid his fingers back inside, all three at once.

Tamryn's eyes slammed closed as pleasure and pain fought to fill her, and she tilted her head back, arching her hips into Reed's face when his mouth closed over her. She reached for his hair, grabbing a handful and rocking with the motion of his tongue on her clit and his fingers inside her.

When he paused again, she nearly crumpled as he withdrew his fingers, but he quickly pushed his pants to his knees, unwrapped a condom and covered his shaft in nearly one fell swoop, then reached for her. With his hands gripping her lower back, he eased her down, wrapping her legs around his waist.

With the tip of his cock pressing against her, Tamryn moaned as wetness pooled. Shivering with anticipation, she wiggled, her body aching for him to make the final move and slide inside. She wrapped her arms around his neck, then pushed down, gasping as he glided his way inside. She pressed further, forcing him to fill her without hesitation, without the tedious delay of caution. She whimpered, but gripped Reed tighter, hoping he wouldn't stop.

She was not a delicate flower. She was not a little girl.

Not tonight. *Especially* not tonight.

Tamryn held tight as Reed pushed all the way into her, pleasure and pain blending to a heady, intoxicating combination. She moaned, head thrown back as her body stretched around him.

Jake's face flashed across her mind, and she almost pushed the image aside, ashamed to picture one man while embracing another. But she wasn't a fool—Reed likely pictured Gennie in her place.

Mutually fucking to forget.

Clinging to Jake's face in her mind, and Reed's shoulders in reality, Tamryn pretended it was Jake's cock inside her, Jake making love to her. She imagined Jake's naked chest against hers and gripped tighter to Reed, her nipples rubbing against his warm chest, hard and hot, and just the right amount of friction.

"TB?"

In a drunken haze, she even imagined she heard Jake's voice, thought she heard him calling her name, but the waters of her mind were murky at best, tequila soaked and lust-drunk. Still, she clung to the sound, the image, the fantasy.

She clung to Reed and made him Jake, a loud moan escaping her lips as she bobbed up and down on his shaft, faster and faster, closer and closer to release—

"What the fuck!"

Reed jumped back, dropping Tamryn in his haste to get away from her, sliding across the room as Jake thundered inside, the door slamming against the wall as he tore through the doorway.

Tamryn curled into a ball, frantically wrapping the blanket around her exposed body. *Holy shit, holy shit, holy shit*...but he only had eyes for Reed. Tamryn scrambled backward until she hit the opposite wall, then pulled her knees up to her chest and tried to disappear. Of all the people to catch them—

"What the fuck!" he shouted again. "TB, Reed? Seriously? How could you fuck TB?" Jake stormed across the wooden floor, then reached down for Reed and pulled him up by his throat.

Reed stumbled, but if the adrenaline ripping through Tamryn's veins was anything like what Reed felt right now, his tequila-induced intoxication was ancient history. *Long* gone. He squared his shoulders and raised his hands in surrender, opening his mouth to—

The *crack* of Jake's fist across Reed's jaw echoed through the room. Tamryn shrieked, then stumbled to get up, dropping the blanket in her haste to rush to Reed's aid. They hadn't done anything wrong!

Jake cocked back to swing again, but Tamryn grabbed his arm and pulled it behind him, holding it tight to her body with all the strength she could muster.

Jake spun around, his face pulled into a sneer as he focused on Tamryn. She let go of his arm and backed up, shrinking beneath his angry gaze.

He opened his mouth to speak, but only panted, his head shaking slightly as he held her captive with his eyes.

Was he mad because he wanted her for himself? Or because she was still, and would forever be, Colby's kid sister? A little girl destined to remain that way.

She had to know.

"What?" she asked after a few torturously long seconds. "What can you possibly say?"

He opened and closed his mouth several times, his bare chest heaving, then his gaze fell to Tamryn's exposed breasts, then lower, and he bowed slightly in the middle as though he'd lost the air from his lungs. He brought his gaze back to hers, his brows drawn down over his eyes. "Is this why you wanted the key?"

Torn between covering up and apologizing—begging him to forgive her, explaining that this was a mistake, an accident—or standing tall, Tamryn chose the latter. Sticking out her chin, she straightened, allowing him an uninhibited view of her breasts, her body, the wetness still glistening on her thighs.

She met his gaze, her eyes hard. *Call me a child now.*

Jake shook his head, frowning.

Tamryn allowed herself a quick glance at his shirtless chest, his unbuttoned pants that rested just low enough that a dusting of brown hair peeked over the button fly. She lifted her gaze to messy, disheveled hair—like someone's hands had been in it just moments ago.

Tamryn closed her eyes, remembering the sound of him fucking Gennie, his headboard punctuating each thrust. They'd shared that heavy moment in the hallway, Jake's desire for Tamryn so obvious you could choke on it, then went right back to fucking Gennie. That's what drove her into Reed's arms.

And now he had the audacity to act like he gave two shits about who Tamryn fucked?

Anger quickly replaced the pain, her muscles tightening. She opened her eyes and met his gaze.

He rocked back slightly.

"What is it, Jake? Only the boss can fuck coworkers?"

He blinked once, twice, clearly stunned by her words, but then he smiled, nodding, turning on that Johnson charm he'd mastered so long ago, careful—as always—not to give away any indication of what he really felt. "Touché, little Baker." He turned his back on Tamryn and pointed at Reed. "We're not finished, you and me."

Reed massaged his jaw and nodded.

Jake stomped out of the room, dust plumes following in his wake. "Put some fucking clothes on! Both of you!"

Chapter Six

Jake paced a trench in the dance floor, but he couldn't sit still with all the emotion flowing through him. He hadn't slept. Hadn't eaten.

His hands itched for something to hit.

He'd already punched Reed last night and at least two walls this morning, but despite his bloodied and bruised hand, he still had way too much anger burning through his veins. Maybe he'd install a punching bag next door, make that space a gym, rather than a spot for singing lessons and fucking.

The front door swung open, and Jake squinted against the rush of sunlight. "We're closed!"

Reed stepped inside and shut the door behind him. "I work here."

Jake's fists curled in on themselves, and he crossed his arms to keep from swinging at Reed. "Get the fuck out, man."

"Are you pissed off because she's Colby's sister, or *your* TB?"

Jake's body went rigid. "The fuck is that supposed to mean?" He spun and headed toward the cooler.

Reed scoffed. "Oh, I think you know exactly what that means, except you're too damn chicken shit to admit it."

Jake whipped around and took three long strides forward to corner Reed. "Admit *what*, exactly?"

Reed straightened his shoulders and leaned toward Jake, eyes narrowed. "That you have feelings for that girl in there." He pointed toward the wall between the empty space and The Bar.

Jake rocked on his heels. "What?" He ran a hand through his hair. "That's Colby's kid sister."

Reed shook his head with a mocking laugh, bringing a pack of frozen peas back up to his chin. He pushed past Jake, walking toward the bar, then paused and swiveled his head to pin Jake with a hard stare.

Jake straightened, expecting another fight.

"Colby's dead, Johnson." He pointed to the empty half of the building again. "But she's not. And she's not *your* kid sister. You'd do well to remember that."

What did that even mean? Of course he knew TB wasn't dead. Reed was off his rocker. Jake scoffed, but remained silent—maybe he'd clocked Reed too hard. They both needed to cool off. After the dirty thoughts he'd had about TB last night, and then catching her with Reed, Jake didn't know which end was up anymore. But he didn't have feelings for her—that much he was certain of. He was just a horny piece of shit as usual and saw a hot piece of ass.

He slammed his hand to his forehead. *A hot piece of ass?* Colby should smite Jake from heaven right where he stood.

He shook his head, then stomped outside for some fresh air.

Shoving a wad of tobacco into his mouth, he paced the wooden porch, kicking up dust and mumbling to himself. How could Reed take advantage of TB like that? She was just a kid! He expected so much more from Reed.

Drunken chicks and random sex was Jake's thing.

The image of Reed balls deep inside her wouldn't cease, burned into the back of his eyes so that every time he blinked, he saw them fucking all over again. He'd stood there too long last night, too stunned by what he saw, and by the time his brain caught up to his eyes, he'd seen far too much to forget. He rubbed at his eyes, wishing he could scrub her naked body from his mind.

But then, hadn't that been why he'd gone in search of her in the first place? Her over-exposed body, the intoxicating feeling between them, the desire buzzing on the air...the way all oxygen seemed to leave the hallway in a whoosh when her gaze met his.

It was her innocence, her youth that always endeared her to him, made him long to be near her, to protect her. It was his promise to Colby that gave him the opportunity to do just that. But the way she stood there in her panties, so bold... the way she openly observed him, confident, free, daring him to touch her.

He closed his eyes, imagining TB's heavy gaze on him once more. His dick twitched at the vision, hungry for her.

"Fuck!" Jake slammed his fist into a wooden post, then shook his hand as pain seared up his arm into his shoulder. He couldn't think about TB like that. Colby had been his best friend since birth. He stomped around the building toward the house, then tore inside.

TB stilled in the entryway, having just walked from the kitchen.

Jake froze as the front door slid closed behind him.

Her wavy blonde hair cascaded down around her shoulders, the usual childlike ponytail gone. She quickly met his gaze, then looked away, eyes downcast.

He waited with bated breath for her to look up at him again.

"Are you okay?" she asked, still avoiding his gaze.

Jake lifted his hands up into the air, scoffing, then let his arms fall to his sides. Was *he* okay? Was she serious? He shook his head, but had no words. He was far from okay, but what could he tell her? That the man who was supposed to protect her and keep her safe from guys like him was suddenly lusting after her?

TB met his gaze, frowning. "I'm sorry, I…"

She's sorry? He closed the distance between them and peered down into frightened blue eyes. "For what? What are *you* sorry for? He should be sorry, TB, he took advantage of you—"

"What did you say?" TB stood taller, squaring her shoulders. "I'm not a fucking helpless infant, Jake, maybe I took advantage of him; did you ever think of that?" She poked his chest, hard, the pain searing straight to his heart.

He opened his mouth to argue, but then his brain conjured images of TB coming on to Reed.

TB, the seductress.

Jake shook his head. No. *Hell no.* "There's no way—"

Her eyes widened and her mouth dropped open. "Don't, Jake." She stared at the ground between them, head shaking slightly.

"Don't what, TB?"

Her pink lips curled back. "You know what, Jake? Fuck you. I'm *not* sorry. Fuck. *You.*"

"Don't you talk to me like that," he snarled. He clenched his aching right hand into a fist, ready to punch another wall as soon as he had the chance.

TB squared her shoulders and took a step toward him. Her robe fell loosely above the belted sash, exposing the soft crowns of her pale breasts. "Don't pitch a fit, Jake." She took another step toward him. "I can say whatever I want."

He took a step back.

She advanced on him once more. "And, not that it's any of your business, but I can fuck whoever I want. Maybe I'll pick someone up tonight and bring him home. Get *real* loud with it."

He sucked in a breath.

She narrowed her eyes and stepped so close she had to crane her neck to look up at him. "I'm not yours to control."

Jake grimaced. "I…I don't want to control you."

TB's face relaxed slightly, the anger dissipating, but she didn't say anything for a long, uncomfortable few seconds.

"Why Reed?" he asked, voicing his thoughts before he could stop himself.

"Why *not* Reed?" She searched his gaze, looking for something he didn't know. When she apparently didn't find it, she smirked. "Yeah, I figured. You don't really care who or what I do, you just didn't have any damn control over it and that makes you madder than a wet panther."

Jake frowned. Was she right? Was that all he was pissed about? "What would Colby think?"

She laughed, a bitter, scornful sound that sent ice down Jake's spine. "Colby is dead, Jake. He's *dead*."

Jake shook his head, each word a knife through his heart. "I promised him I'd take care of you."

She sneered. "I can take care of myself."

"Oh yeah? Is that"—he pointed to the center of the empty room— "is that how you *take care* of yourself? Fucking random guys in my bar? Colby would be so proud."

Too caught off by her soft gasp and the sudden shimmer in her eyes, Jake missed the movement of her hand as she cocked it back, registering the motion a second too late. The slap sent his head reeling, the sharp sound echoing through the room.

"Fuck. You. Jake Johnson."

She ran out the door, and his heart went right along with her, the echo of her sobs cutting far deeper than the sting of her palm.

"What did you do to her?" Reed roared, crossing the bar to meet Jake as he entered. "I heard her crying all the way in the kitchen!"

Jake fisted his right hand; a wooden post just wouldn't cut it this time.

Reed caught the motion and his gaze fell quickly to Jake's hand, then he stepped forward and met Jake's gaze with matched anger. "I allowed you one punch last night, Johnson. That won't happen twice."

Jake clenched his jaw, staring hard into his friend's eyes for a long moment, then sighed. "How could you fuck *her*, Reed? She's TB."

Reed lifted his hands, his shoulders still tense, ready for a fight. "It wasn't planned. We were drunk."

"That makes it worse. You don't even care for her."

Reed smirked. "That's just it, Jake. She doesn't care for me either."

Jake shook his head. "No. That's not the way she is. TB doesn't just fuck for fun. She must have a thing for you."

Reed stepped away, head tilted, then returned to the bar. "What do you know about her sex life, Jake? You've never even noticed that Tamryn's not fourteen anymore."

Jake opened his mouth, then slammed it shut. That wasn't true, he knew she wasn't fourteen. She was—

"She's not, you know."

"Not what?" Jake snapped.

"Fourteen." Reed shrugged as he unloaded a freshly cleaned set of glasses, steam filling the air from the open industrial dishwasher— Jake's latest upgrade to The Bar. "Why can't you see that?"

"I know she's not fourteen. She's twenty-one."

Reed cocked an eyebrow. "She's twenty-two and some change."

Twenty-two? Jake slumped onto a barstool and met his friend's gaze. "She's just a kid."

"Who are you trying to convince?" Reed popped open a Budweiser and handed it to Jake.

He frowned at the beer.

"You haven't slept yet, and you don't look like you're going to until you're good and drunk."

No arguing that. Jake chugged the entire bottle in one long pull, then met Reed's gaze. "She's Colby's little sister, man."

Reed sighed. "I know, bro. And if he were here, I'd let him kick my ass into next Tuesday. But he's not. And she's a grown woman."

Jake glowered. "Don't do it again."

"For you or for Colby?" Reed's eyebrow shot up.

Jake ran his tongue over his teeth, squinting at his friend. "Just don't do it again."

Reed lifted his hands in the air. "Hadn't planned on it, buddy."

Good. Jake slammed the bottle down and stormed out the back.

Chapter Seven

Tamryn's stomach hadn't stopped aching, and she'd chewed her poor cuticles to bleeding, but she stepped into The Bar at five o'clock on the dot for her shift. Jake would never look at her the same way again and, frankly, she couldn't decide if that was bad or good, and this in between feeling sucked. She'd tried to reach Luce all day, but without any luck, which meant Tamryn was on her own. Her heart ached almost as much as her stomach, and for heaven's sake, if that wasn't enough, she felt like she'd delivered a baby last night.

Eyes burning from lack of sleep and too many tears shed, she went through the motions, taking orders, delivering drinks, chatting up customers who were in the mood for connection, all the while avoiding Reed's watchful gaze—which took every ounce of energy she had.

When the bar quieted down during the eight o'clock lull, when folks either left for dinner or hadn't yet made it to the bar after dinner, and Jake still hadn't shown up, Tamryn slipped outside and walked over to the building next door. She still had her key, so until Jake revoked her privilege, she wanted one last look at the space she'd had and lost long before she could even start bringing her dreams to fruition.

As she approached the empty storefront, a commotion sounded from inside. She paused at the slightly open door, tilted her head and listened for more noise. Heart beating rapidly, she waited. Had someone broken in? She should go get Jake, but she wasn't ready to see him.

Quietly, she poked her head in, curiosity getting the better of her.

Engulfed in a cloud of dust, Jake danced back and forth across the floor, broom in hand, shirt off, and headphones on. The vacant space had been completely transformed since this morning—boxes had been moved, mirrors cleaned; the shelving along the walls had been emptied and organized. A large trash pile sat off to the side of the back door.

So this is where he'd disappeared to all day.

Tamryn inhaled a ragged breath through her nose, allowing herself this private moment to watch Jake. His back glistened with sweat, and his running pants sat just below the rounded tops of his cheeks. As he swept and spun, the muscles of his back worked and relaxed, and Tamryn found herself holding her breath as she studied him.

Jake stopped, chest heaving, eyes on Tamryn, and hauled his pants up with one hand, then pulled his earbuds from his ears.

She blushed, quickly searching for something to say, anything to explain why she was just caught staring at his ass, but nothing came to mind. Her throat was thick, her breathing heavy, and all she could think about was touching him.

He grinned. "Well, come in then."

Tamryn stepped inside, surveying the area as she approached him.

Jake's eyes widened, brightening with excitement. "Oh, check this out!" He darted into a small room in the back right corner and flushed a toilet, reemerging with an even wider smile. "The plumbing works."

"So I hear." Tamryn's voice was soft, her throat thick with emotion.

Jake frowned. "For your customers," he prompted. "You know, the singing customers."

Tamryn shook her head slowly, words escaping her. He hadn't taken away her key, or revoked permission to utilize the space. Instead, he'd spent the day getting the storefront ready for her.

Jake stepped toward her, his crooked grin returning, emphasizing his dimple more than usual. "I know, I know, you didn't want my help. But I couldn't very well let *you* clean this place, TB. What kind of gentleman would do that?"

Tamryn smiled, heart racing. "It's amazing. Thank you."

"It's the least I could do, after..." Jake frowned, searching her gaze, then grinned and brushed his knuckles across her shoulder. "I'm sorry about earlier. Your sex life is none of my business. Maybe I'm a bit overprotective of you..."

"Thanks, Jake."

"What are big brothers for, right?"

Frowning, she dropped her chin, eyes downcast. Big brothers. God, she was so stupid. Even after catching her literally *having sex*, he didn't see her as anything but a child. A little girl. An annoying kid sister.

If seeing her in the nude, completely exposed, didn't change Jake's view of her, nothing would. Time to let that dream die.

"Hey now, why the long face? You still sore at me for earlier?" Jake ducked, trying to meet her gaze. "Look, TB, I'm sorry. I acted like a real jerk. Your sex life is none of my business, okay? I'm sorry. Honest."

Tamryn's eyes welled up, so she closed them, wishing the tears and the agony away. Every second with him grew more unbearable, the room closing in on her. A tear dripped down her cheek.

"Hey, hey, TB? What's wrong?" Jake grabbed her chin and forced her to look up at him. "Why are you crying?"

She shook her head. "It's nothing, I just..."

He swiped his thumb across her cheek and her heart broke into a dozen more pieces from his tender touch. The tender, delicate touch of a loved one, not a lover.

A brother.

Shaking her head, she whispered, "I have to go. I'm sorry." She turned on her heels and ran, not stopping until she was safe in her own room, door locked, and pillow over her head. She cried into her mattress, wishing the action would dislodge the ache and longing from her chest, wishing she could open her mouth wide enough to scream her feelings away.

Because living with this ache, this need...was becoming more than she could handle.

A muffled knock paused her crying, and she listened to see if she'd imagined it. Lifting her pillow, she looked at the door.

Another knock.

"Who is it?" She failed at hiding the waver in her voice. *Please don't be Jake.*

"It's me," Reed whispered. "Can I come in?"

"Oh God," Tamryn groaned, shoving the pillow over her head. "Go away."

She really didn't need to be reminded of her indiscretions right now.

"I'm coming in."

"No."

"Hope you're dressed."

Tamryn sat up, glaring at the door as it opened.

Reed smiled. "Not that I haven't seen it before?" He raised one eyebrow.

She belted her pillow at him. "Not funny."

With a grunt, Reed caught the pillow, pulling it to his chest with a frown. "Too soon?"

"You think?"

"Everything okay?"

Tamryn laughed. "Nope. But what else is new?" Fresh tears formed and spilled from her eyes, cascading down her cheeks.

Reed sat down on the bed, side-eyeing her. "You know, before last night, we were just friends. Really good friends. I hope I didn't ruin that."

Tamryn whipped her head up, and Reed met her gaze, alarm widening his eyes. "You?" she spat. "You hope *you* didn't ruin that? God, Reed, I was there too, remember? I'm not some child you did something to, okay? You're as bad as he is!"

"Whoa, wait, I'm just saying I shouldn't have taken advantage of you, okay?"

Tamryn stood, fuming, and threw her hands to her hips. "Take advantage? Maybe I took advantage of you, did you ever think of that? Maybe, just maybe...ooh, I know! Maybe I waited until I could see that you were really hurting over Gennie, and that's when I zoomed in for the kill. Maybe *I* shouldn't have taken advantage of *you*."

Reed smirked, his lips twitching on the smile he fought. "So, now you're a predator?"

Tamryn straightened, and jutted her chin out. "Maybe I am."

Laughing, Reed tossed the pillow at her face, but too much fury coursed through her veins to be playful. She swatted the pillow aside, then stepped toward Reed and bent at the waist, setting one hand on the tops of each of his thighs. Glaring, she held his gaze for a few long beats, and sucked in a deep breath. "You *fucked* me last night, Reed, with your mouth, your hand, your dick, and you *still* think I'm a child. No wonder Jake can't see me as anything but. You've been inside me and still see pigtails and pimples."

Reed stood, gripping her by the shoulders. "I see a beautiful woman who is desperately in love with my best friend. You were in pain last night, Tamryn. I should not have slept with you." His gaze dropped to her lips, then her chest, as if staring straight through to her heart, the source of her pain, and he sighed. "You are not a child, Tamryn, you are my *friend*. I should not have taken advantage of your pain." Meeting her eyes once more, Reed smiled. "Trust me, Tamryn Baker, you are anything but childish."

Tamryn's cheeks warmed and she looked away, unable to stare into eyes that regarded her so earnestly. Reed knew her better than most, and his unfiltered honesty was so much more than random words from some guy she'd had tequila sex with.

"Look at me."

With his words, Tamryn was reminded of last night, and heat pooled deep in her body. She swallowed hard, then met his gaze.

"If you weren't in love with Jake, and I wasn't so hung up on Gen, well, I'd spend every day convincing you just how damn sexy you are."

Tamryn licked her lips, her gaze falling to his mouth as the memory of his lips on her flooded her brain. She didn't have feelings for Reed, and she was pretty damn sure that was mutual, but sex with him had promised to be mind-blowing. She could attest to that having only had a taste.

Reed chuckled, releasing her. "You're trouble."

Tamryn smiled. "Me?"

"Uh, yeah." Reed stepped back. "I don't want to get my ass kicked by your boyfriend again."

Tamryn laughed, then sighed, the mention of Jake clamping down on her heart like a vice. "He's not my boyfriend."

"Damn that Jake Johnson." Reed sat down on the bed, then patted the spot Tamryn had been occupying earlier. "If he only knew."

"Well, even if he did, I think he'd be more appalled than anything, since, you know, I'm his little sister and everything."

Reed leaned back, crossing his arms behind his head. "Man, I wish Colby was here."

Tamryn snorted. "Yeah, because then you would have had two guys punching you last night. Squad goals."

They both laughed, and Reed reached one arm out. "Come here, little Baker."

Tamryn snuggled down into Reed's body.

"I'm sorry I made you feel like a child."

She shrugged. "It's okay. I'm used to it."

"It's not okay, and I really never wanted to make you feel that way. I just wanted you to know that your friendship matters to me. More than the sex."

"It would have been good sex." She nudged him with her shoulder.

Reed's body shook with a chuckle. "Like I said, trouble."

"Fine. No sex. I'll just return to celibacy and wait for Prince Charming to get his head out of his ass."

"Sounds like a plan. Celibacy is good." He squeezed her shoulder. "I'm going to help you build the bakery."

Tamryn sat up, turning to face him, her eyes wide, and her pulse kicking into full speed. "What? You remember?"

"You heard me. I'm gonna help you. And of course I remember. Jeez, Tam, I didn't black out last night, you know." He winked. "I'll build the display cases, do the heavy lifting, drive you into town for anything you need, whatever. I'm in."

Tamryn tilted her head and cocked one eyebrow. "Behind Jake's back?"

"Why the hell not? What's he gonna do?"

Tamryn looked pointedly at the bruise that ran up one side of Reed's jaw.

"Ah heck, that'll heal." Reed grinned, and Tamryn joined him, her heart soaring with hope.

Maybe The Bakery next to The Bar wasn't such a bad idea after all. And now, with Reed's help, maybe it might actually happen.

Chapter Eight

Standing in the center of what would one day be the customer waiting area of her bakery—should everything go as planned—Tamryn grinned from ear to ear. She'd completed painting the walls last night, a muted pink on top, and a gingham wallpaper beneath the chair rail. Well, the chair rail wasn't installed yet, but Reed promised to do it as soon as the paint had dried.

Jake hadn't stepped foot inside the storefront since he finished cleaning the vacant shop two weeks ago. Tamryn and Reed had been able to get quite a bit done, but an air of sadness hung over their progress. Jake hadn't only stayed away from the empty storefront; he'd avoided Tamryn and Reed completely.

Occasionally Tamryn would hear him clunking around in his bedroom, and she'd stand in the hallway, her hand poised to knock, just waiting for that one little ounce of courage she needed to confront him. So many times she'd imagined cornering him in his room so he couldn't sneak out the back and avoid her. Again. She rarely caught an actual glimpse of him, and when she did, their conversations were short and to the point. One-word answers with limited eye contact, if any, and he made it quite clear that he couldn't get away from her fast enough.

Could he really be that disgusted with her?

Running her hand along the wall, she shook her head. What would happen when he finally stepped inside and realized what she'd been up to? The further along she travelled on this journey, the more her stomach sank. Had this been a stupid idea? Would he flip out because she created a bakery behind his back?

Before the whole Reed thing, she'd felt like she knew Jake well enough to do this, knew he'd love the idea and be proud of her for taking the initiative. But now? Anxiety had made itself at home around her heart, a prickly blanket of doubt that wouldn't allow her a full breath.

Tamryn sighed, looking up at the ceiling. "Well, what do you think, Colby?" She closed her eyes, picturing her brother walking through the store, trailing his fingers along the wall, inspecting her paint job. He'd comment about a spot she missed, even if it didn't exist, or tease her about the blush pink paint and gingham wallpaper combo. He'd run his fingertips over the top of the industrial equipment and smile, but then goad her for the ancient age of her kitchen, free appliances or not.

And then he'd turn around, a smile from ear to ear and those deep blue eyes sparkling.

She focused in on the memory of those eyes as she imagined his words. *"I'm proud of you, little Baker."*

A tear slipped from her eye, and she quickly swiped it away, pushing the image of her brother from her mind. If she focused too long, he'd tell her how royally she screwed things up between Jake and Reed.

She sniffed, swiped at her cheeks again and took a deep breath, then locked up and hurried next door to start her shift.

Stepping inside The Bar, the familiar scent of weathered wood and the faint, lingering scent of booze greeted Tamryn, reminding her of *him*, though a quick scan confirmed he wasn't here. Jake had never stayed away from The Bar this long, even back before he'd taken over ownership. Jake lived for this place.

With her heart in her throat, she surveyed the room, assessing tonight's crowd. Her eyes landed on a group of guys in the corner, and she grinned as the dark-haired soldier in the middle met her gaze.

"Well, hot damn," he drawled, his familiar megawatt smile lighting up the room. "If it isn't Tammy Baker."

She cocked her head to the side. "Charlie Morris. As I live and breathe." She bit her lip to fight a wild grin as he stood, stepped out of the booth, then strolled across the dancefloor, his Levis and cowboy boots just as perfectly worn-in as she remembered, the denim snug in all the right places.

He peered down at her, brown eyes sparkling. "You look better than I remember."

"Same." He'd grown in the past four years.

Charlie picked her up in a fierce hug and spun her around in a circle.

When her feet landed back on the floor, his arms still around her waist, Tamryn leaned back, placing her hands on his chest, smiling widely. "You look great, Charlie. When did you get back?"

"Just last week. I got a place with Roc." He hooked a thumb over his shoulder and Tamryn followed the motion, smiling at Charlie's two best buddies, Steven and Rockford "Roc" Hughes. The brothers hadn't gone far, just off to college a few towns over, but Tamryn hadn't seen them in months. Charlie, however, had been gone since right after graduation, continuing the longstanding Morris tradition of joining up right out of high school. "We're staying right outside of town, the old Mills' place?"

Tamryn met his gaze, stomach fluttering as her cheeks warmed.

He focused in on the blush. "Ah, so you do remember."

She pushed him gently. "How could I forget?"

Losing her virginity back behind the old Mills' farm, hidden away beneath a giant maple that hung out over the water, on a tiny little boat meant for one, had been, well, interesting, to say the least. But Charlie was the kind of guy who lit up a room, made every situation fun. And sex—as awkward as the circumstances had been—had been no exception. She'd loved Charlie once, in her own way, as much as a girl could love the boy who didn't hold the key to her heart.

Charlie rubbed her upper arms. "You married off yet, Tammy?"

Tamryn snorted. "Yeah right."

Charlie tipped his head back on a laugh, then scanned the room. "Yeah, I guess your pickins' are slim around this old town." He winked. "It's my lucky day."

She blushed again—couldn't help it; Charlie had always been a charmer.

"What time do you get off tonight?"

Tamryn glanced to her right, movement catching her eye as Jake strolled toward them, shoulders back and head high. After two weeks of barely a glimpse of him, her pulse sped at his sudden and surprising appearance, but her stomach sank from the way he approached them. Was he going to punch Charlie like he'd hit Reed?

She shot him a glare that she hoped said "back off", then looked back up at Charlie. "Eleven. Why? I know you're not trying to get me back out on Mills' Lake, Charlie Morris; I'm not that girl anymore."

"What's this about Mills' Lake?" Jake stood too close, practically maneuvering between them. He pinned Charlie with an icy stare. "And who are you?"

"Jake Johnson?" Charlie took a step back, running his hand over his brown, buzzed-cut hair. "Dang, man, you got huge. You runnin' your dad's place now?"

Jake tilted his head, narrowing his gaze. "Do I know you?"

Tamryn sighed. "Jake, this is Charlie Morris. Remember? My old—"

"I'm Tammy's ex-boyfriend. I used to come around her house a lot. You'd be gettin' into shit with Colby, and..." Charlie's words trailed off and he met Tamryn's gaze, eyebrows drawn. "Man, I'm so sorry, Tammy. I heard about your brother. I wanted to come back for the funeral, really I did, but—"

"Why didn't you?" Jake crossed his arms.

"Jake." Tamryn placed a hand on his arm. "It's okay, really. Charlie was stationed in the middle of the desert."

"Nah, he's right, Tammy. I shoulda called, done somethin'."

Jake grunted. "I was here."

She shot a glare at Jake—what was his problem?—then tried to guide Charlie away from Jake without being too obvious. "It's really okay, Charlie. I got through it. And it's Tamryn now. Not Tammy." She glared at Jake—*and not TB!*—then quickly looked back at Charlie and smiled. "Anyway, enough about that. Let's get you boys some drinks." She pushed Charlie toward his table, then glanced over her shoulder at Jake. He didn't have to be so damn rude.

He remained locked in place, stance rigid and arms crossed, his gaze boring into the back of Charlie's head. Tamryn shook her head and focused on the boys at the table. "Hey, Steve, Roc. How are you guys? What can I get you, a pitcher? Shots?"

Some ex-boyfriend. Jake remembered him all right, always hanging around the Baker house and trying to shoot the shit with Colby's friends. He'd been around TB for a number of years, yet didn't even reach out to her when Colby died?

"Something wrong, pal?" Reed ran a cloth around the lip of a pint glass.

"What? Nah. Nothing." Jake shrugged, fighting the urge to turn his head back to the table where TB still stood. Did she forget she had other customers? Maybe he should remind her of her other tables; she had responsibilities as his employee.

"So, Charlie Morris is back in town, eh?" Reed glanced over at the table of boys, and Jake followed his gaze.

"Guess so. Can't say I remember him, though."

Reed chuckled. "Of course not."

"What's that supposed to mean?"

Reed shook his head. "Nothin', bro. Just that you've had your head up your ass for as long as I can remember when it comes to that girl over there."

Jake scoffed. "How do you figure? I've always watched out for TB."

"Yeah. You're right. What do I know?" Reed shook his head, then slipped into the back as Gennie returned.

"Hey, boys." She patted Reed's ass as he passed, winking at Jake. "Jake, doll, where've you been?"

"Around." Jake looked away from Gennie, his thoughts too focused on TB and her table of douchebags. Had she dated those other two losers as well?

"Maybe I'll just have to go home with Reed if you keep ignoring me like you've been doing, sugar."

"What?" Jake watched Charlie, his blood boiling as the kid placed his hand on TB's lower back.

TB met his gaze, then smiled and slid in beside her ex.

"A woman has needs."

Jake shook his head. What was Gennie rambling about?

"Oh my Lord, is that Megan Morris' little brother?" Gennie sighed. "My my, all grown up, isn't he? That's one fine piece of—"

Jake turned to her, jaw clenched.

She smiled, then ran her fingertips over his beard stubble. "There's my pretty baby blues. What's eatin' you, Jake? You've barely been around for weeks. And, in case you haven't noticed—though I can't see how you could have missed it—I'm wearing a corset that's one size too small. My girls have been desperate to get out of it all night."

Jake dropped his gaze to the soft, freckled mounds of flesh spilling out of Gennie's shirt, then nodded approval.

She leaned toward him, her floral perfume a bit too strong. "Maybe you can help me out of it later, hmm?"

Jake licked his lips, focusing on the woman before him, not the girl behind him. The girl he pledged to protect, care for. The girl who currently had some other guy's hands all over her. Should he step in? Just how far did his promise to Colby reach? Surely, Colby wouldn't sit back and let his little sister get groped all night.

He squeezed his eyes shut against the ludicrous thoughts. Who TB allowed to touch her was none of his damn business.

Unless that Charlie Morris kid hurt her. Then he'd make it his business. As a big brother should, of course.

Gennie's lips brushed against his, and he opened his eyes.

"Whatever it is that's buggin' you, hon, I'll help you forget after work tonight." She winked, then turned away from him, putting a little extra oomph into her steps.

Even with the way her ass swayed with each step, Gennie was far from the distraction Jake needed to get his mind off Charlie Morris.

What   had   happened   at   Mills'   Lake,   anyway?

Chapter Nine

Tamryn leaned against the bar, watching Jake watch Charlie. Jake hadn't relaxed in the two hours Charlie and his friends had been in that booth, but truth be told, Colby had never cared for Charlie either, so Tamryn couldn't say she was surprised. Jake must have been going off of old opinions from Colby back when she'd dated Charlie.

But, damn, Jake was worse than Colby had ever been. Would she ever outgrow the protective older brother thing?

"Hey, beautiful, we're headin' out." Charlie pressed up behind her, sliding his arms around her waist and pinning her to the bar with his frame. "But I have something for you."

"Get a load of you all grown up. Meg didn't tell me you were back in town." Gennie leaned over the bar, giving Charlie an eyeful of her double d's as she dragged her gaze seductively from his feet to his head. "Mmm, *all* grown up."

Charlie straightened his shoulders, his grin slightly more languorous than usual. "How are ya, Gen?"

"Not as good as my girl here's about to be, I imagine." Gennie winked at Tamryn, then moved to the other side of the bar, giving them privacy.

Shaking her head, Tamryn turned in Charlie's arms to face him. Beer breath hit her hard, but she tried to ignore it. He focused on her lips.

"You better not try to kiss me with that breath."

Charlie feigned shock. "I don't have bad breath, I'm a gentleman."

Tamryn raised an eyebrow. "Mhm. You said you have something to give me?"

"This." He reached into his back pocket and pulled out a key on a twisted piece of leather.

"Charlie Morris, is that the key to your heart?"

He grinned, then gave a quick shrug. "Basically. It's the key to our place. In case you ever need to get out from under your *dad's* watchful eye." He cocked his head toward Jake, who still watched them. "You know, or if you're missin' me real bad some night."

"It's a nice gesture, but I can't say I'll ever use it." She pulled out of his arms, but he slid the key into her back pocket, then patted her ass.

"Keep it anyway. I really want you to use it."

She met his gaze, curious at the sudden change in his playful tone. She tilted her head. "What's up, Charlie?"

He frowned, shoving his hands into his pockets. "Nothin'. I just shoulda been there for you before. We've been through a lot together, you and me, and, well, I'm here for you now. If you'll have me."

She pushed up on her toes and placed a kiss on his cheek. "You've always had a place in my life. I don't need the key to your house to prove that."

He winked, then stepped away from her, meeting up with Steve and Roc at the door. "Keep it in case I ever lock myself out!" He tripped over the small lip of the doorway, then grinned and waved as he stumbled out onto the wood landing.

Tamryn retrieved the key from her pocket, turning it over in her hand. She didn't want or need the key to her ex-boyfriend's house, but Charlie wasn't in a state to argue with right now. She'd return it the next time she saw him.

Jake stepped up to the other side of the bar, peering into her hand. "Is that his *house* key?"

Tamryn closed her fist around the metal. "Yep."

He scowled. "Why?"

Tamryn tilted her head. "Why not, Jake?"

Running a hand through his hair, Jake shook his head. "Um, maybe because you haven't seen that guy in five years?"

"How do you know how long it's been?" She crossed her arms. "Were you listening to our conversation?"

"It's not like your friends were very quiet." Jake mimicked her stance. "How many pitchers did you serve them, anyway?"

"They paid for every single one, if that's what you're worried about. I don't give drinks away."

"Good. It'd come out of your paycheck." He crossed his arms over his chest and stared down at her.

"I just said that I don't give free drinks away." She picked her tips off her tray, untied her apron and set it down. "What's with you lately, anyway?" She shook her head, then turned and strode toward the door.

"Hey, your shift ain't over yet!" Jake called.

"Fire me." She stepped past some late night customers just arriving, then ducked into the shop next door as quickly and quietly as she could, shutting the door behind her and standing in the darkness.

With her head leaned back against the door, she listened for Jake's footsteps on the old wooden porch outside. She didn't have to wait long.

"TB!" He thundered to one end of the porch, then the other, stopping to peer inside the window of the old storefront, but she knew he couldn't see anything with the curtains she'd hung. "Ah, hell," he muttered, the sound of his footsteps walking away and disappearing when he reentered The Bar.

Tamryn slid down to the floor, resting her elbows on her knees. "What the hell," she whispered.

Jake strode through the bar, ignoring his customers as they called out for him. Someone requested a show, but Jake couldn't be bothered to sing tonight.

"Everything all right, sugar?"

Gennie's voice cut through the haze of anger and he turned to face her. "Let's go."

Her eyes widened, and she looked at the clock on the wall.

Jake's chest tightened. "It's my bar, and I said let's go."

Gennie grinned as she shrugged out of her apron. "You don't have to tell me twice." She hurried out from behind the bar, sidling up next to Jake. "What's eatin' you?"

"Nothing," he snapped. He didn't actually know why he was so mad. So what if TB had a key to some dude's house? Wasn't like she'd ever use it. TB wasn't that kind of girl. Jake pushed through the back door of the bar, the screen slamming against the outer wall.

"Jeez, Jake, what's got you in such a hissy?"

"I said nothing was wrong, Gen." He rounded on her and she took a step back. "Are we doing this thing or not?"

"This *thing*?" Gennie crossed her arms, staring up at him defiantly. "Not."

Jake sucked in a breath. "What?" He needed to let off some steam, and sex was his favorite way of relaxing.

"I'm not fixin' to fuck you tonight, Jake Johnson. You're angry and I don't like angry sex."

"I'm not..." Jake shook his head, then ran a hand through his hair. "Ah, hell."

"You're shouting orders and acting like a real ass, and I'm the farthest from turned on I think I've ever been around you." She turned on her heels and stepped back into the bar, leaving Jake standing in the dark.

He kicked at the dirt, then stomped inside his house. All the lights were off, and TB's door was open, so she obviously hadn't come home yet.

"Dammit," he whispered into her empty bedroom. "What have you done to me, kid?"

Chapter Ten

Tamryn slipped quietly into the house, tiptoeing to keep from waking Jake and Gennie. She fumbled with the kitchen light switch, nearly knocking down someone's glass of water left precariously on the edge of the counter. She steadied it, then opened the fridge.

"Where have you been?"

She gasped, whipping around toward the living room and squinting into the shadows. "Jake?" She searched the darkness for him, then tilted her head. "What are you doing?"

"Were you with your ex?"

"No, Jake," she said on a sigh. "I was with Reed."

A small grunt sounded deep in his throat.

"God, not like that." Tamryn stepped forward and reached into the living room, running her hand along the wall. She flipped up the light switch and bathed Jake in the amber glow from the lamp within the ceiling fan. "What are you doing?"

Jake pushed up off the couch, his muscles rigid.

Did he even *own* a shirt?

"What do you think I'm doing? Do you know what time it is?"

Tamryn took a step back, chuckling softly. "You're kidding, right?" She turned and started back to the kitchen. He was obviously joking—

He stepped in front of her, blocking her path. "Do I look like I'm kidding?" He peered down at her, his blue eyes intense.

Tamryn bit her lip, wary of his tone. He'd never acted like this before, so protective it bordered on possessive, which was off-putting and sexy all at the same time, but the fact that this sudden show of possessiveness had sprung up seemingly out of nowhere was borderline alarming.

His gaze dropped to her mouth, so she released her lip and sucked in a deep breath. Dammit, being this close to him was intoxicating. "Jake, I'm...I don't understand. You've never cared about what time I came home before. Why now?"

He leaned closer, his lips just a few inches away from her face. "I..." He searched her gaze. "I was worried, that's all."

She raised an eyebrow, breathing through her mouth as subtly as possible so his scent wouldn't knock her legs out from under her. "Where's Gennie?"

"What?" He ran his hand through his hair. "How the fuck should I know?"

Tamryn took a step back, eyes narrowed. "You're acting weird. I have baking to do." Truthfully, she just needed to get away from Jake and keep her hands busy, lest she jump on him and do things she'd only ever dreamed of. She turned her back and walked further into the kitchen, reaching for the pantry.

"Don't you walk away from me," he growled.

"Excuse me?" She spun to face him. "You think the sun rises each day just to hear you crow, don't you?"

His lip twitched, but he remained silent.

She threw her hands up. "God, Jake, what is your *problem*? I was at the bar. With Reed. Like every other night after work on every other day."

"You left the bar."

"And then I came back," she stated, slowly drawing out the words. "To finish my shift, because, unlike some people, I'm not an asshole."

His eyes narrowed. "What's that supposed to mean?"

Tamryn crossed her arms and leaned back against the counter. "I think you know exactly what that means."

Jake's gaze flicked to the microwave then back to her. "It's almost four o'clock."

"Yep."

"What were you...?" Jake's jaw clenched, and he straightened. "Did you and Reed...?" His bright eyes flicked back and forth between hers frantically.

Tamryn exhaled a breath and rolled her eyes. "I wasn't fucking Reed. That was a drunken mistake and won't happen again. And I wasn't with Charlie." She stepped toward him. "Although, I'm quite confused why it's suddenly any of your business."

Jealousy was a good sign, but she refused to get her hopes up.

Maybe it wasn't even jealousy.

"It's always been my business. I promised your brother I'd look out for you."

Not jealousy then. Obligation. Tamryn's shoulders fell and she shook her head. She turned back to the pantry and gathered the dry ingredients in her arms. "My sex life was never Colby's business, Jake, and it's definitely not yours." The sack of flour teetered on her forearm. She reached for it, the other ingredients wobbling with the motion.

"Whoa, let me help you—"

The flour crashed to the flour, spilling out across the linoleum in a white wave.

Tamryn laughed. "Too late." She plopped down to her knees and righted the flour sack to prevent any more from spilling out, though most of it was already coating the floor.

Jake pushed the flour sack aside with his foot, then lowered himself to his knees in front of her. Too close, way too close.

Tamryn sucked in a breath, eyelevel with pecs so hard she wanted to run her tongue along the ridges.

"You're making me crazy, TB. I'm not sure what's going on in my head anymore."

"You make me crazy too, Jake." She closed her eyes, unable to look into his gorgeous blue gaze another second.

Jake ran his thumb across her cheek as a single tear escaped, then chuckled softly.

She opened her eyes warily. "What's so funny?"

He held up his thumb to show the smeared flour paste he'd just made by wiping her tear. "You spilled the flour," he whispered.

She licked her lips. "You sat in it."

"I did."

"You're covered in it," she whispered.

"Not yet."

Tamryn smirked, then picked up a handful of flour. She rose up on her knees to better even out the height difference, holding his gaze as her heart ran a marathon within her chest, then started at his shoulder, smearing the flour downward.

His hand flew up and he caught her wrist, then pressed it against his chest. His heartbeat pounded beneath her palm.

Tamryn's eyes widened and she inhaled through her nose, finally allowing herself to breathe him in. Her pulse kicked into overdrive.

"I'm sorry I've acted like such a jerk." Jake leaned forward, bringing his lips to hers, tentatively at first, a feather soft kiss that sent tingles out across her face. "I don't know what's wrong with me."

Nothing. She pushed toward him, wrapping her arms around his neck and pressing her lips to his. He opened his mouth and she followed, then he ran his tongue along the length of hers, the heady scent of whiskey on his breath. Tasting her, suckling her tongue and then repeating the motion, Jake drove every doubt from her mind. He wrapped his arms around her back, hands on each shoulder blade, holding her tightly to the length of his torso.

Spicy and warm, his kiss was everything she'd imagined it would be, a whiskey burn that curled around her heart and warmed every inch of her body.

Tamryn's pulse sped, the rhythm an ecstatic song of *finally.*

Finally, Jake's lips were on hers.

Finally, Jake's body pressed against hers.

Finally, Jake's arms holding her close.

Finally, *Jake.*

She held him tighter, pressing her hips into his, her patience wavering. Savor the moment she's waited for all her life and make it last as long as possible, or rip his clothes off and jump his bones right here on the kitchen floor?

Decisions, decisions.

Jake rocked his hips, pressing his hardness into her, and a moan escaped his lips. He pulled back, gripping her biceps and holding her at arms' length, his eyes wide. "Oh, shit, TB. I'm so sorry. I shouldn't—"

Tamryn opened her mouth to speak, to tell him 'yes, yes you absolutely should', but he stood without a word and raced from the room, leaving her in a stupor.

She touched her fingers to her lips, then shook herself from the haze. "Jake! Wait!" She stumbled on weakened legs to stand, slipped on the flour, then ran into the living room, searching for him, hoping he'd turn around and talk to her. If he would give her a chance, she could tell him she's always wanted this, always wanted him. She'd tell him he'd had her heart since long before he even knew she existed. No apologies.

"Jake!" She ran to his room and flung the door open. Empty. She stepped into the master bathroom, empty as well. Had he rushed to The Bar? She dusted the flour from her knees and hands, then the roar of the bike shook the house, and she ran outside in time to watch dust kick up behind him as he sped off into the night.

"Jake!" she shouted after him, but it was too little, too late, and he was too far gone.

Chapter Eleven

Jake had been a ghost for three days. She'd smell him in the morning, a hint of his cologne tainting the air of the house, teasing her with the promise that he'd been there, but he left before she awoke and returned after she went to bed. She'd stayed up for him that first night, but he hadn't returned, his absence resulting in images of him running to Gennie.

Tonight was the first time Tamryn had seen him since their kiss, but he hadn't said a word to her. The only acknowledgement he'd given that she actually existed at all was the occasional glance he'd send her way. Unreadable glances. Did he regret their kiss?

Obviously. *What a dumb question.*

But she wished he'd talk to her, explain his feelings so she could explain hers, finally get it all out in the open so she wouldn't continue to drown in her love for him.

She eyed the shiny new digital jukebox mounted to the wall by the stage—another upgrade Jake hated, but she was secretly excited about.

"Just pretend it isn't there, hon. You know how Randy is with his love of all things Nascar," Gennie said on a sigh. "We'll never get to play any songs at this rate." She returned her attention to the playlist they'd been jotting down all evening.

It was almost closing time, and they had yet to play even one track on the new machine.

Glancing over at Randy, who now one-eyed the television, Tamryn shook her head. "I think there's a chance we may get our way sooner rather than later. Hand me another beer." She accidentally let her eyes wander to Jake, who watched her like a hawk, his face completely void of emotion.

Gennie chuckled as Randy nearly ran his cue through the felt. "I like your style, hon. This one's on the house. For the music's sake, of course." Gennie winked, then cracked open a Bud and pushed it across the well, stopping just inches from Tamryn's waiting hand. Tamryn looked up to find Gennie's mouth dropped open and her eyes wide.

"Gen?"

Jake whistled through his teeth.

The customers all fell silent, and Tamryn turned to follow Jake's gaze to the gorgeous blonde strolling into The Bar.

"Hot damn, I love city girls," Reed whispered.

"I love city girls with tits the size of—"

"Randy!" Tamryn hissed.

Jake straightened, ignoring his friends.

"She's probably a yank, anyway." Randy took a swig of his beer. "An uppity city girl. I ain't got time for stress like that."

Tamryn watched Jake as he assessed the newcomer, his eyes wide and his lips pulling into a slow smile.

Look at me. Look at me*, Jake.*

Hell, he could look over at Gennie, for all Tamryn cared, and it would be a heck of a lot better than the way he watched this stranger.

Heart on the floor, Tamryn finally tore her gaze away from Jake and focused on the customer. Blonde hair pulled up into a loose bun— messily sexy—and curves that would make Jessica Rabbit green with envy.

"Motherfucker," Gennie hissed.

Tamryn closed her eyes and inhaled a deep breath, composing herself. She had no room to be upset; Jake wasn't hers. Frankly, Gennie had more claim to the man than she ever would. She turned to Gennie, mustering some sort of compassion for the woman who frequently slept with the man of Tamryn's dreams. They'd kissed. Once. And that probably didn't even count since he'd hightailed it away from her afterwards. Gennie had been sleeping with him for the past year at least. "I'm sure he hasn't even noticed her, Gen." Tamryn's stomach sank further with every word.

Gennie met Tamryn's gaze, her eyebrows raised. "Are you kidding me? Them two have already eye-fucked the livin' daylights out of each other. I'm just hopin' I can join them." Gennie ran her tongue along her plum bottom lip. "That skirt's so tight you can see her religion."

Tamryn frowned, swallowing the giant lump in her throat.

"Damn. Looks like Jake's fixin' to go to church."

Tamryn whipped her head around, knowing she should leave, should look away, but unable to move.

Jake and the woman were in a stand-off, clearly, and the hush in the room was heady enough to swipe a knife through.

Tamryn felt the heavy weight of Reed's gaze and turned to face him. He frowned in sympathy and she clenched her jaw, counted to ten, then looked back at the bar and straightened her shoulders. Imagine how much pity those knowing eyes would hold if she'd told him about the kiss.

She'd seen Jake with plenty of women; why should this one be any different?

The blonde tore her gaze away from Jake long enough to flag Tamryn over.

"What are you waiting for? Go take that woman's drink order and hopefully she'll order for her husband, too." Gennie glanced at the door. "Maybe he's right behind her." She closed her eyes. "Lord in heaven, let him be right behind her."

Tamryn watched Gennie mutter a silent prayer—maybe she wasn't as cool with this as she wanted to seem—then grabbed her tray and headed over to the table, her gaze on Colby's dog tags hanging just above the woman's head. *Of course* she'd sit in *that* booth. Tamryn stopped a foot away, ran her tongue over her teeth, and met the woman's fierce green eyes, forcing a fake smile. "Waiting for someone, Ma'am?"

The woman forced a smile that didn't reach her eyes. "Gin martini. Dry. Shaken. Two olives. Skewered, not just tossed into the glass." She held Tamryn's gaze for much too long, unwavering.

Tamryn raised her eyebrows and considered asking the customer to clarify her gin preference, or nudging her about her absent husband, but the woman raised one eyebrow in silent challenge and Tamryn turned on her heels and left.

Gennie's narrowed gaze followed Tamryn's every move as she returned to the bar. She waved her hands, motioning for Tamryn to hurry. "Well? Is she alone?"

"She only ordered one martini, so…"

Gennie snickered.

Tamryn squinted. "What?"

"Randy was right; she's a highfalutin' city girl. Jake will lose interest. Always has been a sucker for a good whiskey girl." She turned away from Tamryn and made the martini. With vodka.

Whoops.

Careful not to slosh any liquid over the lip of the glass, Tamryn approached the corner table once more as the woman unbuttoned the top button of her blouse, then reached for the martini before Tamryn could even set it down.

Tamryn's lungs tightened.

"What can you tell me about him?" the woman asked, her gaze still locked on Jake.

Tamryn turned, her cheeks flushing and her heart breaking in her chest, met Reed's knowing gaze again, ignoring Jake completely so she wouldn't have to witness the way he eye-fucked this customer. Every cell in her body begged her to run to Jake, to shield him, wrap herself around him like a cocoon, but that was crazy.

Tamryn turned back around, deciding to play dumb. "Who do you mean?"

The woman flicked her gaze to Tamryn, glancing at her cheeks, then smirked. "I think you know exactly who I mean. Tall, gorgeous, and deadly over there."

"Oh." Of course. Why couldn't she want Reed? Or Randy? "That's Jake Johnson. He's lived here all his life."

"Jake Johnson," she said slowly, tasting the words.

Tamryn's skin crawled. "Yes, Ma'am. He's the—"

The woman raised her hand. "I'll stop you right there. Married?"

"No, Ma'am, but—"

"Thank you. I'll need another of these in about ten minutes, please." She pinned her gaze on Jake, and Tamryn couldn't move. She should say something, do something, anything…

Anyone who knew Jake could guess what would happen next.

Chapter Eleven

Jake hadn't yet been able to tear his eyes away from her. As Randy so indecently noted, she was gifted up top, but that wasn't what mesmerized Jake. The woman's hips spread out beneath her tiny waist like an hourglass, and with each stride across his bar, they'd called to Jake, drawing his attention to the perfected swing in her step and the fullness of her ass, whispering a promise.

A promise of forgetting.

He'd do anything—any*one*—if that would get his mind off TB and that damned kiss.

He'd given her space the last few days. Or maybe he'd needed the space. He'd kissed Colby's little sister. After he'd grilled her, of course, because nothing spells romance like interrogating someone about their ex-boyfriend.

But, damn, he'd *kissed* her. Really kissed her. The kind of kiss that would have led to fucking her right there on the kitchen floor.

That was the opposite of watching out for her. How could he do such a thing? He couldn't have feelings for her. It wasn't right. She deserved more than a guy like him. A guy who fucked for fun and rarely stayed long enough to get a girl's name.

TB deserved far more than that.

Dipshit.

What the fuck was wrong with him?

This was TB. Colby's sister. You don't kiss TB.

When this woman slid into his favorite booth, he couldn't help but smile, as if her random seating choice was some sort of sign, Colby's way of telling him to stay the fuck away from such dangerous thoughts about TB. Jake bent over the pool table, pretending to position himself for a shot, and waited for her to search him out, his breath held in anticipation. He wanted a chance with her tonight. Just one. No strings. Just a taste to get the taste of TB's mouth out of his mind.

Finally, the blonde unabashedly assessed his every inch as though she thought she weren't under the scrutiny of everyone in his bar. Or maybe that didn't bother her one bit. The thought intrigued Jake even further.

Slowly, her gaze travelled up, up, up…

Bingo.

Her eyes widened.

Jake smirked.

"And another one bites the dust," Reed whispered, chuckling under his breath.

"Damn that Johnson charm," Randy slurred.

"It's all in the eyes, Randy. Gets 'em every time, huh, Jake?"

His friends disappeared into the surroundings, his focus tunneled. She took a long pull of her martini, then raised one eyebrow. Jake smiled, hung up his cue, and stepped forward. Motion beneath the table caught his attention as she very deliberately uncrossed and re-crossed her legs. This woman meant business.

Her attention now focused on the moisture beading up at the base of her glass, she didn't catch him adjust the tightening in his pants, and he hoped she also didn't catch Randy slap him on the back as he stepped away from the pool table.

Gennie might be watching, but knowing her, she'd want to join in. Jake imagined a scenario with the feisty redhead and this sultry blonde. He smiled. Not a bad idea.

TB might be watching, but—

He shook his head. Colby's little sister was none of Jake's concern, and he wasn't hers. They'd made a mistake; one that would never happen again. Jake would watch after TB, make sure that Charlie kid didn't hurt her, but that's where his involvement stopped. Where it had to stop.

Regardless of how that resolve tightened a confusing grip around his heart.

Jake slid his way into the booth, resting his forearms on the table, the wood creaking beneath his weight. She smelled like honeyed flowers, if that was a thing.

She met his gaze, and a faint gasp followed. "Took you long enough."

Jake licked his lips, grinning. "You've only been here ten minutes."

"You noticed."

"The air shifted when you walked in." He'd heard the line from a customer who later left with the woman he'd been hitting on. If it worked for that guy...

She tilted her head.

"I'm Jake."

"Johnson. I know. Sage."

Hmm. He was at a disadvantage. Had this woman asked TB about him? He fought the urge to glance over at TB. "Just Sage?"

"Yep." She toyed with the next button of her blouse, exposing more of the soft crests of her breasts. "May I steal you away from your game for ten minutes?"

He smiled.

She licked her lips and met his gaze once more.

"Ten minutes?" He shook his head, then stood, extending his hand. "I have all the time in the world."

If she'd help cleanse him of his dangerous thoughts about his best friend's little sister, he'd give her all the time she wanted. He'd fuck TB right out of his mind.

He pulled the woman from the booth, helping her to her feet. When she looked past him at TB, his stomach sank. He knew TB watched them, but he'd been trying to ignore the weight of her gaze, and the way it intensified the sinking feeling in his gut that he couldn't shake to save his life.

"Excuse me for a moment," the woman whispered. She turned, brushing her breasts against his arm in the process.

The blonde chick released Jake's hand and strolled across the floor.

Tamryn's heart froze in her chest.

The woman grabbed her cocktail, finished it in one long gulp, then set the empty martini glass back on Tamryn's tray. She leaned forward, bringing her mouth just shy of Tamryn's ear. "There's a difference between vodka and gin, honey." She started to turn away, then paused. "Close your mouth; you look like a tourist."

Tamryn slammed her mouth shut, and as she watched the woman sashay back to Jake, it took everything in Tamryn to keep from crying right there on the empty dancefloor. She inhaled a breath, jumping as the door banged shut behind Jake and the beautiful stranger.

Tamryn turned on her heels and raced to the bar, slamming her tray down a bit louder than she intended. She quickly glanced around the room, sadly noting all eyes on her. Was there anyone left that didn't know about her feelings for Jake?

"Oh, honey." Gennie placed her hand over Tamryn's and rubbed her thumb back and forth over Tamryn's knuckles. "I had no idea. I mean"—she glanced around the bar as Tamryn had just seconds before—"it seems I'm the only one who didn't know. But I had no idea."

Tamryn yanked her hand out from beneath Gennie's. "I don't know what you're talking about."

"How long?"

"What?"

"How long have you been in love with Jake, Tamryn?"

Tamryn squared her shoulders. "I have tables—"

Gennie cringed. "All those nights—"

"Were none of my business." Tamryn grabbed her tray and Randy's pack of cigarettes, then raced through the swinging kitchen doors, knocking a dusty plate off the counter as she did so. The shattering sound of ceramic hitting the linoleum floor did nothing to pause her escape—she couldn't breathe.

Pushing through the back door of the building, she stopped to inhale a deep lungful of air, trying to catch her breath as her heart tightened in her chest. Tears burned her eyes.

"Fuck, you feel so good," Jake whispered.

Tamryn's heart stopped. She sucked in a breath, then quickly threw her hand over her mouth to mask the sound.

Right out there in the open, Jake had that woman pressed up against the bar, her skirt around her waist and his hands...

Tamryn ducked into the dark shadows behind the building and hurried to the house she shared with Jake, praying he hadn't heard or seen her lurking in the shadows, some creep watching him fuck a stranger.

Chapter Twelve

Jake smiled at the familiar cacophony of pots banging in his kitchen. TB must be baking. He hadn't had a Baker muffin in weeks; she hadn't cooked for him since the whole Reed thing. Then, that night he'd kissed her, she'd been about to bake when all hell broke loose. The spilled flour had been cleaned up by the time he got back, making the whole thing feel even more surreal; a kiss that hadn't happened.

He hoped the ruckus in the kitchen meant they were finally moving forward.

His stomach growled as he imagined her hustling around the kitchen to make his favorite muffins. His mind took it a step too far, conjuring an image of TB in that lace bra, covered in flour, reaching up to the top shelf—

Damn. Jake groaned. Fucking that customer hadn't dampened his dirty thoughts about TB at all. In fact, his latest discretion had only fueled his desire for her. Something was missing with that woman. But not just sexually. He had a connection with TB. He'd spent years with her.

He missed their easy banter. Missed the glint in her eyes when he annoyed her or tugged her ponytail. He missed *her*. This silent treatment thing was bullshit.

He should tell her that.

Jake sauntered through the living room, ready to chastise TB for ignoring him, and debating how best to bring up their kiss, then paused as his brain caught up to his eyes and he finally recognized the chaotic state of his home. Flour covered every inch of the small dining room that conjoined the living area and kitchen. He ducked, narrowly escaping a cookie cutter that ricocheted off the wall and flew just past his head.

What the...?

Eyes wide and heart racing, Jake sprinted through the small dining room, turning the corner into the kitchen and skidding to a stop when he discovered TB hurling baking supplies around. A tiny human tornado.

Confused, he surveyed the area, a half-smile on his lips. "Hey now, what the hell happened in here?"

TB paused, met his gaze, then whipped a cookbook at his head.

He dodged, narrowly avoiding a collision, then ran a hand through his hair. "What the hell was that?"

"Well, bless your heart, Jake Johnson, that was a cookbook." She picked up a large sack of sugar and dumped it on its head, granules rushing out over the linoleum in a white wave.

Watching the fine sugar spread across his floor like liquid, blending with the flour, Jake couldn't decide if he was pissed or amused. At least she was talking to him. He looked back up, meeting TB's fiery gaze.

Her eyes narrowed further. "Something about this funny to you? Because I'm only getting started." TB picked up an oversized mason jar full of cupcake wrappers and lifted it over her head. "I'd run, if I were you, Jake Johnson."

"Whoa..." Jake raced across the kitchen, grabbing her arm at the wrist and taking the mason jar from her hand before she could toss it and shatter the glass. "What are you so fired up about?" Jake stared hard into her eyes, searching for the reason behind the sudden madness. In all their years together, he'd never seen TB so livid. "What happened?"

"What happened?" She pulled free of his grasp, then reached for a rolling pin. "You happened!" TB screamed. She waved the rolling pin toward him. "You, Jake! You and that...that *thing* you can't seem to keep in your pants!"

She pointed the pin below his waist, circling it at his crotch.

He took a step back. "What?" When she continued to point the rolling pin toward his dick, he reflexively brought his hands to his crotch.

She glowered. "Fuck, you feel so good," she growled, her voice strangely deep, like she was mimicking a man—

Jake's brow furrowed.

"Did you even get her name?" she spat.

He frowned. Her name? *The blonde's?* He narrowed his eyes, studying TB, and tilted his head. "You've never cared who I hooked up with before, why the sudden change?"

That kiss. The answer whispered through his mind, but he pushed it aside. That had been a mistake. She had to know that. Logically, she had to know. He was Colby's best friend, someone entrusted to look after TB. They'd crossed a line, and they both understood the mistake made in doing so.

Right?

TB laughed mirthlessly, throwing her head back, then pinned him with angry blue eyes. "Is the mighty Jake Johnson speechless? How fucking *perfect*." She shook her head rapidly, teeth clenched, her lips in a straight line. Jake watched, held her gaze, waited for an explanation, but she just shook her head over and over again, fighting some private battle he wasn't privy to.

He grabbed her shoulders and peered into her eyes. "Stop doing that! Stop shaking. Talk to me. Is this about that kiss?"

She froze, her breath catching audibly in her throat; a vein pulsed in her eyelid.

"I told you I was sorry, TB. What more can I say?"

"Ugh!" She pushed herself free of his grasp. "You're completely oblivious!"

He searched her gaze, desperately trying to follow her thought process. "I don't understand."

She untied her apron and threw it on the floor, then fled from the kitchen.

"Fuck!" he growled, tearing down the hall after her. This was nuts! "TB!"

Tamryn pushed her door closed, but he was stronger and managed to slide it open without much exertion. He stood in front of it and looked down at her. She crossed her arms and glared at him. "Get out, Jake."

"No. Not until you tell me what the hell is wrong with you right now. Are you...on your period, or something?"

Her mouth fell open. "Get out."

Oh shit. He'd really gone and done it this time. Jake squared his shoulders and crossed his arms. "No."

"This is *my* room."

"This is *my* house." A low blow, but he wasn't in the mood for the high road.

TB's eyes widened, then she promptly composed herself. All emotion drained from her face, the angry flush replaced with an icy pale.

Jake's stomach sank.

"You're right. This isn't mine." She waved her hand around the small room. "None of this is mine."

"No," he argued, "that's not what I meant." Jake struggled against the confusion in his mind, sorting through all the words he wanted to say to her. "How can you say that? This is your home."

"No, it's not, Jake. I sleep here, and I bake in that kitchen, but I don't even sit on that couch for fear of all the women you've fucked on it."

He slammed his mouth shut, her words a punch to the gut. "I don't, I've never—"

TB closed her eyes and raised her hand. "Stop. It's not my business. That's the whole point." She met his gaze once more, her eyes glossy, and Jake's lungs fought for air that no longer existed in this room. "This isn't my home. You're not my family. I don't belong here."

She turned, but Jake panicked, reaching out for her and spinning her around. "All of this is yours. This house, this room, the kitchen"— he paused before the last word fell from his lips: *me*—"I'll go. I'll sleep at the bar. You stay here. If I. . .if you're so disgusted by me, I'll go. You can have the house."

"Jake, that's ridiculous."

"It's what Colby would have wanted."

"Colby isn't here." TB closed her eyes, as a tear dripped down her cheek. Jake watched its descent, but couldn't move. She inhaled a ragged breath, opened her eyes, then turned around and pulled a suitcase out from under her bed. She popped it open, and—

Jake sucked in a gasp. "You're already packed?"

She looked back at him and smiled sweetly. "Sure, Jake. I mean, I didn't want this either, and think of all the fun you can have without your dead best friend's little sister bringing you down all the time."

The words battered Jake like physical blows, his heart crawling up his throat to escape the painful ache growing in his chest. "Is that what you think? That you bring me down?"

She turned around, narrowing her gaze. "Look, Jake, whatever promises you made to Colby, I'm letting you off the hook. I'm twenty-two years old now. I can take care of myself, okay? You're free."

Free? The word made his chest constrict tighter. Jake was desperate for some crack in the façade, some hint that she didn't really want to leave him, but she remained stoic, reserved, giving him nothing but an icy stare.

She really did want to leave. What could he do?

He pulled in a deep breath, then gave a quick nod. "Fine. Okay. Whatever you want. I would never make you stay here if you were that unhappy."

"I am. I am that unhappy, Jake. Let's face it…you were Colby's friend, not mine."

The finality of that statement stole the air from his lungs. Jake dug his fingernails into his palms to keep from crumbling as her words tore through his brain. He'd cherished her all this time, grown so comforted by her presence, so accustomed to it, while all along, she'd wanted to get away from him. He'd tricked himself into believing they needed each other when that dependency had been one-sided. He'd imagined little moments between them, conjured stolen glances that didn't exist.

He'd fallen in love with a girl who didn't even want to *know* him.

Shit. He'd fallen in love with TB and he didn't even know when exactly that had happened.

In his stupor, he watched her shove pictures and books into a quickly-overflowing suitcase, helpless to stop her, his mind only able to focus on the searing rush of agony consuming his every cell.

She'd been miserable all this time. He'd held her captive.

She hated him, and he loved her. *What have I done?*

This wasn't what Colby wanted, not in a million years.

God, he'd failed both of them.

"Goodbye, Jake."

He blinked, bringing her back into focus. He searched those familiar blue eyes one last time, but nothing had changed. She was really leaving.

"Goodbye, Tamryn."

Her eyes widened slightly, then she nodded and passed him, and though his heart begged to follow her, to chase her, to stop her, his feet wouldn't budge. He'd gone numb, save for his cheeks, where the warm, unfamiliar sensation of tears was all too surreal.

"Oh, and Jake?" She looked back, and his heart soared. He blinked the wetness away, but she didn't meet his eyes, only looked him up and down, her lip curled in disgust. "You might want to stop fucking the woman your best friend is in love with."

Tears streamed down Tamryn's cheeks, but she held steadfast to her exit. How fitting that Jake had finally ditched her childish nickname as she walked out of his life, as if leaving was the act that finally grew her up in his eyes.

She ran into The Bar, her tears now accompanied by sobs. "Reed!" She scanned the empty saloon, but he was nowhere to be found. Panic bloomed in her chest beside the ragged-edged, gaping hole where her heart once lived. The old Mills' place was too far to walk, and Tamryn didn't have a car, so if Reed had left for the night, she'd be screwed. "Reed!"

She'd just left Jake. This was real. Her heart fought against its cage, frantic to flee and run back to him. Her suitcase hit the floor with a loud *thud* that mimicked the roar of realization as it slammed into her soul. Agony ripped her heart in two. She cried out, slamming her hands to her chest.

Reed appeared from the kitchen, eyes wide. "What is it? What's wrong?" He ran to her, stopping a foot away.

She looked up at him, her hands out, palms up, a silent question begging to be answered. Why? How? What had she done? She sobbed, then clasped her hands to her face.

"Oh, Tamryn." Reed wrapped her in his arms as she collapsed from the weight of her pain, lowering them both to the ground. "What happened?" He pulled her away enough to look down at her, swiping tears from her cheeks. "Tamryn?"

She curled into his chest. "I think I just moved out," she sobbed.

"Oh shit. How'd he take it?"

Tamryn cried harder. *How'd he take it? Like a champ.* "He didn't even follow me."

Reed held her until the tears subsided, maybe minutes or hours later.

Jake never came. In the back of her mind she'd been waiting for him, giving him this one last chance to catch up to her—physically and emotionally. There was no point wasting another minute of her life waiting for Jake.

She sniffed, then pushed back and wiped her face with her sleeves. She stood, and Reed rose with her. She gave a curt nod. "I'm okay."

He sighed, then gathered her suitcase. "I'm thinking you need a place to crash?"

"No. But I do need a ride."

"Care to tell me where we're going?"

Tamryn smiled sheepishly; there was no way in hell Reed would think this was a good plan. "The old Mills' place?"

Reed shook his head, eyebrows raised. "Do you think that's the best idea?"

"Save the lecture, Reed. Are you going to take me or not?"

Reed sighed. "Damn, Tamryn. I hope he doesn't kick my ass for this."

She wiped her eyes. "Oh, please. He's probably already calling a bunch of girls to come over right now and christen his empty house with a quick romp in the flour."

"Somehow I doubt that." He cocked his head. "Wait. The flour?"

"I might have made a little mess on my way out."

"Should I ask?"

"Nope."

She wiped her face, straightened her shoulders, and stepped outside. It was time, long overdue, that she get over Jake Johnson.

Charlie's sudden reappearance in her life couldn't have been more perfectly timed.

Even as she thought the words, her heart broke further. Charlie wasn't the answer, but at least she had somewhere to go while she sorted her life out and decided on her next move. Old friends seemed like exactly what the doctor ordered.

Chapter Thirteen

Charlie opened the door in unbuttoned jeans hung low on his hips, eyes puffy with sleep and his dog tags hanging off one bare shoulder. "Tammy? What's wrong?"

Tamryn wiped her eyes, then shook her head. "Nothing. I'm good. I mean..." She wasn't good. She was broken. She shook her head again, unable to find the words. What was she doing here? Had she really just left Jake? "Remember what you said about getting out from under Jake's watchful eye?" She laughed, but the tears gave away the pain in her words. "I just did that."

"Come in, come in." Charlie opened the door all the way, stepping aside for her.

She waved to Reed and he pulled slowly down the gravel road, pissed off, Tamryn knew, but dammit, she was done being treated like a child by Colby's boys. She'd *had* a protective older brother, but he was dead. She didn't need them to step into his place. They'd never had a chance of filling those shoes, though she'd appreciated their concern...to a point.

She paused in the entryway, one eyebrow raised; beer bottles decorated the living room, spotted among pizza boxes, beer cases, and dirty clothes draped over half-emptied moving boxes. "Oh my."

Charlie rubbed his chin, smiling. "Yeah, well, I didn't think you'd use your key so soon."

"I didn't."

"You're right. Why not?"

Tamryn shrugged. "It felt weird? I haven't seen you since high school, Charlie. I can't just walk in like I own the place."

He looked down at her suitcase when he closed the door. "Yet you brought a suitcase. Staying for a while?"

"Yes. No. I don't know. Do you mind?"

He grasped her shoulders. "I gave you that key for a reason. I want you here." His brown eyes searched hers, his eyebrows bunching. "What's wrong? You've been crying."

Tamryn took a step backward. "This was a mistake. I'm sorry, I shouldn't have come." Tears filled her eyes, and she took another step backward toward the door.

"Whoa, wait." He held his hands up, palms out. "Whatever's going on, I'm your friend. I just, well, when I saw you again, it was like yesterday. Like time hadn't passed."

"Four years passed."

"I know, and...I don't know, I guess I felt like I was home again. With you."

"You are home again, but you're not *with* me."

"Yet." He smiled his crooked smile, and Tamryn warmed at the memories of him, of the two of them, the only boy she'd ever tried to love outside of Jake Johnson.

But that was just it. She'd had to *try*.

"I'm in love with Jake, Charlie."

His eyes widened, and he rocked back a bit. "No shit?"

She shook her head. "No shit."

"And you told him tonight? That's why you're here?"

"No. I didn't tell him. I've never told him. He has no idea."

Charlie grabbed her suitcase, pulling it from her grasp. "Come on. Sit. I'll get you something to drink." He kicked Roc's foot on his way to the kitchen. "Move your fat ass to bed, Roc, we have company."

Roc grumbled but didn't fully wake, curling up into a ball between the couch and the coffee table.

Charlie returned to the living room, making a face when he saw Roc still in the same place he left him. "I said git!" He nudged him again, harder this time, then tilted a beer bottle over his face. "You'll be covered in a golden shower in five, four, three—"

"I'm gettin', I'm gettin'. Damn, Chuck, you're mean these days." Roc stood, stumbling over an afghan as he turned down the hall. "And that's not a golden shower, dipshit."

"Say hi to Tammy, Roc."

Roc turned around, eyes wide. "Oh, shit, Tammy, I didn't know you were here." He stood straighter, pulling his shirt down around a protruding belly, his pale cheeks flushing. "And here I was talking about golden showers. Shit. Sorry. Was I snoring?"

Tamryn giggled. "Not since I've been here, Roc."

"Ah, cool. I'll see you two lovebirds later."

Tamryn's eyes widened. "It's not like that." But he'd already disappeared into a room down the hall. She turned to Charlie, whispering, "It's not like that."

"I know. Here." He handed her a cold beer. "Sit down." He stepped toward the couch, pushing aside magazines and rental insurance paperwork, clearing a space for her.

When she sat down, she took a long pull of the beer, then fiddled with the label. "I probably shouldn't have come here."

"Tammy—"

"Tamryn."

"Tamryn, sorry, I'll get used to that, I swear. Old habits, and all. Look, you're welcome here anytime you want, for as long as you want. We're your boys, remember? I won't push you to date me again, especially if you're in love with someone else. I'm not that guy."

She smiled, then met his gaze. "Thank you."

"Wanna tell me what happened?"

"I wouldn't even know where to begin."

"The beginning." He settled into the couch, took a sip of his beer, then pinned her with an all-too-familiar brown gaze she knew would pull the truth from her.

But if she went back to the *very* beginning, she'd break his heart. So she started her story after high school, just after Charlie left.

He didn't need to know she'd only ever loved Jake Johnson.

Jake ached like someone had physically extracted his heart, left his chest open and exposed, then poured burning embers inside the raw cavity...an alien sensation he couldn't remember having experienced in all his twenty-six years. Had he ever cared about anyone as much as TB? He didn't think so. Not with the way this raw ache consumed his every muscle.

Noon had come and gone by the time he'd cleaned up his kitchen, though he knew he'd find flour in obscure places for weeks, possibly months to come. Little reminders of the girl he'd loved and lost before he ever even recognized that he loved her.

He'd realized it all too late. And now she was gone.

"What a fool."

"Talking to yourself, Johnson?" Reed stood in his doorway, a box of pizza and a case of Buds in hand.

Randy leaned against the kitchen table, sipping on a bottle of Gentleman Jack.

Jake crumpled to the floor. "She left me."

"I know, buddy." Reed crossed the kitchen and slid down the cabinet to sit beside Jake. He popped open a beer and handed it to him, then opened the pizza box. "What are you gonna do about it?"

Jake looked up at Reed. "What do you mean? She hates me. She said she was never happy here, never wanted to be here."

Reed tilted his head. "And you believe that?"

"It's what she said."

"Then you're dumber than you look."

Randy sat down across from Jake and Reed, stretching his legs out and crossing them at the ankles. He leaned back against the cabinet and shoved half a piece of pizza into his mouth. "You know, you're about as sharp as a cue ball, Johnson." Randy grinned his lopsided smile, exposing the missing molars he'd lost after a football game over a decade ago, and a mouthful of half-chewed food.

"What am I missing?" Jake grabbed a slice, biting into the cheesy goodness.

"That girl loves you. She's loved you since she was still in a training bra."

Jake met Randy's gaze. "Let's not discuss TB's bras."

"I'm just sayin', man, that girl looks at you like you hung the moon. Everyone knows it."

Jake tilted his head, eyes narrowing.

"Everyone but you, Johnson." Reed smacked his shoulder. "Everyone but you."

"Nah." Jake rubbed his hand through his hair, shaking his head. "She was already packed and ready to go."

"All right, buddy. Get up. You need to see something." Reed pulled Jake up by his armpit. "Randy, grab the grub; we've got work to do."

Jake followed the guys next door, raising an eyebrow when Reed pulled a key from his own pocket. The muscles in his arms tensed. "Don't remember giving you a key, bro."

Reed nodded. "No shit. Had to get one made."

Jake's chest constricted. He really didn't want to kick Reed's ass again—

"Now, before you start swinging at me again, it's not what you think." Reed unlocked the door, pushed it open, then motioned inside. "Go on, see for yourself."

Jake narrowed his gaze, watching Reed as he stepped past him.

"It happened *one time,* buddy."

Jake snorted. "One time too damn many," he muttered under his breath.

Reed stepped in behind him and flicked on the lights.

Eyes wide, Jake stepped into the center of the room, then spun in a slow circle, left hand on his hip and the other rubbing back and forth through his mop of hair as he tried to make sense of everything before him. Pale pink paint covered the top half of the walls, some striped plaid wallpaper beneath. There was a chair rail installed through one section of the room, halfway finished. Beside a glass display case, a countertop had been installed, a vintage-looking cash register resting atop.

"What...what is all this?"

"You really don't know, do you? What *do* you know about Tamryn Baker?"

Jake rounded on Reed, meeting his gaze with narrowed eyes. "I know TB. She likes to sing, and bake, and—" His eyes widened, and he surveyed the small storefront once more, realization hitting him like a brick. "She likes to bake," he whispered.

"Yep."

Randy snorted.

Jake shot him a glare, then looked back at Reed. "She really doesn't want to go to college, does she? Shit, man, all this time, I just thought she was digging her heels in to spite me."

Reed smirked, shaking his head.

"She wants a bakery."

"Quick wit for the win," Randy murmured, fingering the keys on the cash machine.

"She wants her own business." Jake slowly looked around the room again as things reluctantly fell into place. How had he missed this?

"Not just her own business, Jake. Not just a bakery. She wants a bakery next door to *you.* Her dreams aren't just for *her.*"

Jake scratched his beard stubble, struggling with this new information, still trying to make sense of everything. He looked back at Reed for further explanation, brow furrowed. "Help me out here, man."

Reed shook his head, smirking. "You really don't get it, do you? This is *The Bakery*. Next to *The Bar*. Your bar. She wants to set up shop beside you. Live in your home. With you. All of her dreams *include you*."

Jake shook his head, unable to process Reed's words.

"Even after loving you all this time with not a whole heck of a lot in return, she wanted to set up shop beside you. Like it or not, man, that girl is the very best thing you've ever had in your life."

"And you fucked it up right good," Randy said.

TB wanted to live with him? But that couldn't be right...she'd been very clear in her exit speech. "She said I should be free." He shook his head again. "She felt like she was stuck with me 'cause of Colby. That's all."

Reed sighed. "She's not stuck with you, asshole, she's in love with you."

Chapter Fourteen

Jake scowled. Everyone he'd ever loved had left.

Reed watched him, eyebrows raised, waiting.

Jake shook his head. "Nah, man. She doesn't feel that way about me." But even as he said the words aloud, something tugged at his chest. He spun in another slow circle, still processing the sight before him, from the new girly curtains to the Barbie pink walls.

"A bakery?"

"Yes, Jake, a bakery. She wanted to surprise you."

"But she left."

"Yes, Jake. Because you're an asshole."

Jake glared at Reed.

Reed shrugged. "Sorry. But you know it's true. How many women have you paraded in front of her?"

Jake threw his hands up. "I didn't know!"

Randy snorted again, then took a long swig of his beer, following it up with a loud belch. "Sure you didn't. Everyone knew."

Jake barked out a sharp laugh. "Apparently not everyone."

Reed slapped his hand on Jake's shoulder, so Jake turned back to meet his gaze.

"Well, now that you know, what are you going to do about it?"

Jake inhaled deeply, straightening his shoulders, then puffed out a large breath of air, sagging beneath Reed's hand on his shoulder. "Not a fucking clue, man."

Reed frowned. "Yeah, I figured."

"For all the ladies you've been with, I'd have thought you'd have a better understanding by now." Randy smirked as he bit into another slice of pizza. "Turns out, you're even dumber than the rest of us."

Jake raised an eyebrow. "Get a woman—*any* woman—naked, boys, and I'll know exactly what to do. Not sure that's going to work in this case, though."

Reed chuckled. "No, I'd think not."

"I'm open to suggestions."

Reed dropped his hand, then reached for a beer, popping the top off and handing it to Jake. "That, my friend, is on you. If I tell you how to get Tamryn back here, it won't be sincere."

Jake exhaled, then chugged the beer in one long swig. "Y'all are worthless, you know it?"

Reed shrugged. "We'll leave ya to it," he said as he headed out behind Randy.

Jake paced around the newly transformed space, still dumbfounded by it all. Everything he knew about TB had shifted. She loved him? He couldn't wrap his mind around it.

Everyone else had known, but he'd been oblivious. Maybe that meant they were wrong, then. Maybe she wasn't really in love with him. Just because she wanted a bakery next to his bar didn't mean she wanted *him*. Not like that anyway. They were practically family. And even if she had wanted him, she'd made it clear by leaving that her feelings had changed. He'd do well to remember that.

And hell, Jake Johnson wasn't boyfriend material anyway.

Just ask the army of women who hated him.

Tamryn awoke to the unmistakable scent of bacon, the sizzle of meat in a pan, and the clank and bang chorus of boys in the kitchen. She opened her eyes, squinting against the sliver of sunlight seeping in through the living room windows, turned over on the couch and inhaled deeply. "Mmm."

"Good morning, beautiful." Charlie popped his head through the doorway to the kitchen, smiling widely. "I hope you're hungry."

"You cook?"

"Bacon? Hell yeah. Who can't cook bacon?"

Tamryn laughed. "Does it come with eggs or toast, or are you about to feed me a plate of animal product covered in animal product, topped with more animal product?"

Roc emerged from the kitchen doorway. "Sounds legit to me."

Charlie laughed. "Nah, Tam, I can make toast and eggs, too, believe it or not. How do you want 'em?"

"Over medium, please."

He met her gaze. "Just like I like 'em."

Tamryn smiled, then pulled herself up into a sitting position and tugged her ponytail holder out to redo her hair.

Roc sat beside her, a plate of bacon on bacon in his lap. "Sleep good?" He pushed a slice of crispy goodness into his mouth like a conveyor belt, until the entire piece was gone.

"Yes, actually." *Considering.* "Sorry I showed up and you had to move from the floor." Tamryn winked.

"Yeah, well, for you, Tammy Baker, I'd sleep in a bed any time."

"Are you flirtin' with my girl, you big bastard?" Charlie rounded the corner, plate of steaming food in one hand and a steaming cup of coffee in the other.

"Pretty sure she's not your girl no more," Roc said around a mouthful of bacon.

Tamryn accepted the plate and mug, settling deeper into the couch. Her stomach growled, triggering her mouth to water at the prospect of perfectly cooked eggs—no runny whites in sight.

"So, what's your plan?" Charlie pushed the coffee table back a few feet, then sat cross-legged in front of Tamryn. "Do you have one?"

Tamryn's cheeks flushed and she shook her head.

"No, I figured as much."

Tamryn smiled sheepishly, then took another bite of breakfast; she couldn't talk with a mouthful of food, and staying silent about last night's catastrophe was her only plan thus far.

"Since you left the dude you were living with and also working for, I'm assuming you left your job?"

Tamryn's mouth stalled, mid-chew, and her eyebrows rose as her stomach sank. Her job. She hadn't even considered that part of all of this. "Shit," she mumbled around a mouthful of food.

Charlie smiled, shaking his head. "You always have been quick to act, slow to think things through."

Tamryn threw her napkin at him. "I am not slow!"

"Isn't that the truth? You're one of the hastiest people I know." Charlie laughed, dodging as she whipped a chunk of toast at his head.

"It's no big deal, Tammy, we always loved the way you kept us on our toes." Roc laughed. "Especially my boy, here, huh, Charlie?"

"Whatever, Roc. Eat your bacon." Charlie met Tamryn's gaze again. "We'll find you a job in no time. Just eat. No worries."

Tamryn inhaled a deep breath through her nose, then resumed chewing, nodding at Charlie.

A job. What was she thinking? She'd never worked anywhere but The Bar; she had no other qualifications!

Chapter Fifteen

Two weeks later, Tamryn walked into the local Wynn-Dixie for her third shift as a cake decorator in the bakery. It wasn't baking, exactly, and working for minimum wage at a grocery store was definitely not owning your own bakery, but beggars and choosers, and what not.

Tamryn had made her bed, and now she laid it in. Alone. In an ugly apron and hairnet combo that slayed a little bit of her soul every day that she put it on. No more than she deserved, she figured, for holding onto her idea of Jake for so long, rather than facing reality.

She shook her head and tied the back of her apron.

Her other job wasn't too awful, so she tried to focus on that. Hosting karaoke night at the *other* bar in town, Old Faithful's, was actually a pretty good gig and rarely ever felt like work in the true sense of the word. She drank for free, sang as often as she wanted, made somewhat decent tips, *and* kept every damn cent she earned.

There was also the tiny victory of working at The Bar's only competition.

Take that, Jake Johnson.

Tamryn sighed, her heart tightening in her chest at the thought of him. She straightened her shoulders, washed her hands, then headed back to the main desk to assess the day's work orders. If there weren't too many, she hoped she'd be able to get a little baking in. The manager had been kind, granting Tamryn permission to use the industrial kitchen for baking, but *only* once all store responsibilities were finished.

Which had yet to happen, but a girl could dream.

Her gaze landed on a stack of receipts a half inch high. She groaned; no baking today. What else was new?

"When you gonna come back and bake for me, Little Baker?"

She grinned, looking up from her paperwork to meet Reed's warm gaze. "You aren't supposed to be back here."

"Shit, me? Don't forget I played football with Marty Bankhead. Your WD manager would let me sleep in the meat freezer if I asked."

Tamryn stood, smirking. "That would be an odd request." She tilted her head. "Now, Randy, on the other hand—" Words cut off by a fierce hug, she let Reed lift her into the air, squeezing him back just as fiercely.

"We miss you, Tamryn."

"I miss you, too, Reed."

Reed released her and surveyed the room. "So, you're baking; that's good, at least."

"Yeah. I love it here. I'm baking all the time." Her heart tightened on the lie, but she forced a smile. "It's awesome, everything I've always wanted. I'm so happy here. It's great." She promptly closed her mouth; she'd gone too far.

Reed's eyes narrowed ever so slightly and his lip quirked. "Great."

"Too much?"

Reed nodded. "Just a bit."

She inhaled a deep breath. "So, what brings you by?"

Reed nodded slowly. "Groceries."

Tamryn snorted. "Oh, obviously. How silly of me." She looked down, fiddling with the hem of her apron, then ran her hands over the fabric, straightening out nonexistent wrinkles.

Reed leaned against the doorjamb and crossed his arms. "Tamryn Baker, have we been pushed into fake niceties and bullshit, you and me? Are we really *those* people now?"

She looked up, eyes wide. "No, Reed, of course not, I mean…"

"Then don't bullshit me. This is a shit job in a shit place, and you're miserable."

"Reed."

"Come back to us. The Bar isn't the same without you."

Tamryn opened her mouth, then closed it. She shook her head. "I moved on. You have to, too. It will just never be like it was, you know? Jake's better off without me, and frankly, I'm all the better without him."

"You don't believe that."

"I do." She forced a smile. "I'm quite happy."

Reed glanced pointedly at her stack of orders. "Frosting someone else's cakes?"

Tamryn scowled. "Just go, Reed. You came to convince me to come back to Jake's, and it's just not going to happen."

Besides, Jake had been frosting someone else's cakes for as long as she could remember.

"TB—"

She held up a hand. "Don't call me that."

Reed sighed. "I'm sorry. Please just consider coming home. He misses you."

Her heart pinched, but she pushed away the pain. "Like an old family puppy, Reed, nothing more. I can't keep living like that."

"You're wrong."

"Oh?" She met his dark gaze. "Tell me then. How much does Jake miss me?"

Reed opened his mouth to speak, but Tamryn raised a hand.

"Better yet, tell me how many women he's had in his home since I've left. He still fucking Gennie for you?" She gasped on the question, slamming her hand over her mouth.

Reed's mouth crashed shut, and Tamryn didn't know if the loud *thud* she heard was his jaw closing or her heart plummeting to the floor. How could she have said something so awful? Reed didn't deserve her wrath.

"Reed, oh my gosh, I'm so sorry."

He shook his head, his hazel eyes a little less bright. "It's all good, Tamryn. I'll see you around."

He turned and left the back room, shoulders slightly slumped. Tamryn's eyes welled up, but she squeezed them shut and swiped the wetness away.

Fucking Jake. This was all his fault.

By the end of Tamryn's shift, her shoulders were heavy with ache from both the posture she'd held all day while frosting other people's cakes, and the weight of the words she'd said to Reed.

She had to make things right.

Unfortunately, the only sure place to find Reed at this time of night was at Jake's, and, that wasn't happening. Checking the clock on the dash one more time, she decided to head to his house and leave him a note. It was all she could think to do, and she had to do *something*. There was no way she could sit idle after saying something so awful to Reed today.

She drove Charlie's rickety old truck out past The Bar without consciously assessing the cars parked in front—no sign of Jake's truck—or the people standing outside—was that Gennie?—and she kept right on going until she hit old Highway 45. After a few miles on 45, she turned down the first dirt road she could find, and rattled all the way to the Samuels family farm.

She pulled up alongside Reed's truck; guess he wasn't at work tonight.

Relief and nervousness tickled her belly with butterflies; she'd have to face him instead of writing her apology in a note. Tamryn inhaled a deep breath, then stepped outside, mustering all the courage she could, confident in her words—she'd rehearsed them during the twenty-five minute drive—but unable to ignore the twisting tendrils of fear in her gut. What if he didn't accept her apology?

What if she'd managed to push Reed away, too?

She turned off the engine and looked up as Reed strolled through the doorway, screen banging closed behind him. He took the stairs two at a time, racing toward the truck. Of course he'd heard her arrival; nothing but insect songs filled the still night air.

She took one last, deep breath, then opened the truck door and stepped down.

Now or never.

Chapter Sixteen

"What's wrong? Are you okay?" Reed asked as he quickly approached.

"Nothing. I mean, yeah, I'm okay."

He sighed, stopping a foot away. "You never drive all the way out here, and it's almost midnight." He glanced at the truck, then back at Tamryn. "What's wrong?"

She smiled; these boys were always so worried about her. Had their concern really been so bad? Had being protected and safe been such an awful feeling? "God, you're so much like Colby." She stepped forward and wrapped her arms around Reed's neck. "I'm so sorry for what I said today, Reed."

His shoulders relaxed and he wrapped his arms around her waist, squeezing tightly. He chuckled into her hair. "Damn, Tamryn, is that all? You had me in a panic."

She pulled back, looking up into his eyes. "You're not mad at me?"

"Heck no. You were right to lash out; I shouldn't have pushed you. But, that reminds me...you have to leave." He started to pull back, releasing the grip he had on her waist. "I'm not alone—"

The screen door slammed shut, echoing in the stillness of the night, and startling Tamryn a foot backwards. She gasped, looking up at the doorway, then her breath caught in her throat.

She'd know that silhouette anywhere.

Her stomach collided with the earth at her feet.

Framed in the amber light from inside, so that his face was hidden in darkness, Jake stood on the porch, arms rigid and fists clenched.

"Shit," Tamryn whispered. No wonder she hadn't seen his truck outside his bar. She risked a quick glance around. Sure enough, beneath the old willow tree, next to the big muddy tractor, sat Jake's truck. *I'm so stupid.*

Reed cleared his throat. "I'm sorry. I tried to tell you."

"So, this is why you had to go 'check on the barn', buddy? A secret meeting with TB?" He stepped down each step, slowly, menacingly.

Tamryn's emotions ricocheted between anger, happiness, and guilt. She'd been caught with Reed again, innocently this time, but it wouldn't look like that to Jake. And there'd be no point in arguing. Bull-headed was an understatement when it came to Jake Johnson.

Reed raised his hands, palms out. "It's not what you think."

"Isn't it? Looks like you've snuck off to be with TB, right under my nose. Again." He crossed his arm, stopping at the last step, his face now a bit less covered in shadow, and his gaze unquestionably on Tamryn. "Never really considered you the late night booty call type."

Tamryn opened her mouth on a rebuttal, then stopped herself. What Jake thought of her was no longer her concern. She closed her eyes and counted to ten as she inhaled a deep breath, readying herself to get back into the truck. Reed and Jake could sort this out amongst themselves.

The rumbling growl of a motorcycle approached, echoing loudly in the palpable silence between the three of them, growing louder as it approached the Samuels' family farm. Tamryn opened her eyes and stared down the long drive as one headlight grew larger in the darkness.

"Now who the fuck is this?"

Reed shrugged, then looked at Tamryn as Charlie pulled up on his old dirt bike, an arc of dirt and gravel spraying up behind him as he skidded to a stop a few feet from where she stood with Reed. "Friend of yours?" Reed's voice was hard.

Tamryn looked from Reed to Jake, then back at Reed, before she rushed to meet Charlie. "What are you doing here?" she growled. As if this fire needed any more fuel.

"You never came home after work. I went by The Bar, but Gen said she saw you head out this way just a few minutes before I got there."

"So you thought following me was necessary?" Tamryn shook her head. Did she have to move to another state to get out from beneath all this patronizing concern for her? "I'm fine, Charlie." She threw her hands up into the air, spinning around so she could almost face all three of them. "God, *seriously*? When will every man in my life stop treating me like a fucking child? You guys have to stop! I'm not a little girl anymore! My brother is dead. My addiction-addled excuse for a mother is MIA. My fucking love life is a joke. My career has become a part-time job at the fucking *Dixie*. So what? Who cares? Do I have to leave town to get out from all of your watchful fucking eyes? For how *concerned* you all are for me, it's funny how none of you actually give a shit about what I need or want."

Tamryn stomped to the truck, tears fighting at the back of her eyes, her composure hanging on by a quickly unraveling thread. She'd call Luce in the morning; maybe there was room for one more in that tiny apartment. New York had to be far enough away from these guys.

Jake raced toward her. "TB, wait—"

She rounded on him. "Don't come any closer."

He skidded to a stop, mouth open to argue, hands sort of flapping by his sides.

"You've lost any right to tell me what to do."

Reed reached her side before Jake did, and reached for her arm—

"Don't you touch her," Jake snapped.

Tamryn met Reed's gaze as he lowered his hand. He looked away from her at the ground.

She scoffed. "Seriously? Don't touch me? You're going to listen to that, Reed?"

Charlie stepped off his bike, helmet in hand. He reached Tamryn and placed a hand on her lower back. "Come on. I'll take you home."

Tamryn spun on him. "Don't you get it, Charlie? You don't need to take me anywhere. I'm just fine on my own." She turned back around to climb into the truck. "I can damn well take care of myself—" her words faded as the sharp *smack* of Jake's knuckles slammed against Charlie's cheek.

Tamryn looked over just in time to watch Charlie stumble backward, gripping his jaw.

Tamryn gasped, then turned to Jake, who stood rigid, shaking his hand. Scowling, she closed the distance between them, mustered all of her strength, and pushed him.

He faltered back a step, surprised by her attack, his eyes wide.

"Jake! What the hell is wrong with you?" She rushed to Charlie's side. "Charlie, let me look." She reached for his cheek, but he shrugged away from her hand.

"I'm fine." He nodded toward Jake, his lips curled. "That's your big prize? That's the love of your life?" He scoffed as he slid back onto his bike. "I don't get it, Tammy. I just don't get it. I would never treat you the way he does—"

"She doesn't want you, kid," Jake snarled.

Tamryn closed her eyes, grappling with the fact that Charlie had just said *'love of your life'* out loud. Had Jake heard those words too? She hoped he was still too consumed with rage to have heard the truth fall so blatantly from Charlie's lips.

"Charlie…" She opened her eyes, chewing on her bottom lip as tears streamed down her cheeks.

Charlie's shoulders slumped and he shook his head, the sharp lines of anger fading from his face, replaced with a shadow of defeat. "Get on, Tammy. Me and Roc'll come back for the truck in the morning."

Tamryn's hands shook, but she obeyed, climbing onto Charlie's bike behind him. Her eyes were so full of tears, her vision was blurred. Driving would be a bad idea anyway. He placed his helmet on her head, then frowned as he tightened the strap.

"Don't go," Jake pleaded. "We need to talk."

"I have nothing to say." The words were muffled by the helmet. More tears fell, but she didn't look back at Jake.

Charlie sighed, gave a curt nod, then turned back around. "Hold on tight." He kicked the stroke until the bike growled to life beneath them.

Tamryn wrapped her arms around his waist, turning her head to the side that Jake wasn't standing on so she didn't have to try to discern the look in his eyes, and squeezed tighter when Charlie threw the bike into gear and took off down the road.

She thought she heard Jake call out to her, but couldn't be sure over the roar of the dirt bike. Tears continued to stream, drying on her cheeks from the wind as they raced through town to the other side, as far as she could be from Jake without actually moving to a different town.

Though, in her heart, she'd never felt further from him than at this moment. Physical distance had nothing on the gaping chasm between them now.

"Now you've done it!"

Jake stepped back as Reed rounded on him, hands in the air.

"You're a right fool, you know it?"

Jake frowned, shaking his head, his shoulders still tightly bunched around his neck. "What are you rambling on about, traitor?" His lip curled as that last word lingered on his tongue. Traitor. Reed had betrayed him again. Colby never would have done such a thing to Jake. Not with TB, obviously, but with *any* girl. His heart pinched at the thought, then fell as thoughts of Colby morphed into images of TB, tears on her cheeks, arms wrapped around that Charlie kid and riding off into the night.

Away from Jake. Again.

Reed dropped his hands to his sides. "I slept with her once, Jake, once. It was a mistake. I've apologized."

"What was this little secret meeting about then? She wants round two? Can't get enough of Reed Samuels?"

Reed inhaled, squaring his shoulders. Jake recognized the glint in his best friend's eyes. He braced himself for the truth; that's what that determined glint meant: truth bombs. Whether Jake wanted to hear them or not. He could read his oldest friend like a book, goddammit, and he hated it sometimes.

Times like this.

Jake's mouth opened before he could stop himself from speaking. "All this time you're telling me she loves me, trying to convince me to get her back here…for what? So you could have an easier time fucking her?"

Reed swung, and whether Jake was too tired or too full of self-loathing, he didn't know, but he braced himself for the attack instead of dodging or blocking it.

Knuckles slammed into Jake's jaw, a crack echoing through the field. His head whipped back, and he reached up reflexively to rub his face. He squeezed his eyes shut, pain throbbing through his mouth, his jaw, ringing in his ears. He opened and closed his mouth a few times, stretching the muscles, now tight from assault. After a few long seconds, he opened his eyes, closed his mouth, dropped his hands, and met Reed's glare.

"I deserved that."

Reed exhaled a loud breath. "You're damn right you deserved that." He lowered his arms, shoulders relaxing, then shook his hand out. "I went to see Tamryn at work today; you know that dream job she has over at the WD?" He paused, letting that sink in.

As if Jake had forgotten that TB was now baking for the customers of the local super market instead of for him. In his kitchen. Safe within his home.

"Foolishly," Reed continued, "I tried to fight your fight and get her to come back to work."

Jake smiled, in spite of himself. "Which only pissed her off."

"Yeah. No kidding."

"She doesn't like being told what to do." An image of TB's arms crossed over her chest, and that defiant glint in her eye formed in his mind. "So, what happened then?" He tried to ignore the little flutter of hope in his chest.

"Well, she basically told me to go fuck myself, just not in so many words."

Jake cringed. "What were the words, exactly?"

Reed frowned, pulling his gaze away from Jake's.

Uh oh. "Give it to me straight, man."

"She asked me if you were still fucking Gen for me."

Jake's eyebrows bunched together as he processed the words. "She's mad about Gennie?"

He thought she'd been mad about that blonde chick he'd fucked outside The Bar, but...had she been mad about Gen this whole time, too? He ran his hand through his hair. "I don't..."

Reed shook his head, blowing air through his lips. "She asked if you were still fucking her for me, Jake. *For me.*"

Jake looked back at Reed, taking a deep breath. His eyes widened, and he reached up to rub his hand over his hair, slowly, as each piece of the puzzle settled like bricks in his chest. "You're still in love with Gennie."

Reed raised his shoulders, then dropped them slowly, a long, drawn out shrug of agreement.

"Holy shit, man." Jake started to pace. "I thought that was ancient history." He ran his hand through his hair, as if rubbing his scalp would help his brain work faster.

"It is." Reed smiled sadly. "For her."

"What have I done?" He'd hurt the two most important people in his life, that's what he'd done. Killed two birds with one Gennie.

"You didn't know."

"Some good that did! I should have known. You're my best friend. How could I be so blind?"

Reed laughed. "Johnson, you can't even see that you've been in love with Tamryn Baker since she first sprouted tits; I can't fault you for being blind to who I'm in love with if you can't even figure out your own shit."

Chapter Seventeen

Tamryn's hands still shook when Charlie pulled the bike to a stop in front of the old Mills' place. Tears continued to pool, running over the dried tracks of those that had fallen before them.

She climbed off Charlie's bike in a daze, then turned and began to walk inside.

"Whoa, hold on." Charlie slid his fingers around her wrist and pulled her back. "You're still wearing the helmet."

"Oh."

She stared blankly past him into the darkness in the direction of the pond.

Charlie sighed as he unbuckled the strap and slowly removed the helmet from her head.

Tamryn vaguely registered what a relief it was to have that thing off; her high ponytail should have been taken down before they left, but she hadn't thought of it. Hadn't thought of much of anything except Jake. Now her head throbbed with the release of the tension, and she reached up to pull the rubber band free, her long, blonde hair flowing loosely, her scalp prickling with the release.

Charlie placed the helmet on the seat of his bike, then reached his hands up to cup her cheeks, his fingertips in her hair on either side.

"Hey, hey now, stop crying, Tammy. He's not worth it." He rubbed his thumbs across her cheeks, smearing the tears. "He's not worth it."

His words only made her cry harder, the tears fall faster. That was the thing...Jake *was* worth it; she knew that all too well. With all his faults and all his mistakes, Jake had always been the love of her life, and probably always would be. She knew why he was so afraid to love, to connect, understood his fear...loved him for it, in spite of it, maybe even because of it. They had so much in common, her and Jake, so much loss, so much sadness. They'd gotten through it all, together, had formed a bond she'd once thought was unbreakable.

Had she really lost her best friend through all of this?

A sob escaped her lips, and she squeezed her eyes shut, pushing a flood of tears down her cheeks.

Charlie sucked in a breath. "Hey, look at me."

She met his gaze, caught off guard by his smile. What could he possibly smile about when she stood before him a broken shell of herself?

He swiped at her cheeks, took a quick look around, then lowered his head conspiratorially. "You know what you need?"

A wakeup call. She shook her head.

"A dip in that ol' pond over there. A Mills' style baptism to cure what ails ya."

Tamryn tilted her head and gazed out at the moon's reflection on the surface of the pond. "It's kinda cold for a swim—"

"Bullshit. The Tammy I know would already be naked and racing me to the edge."

Memories of summers spent sneaking through the fence to skinny-dip until Old Man Mills caught them rushed back to the forefront of her mind. Carefree and wild...when had she lost that part of herself?

"There's nothing that a midnight swim can't fix," Charlie whispered.

That might have been true when they were teens, but she doubted that was the case now. With a sigh, she stepped back from Charlie. "Last one in's a rotten egg!" She ducked past him, taking advantage of his momentary shock to get the upper hand and beat him into the water. Sprinting toward the water's edge without looking back, she stripped down to nothing but a bra and panties, leaving a trail of discarded clothing in her wake. As she reached the shore, she leapt into the air. Just as she broke the surface, her brain registered the giant splash to her left.

Damn that Charlie Morris! He always had been faster than grass through a goose!

"Goddammit!" Jake paced through The Bar, across the dancefloor, around the pool table, from one end to the other, over and over. He'd never felt so foolish in all his twenty-six years.

He'd accused his best friend of something awful, punched some kid who was obviously just being a good friend to TB when Lord knows he wasn't, and pushed the person he cared about most in the world even *further* away from him.

"What the hell is wrong with me?"

He needed to run. Or punch things. Or both. Maybe a long ride on the bike.

Or a good fuck.

No, that was the last thing he should do. No more random lays until he figured this shit out.

He stripped off his shirt, slipped on his running shoes, did some jumping jacks for warm up, then strode into the cool, dark night.

After a three mile run, as dawn's violet glow began to peek over the mountain ridge in the east, Jake's desire to punch things had dwindled, but his agony and restlessness hadn't waned.

Gripping the large wooden door of the barn, he slid it open across the dirt, early morning light shining on his baby. "Hey, girl," he whispered, stepping inside the barn and tapping the seat of his dad's '48 Panhead.

He examined his half-face helmet for unwanted critters, tapped on it and shook it a few times for good measure—never could be too sure—then placed it on his head and tightened the strap. As the adrenaline from his run slowly dissipated, goose bumps rose on his exposed skin as a cool breeze brushed past. He opened the door to his pickup, smiling when he found his red plaid Pendleton wadded up behind the seat. He shook it out, pulled it on forgoing the buttons, and climbed onto his bike.

The bike purred beneath him, rumbling low and steady as she warmed up. A peacefulness settled into his bones, his muscles relaxing, ready for the ride he so needed. No better way to clear his head than a ride. Or a good pull of whiskey. Or a woman.

Hell, it was a woman who got him here in the first place and it was too damn early for whiskey. It had been far too long since he'd taken his bike out for a ride. He released the brake and pulled out into The

Bar's dirt lot, then onto the main road, his flannel shirt flapping like a flag behind him as the sun slowly lit the sky.

With the wind on his face and the roar of the engine, he rode straight through town, passing the Dixie with a scowl, the hardware store, Randy's old house, the cemetery where two of the most important men he'd known lay resting, past the high school, the Tastee Freeze, and Syd's coffee shop—the only place with a sign of life at this ungodly hour. He rode right through town, aimlessly letting the road guide him, the wind take him...

Straight to Franklin Mill's place, long ago deserted by the Mill family and only recently rented out.

To Charlie fucking Morris.

He pulled to a stop beside that kid's dirt bike, his heart beating fast. He hadn't planned on coming here; at least, he didn't think so. Clearly, his subconscious had another agenda.

But what now?

Jake looked back in the direction he came, gauging the sun's ascent over the eastern mountains, guessing it was barely six o'clock. What a schmuck; he couldn't just stroll up and knock on the door at the butt crack of dawn.

He sighed, listening to the low rumble of his bike, and wishing TB would just walk outside, make this easier on him.

But, what the hell would he say to her?

Chapter Eighteen

The reverberating idle of a motorcycle stirred Tamryn from a light, restless sleep, drawing her swollen eyes open to the soft, grayish-purple glow of morning light. She rubbed her eyes, glancing at the clock on the DVR; who was making so much noise before even six A.M.?

She listened to the purr of the bike's engine. Had Charlie planned on going somewhere early this morning? She searched her sleep-addled brain, but couldn't remember him telling her anything like that.

She groaned, sitting up on the couch as Charlie's bedroom door opened and he stomped down the hallway.

Oh. Not Charlie then.

Tamryn's tired eyes widened and she sat up straighter. "Is someone stealing your bike?"

Charlie threw a glare over his shoulder. "That ain't my bike." His scowl registered in her mind just as the low, rhythmic rumble finally rang familiar bells.

All at once, her heart soared and her stomach slammed into the floor. She jumped up, dropping her blanket, bringing her fingertips to her lips. He'd come. Fighting a smile, Tamryn stepped around the coffee table, bumping her shin in her haste, then rushed to the door.

Charlie blocked her way, a frown pulling at his full lips, eyebrows drawn down over dark brown eyes. "Don't go out there. I'll handle him."

She sighed, shaking her head, then placed a hand on his arm. "Please let me by. I have to at least hear him out. I owe him that much."

"Why? What could you possibly owe him?" He threw a hand up. "What has he ever done for you?"

Tamryn smiled a sad smile. "More than you'll ever know, Charlie. I'm sorry; I know it's difficult since you've been gone for so long, but Jake...well, he's family." *So much more than family.*

Charlie scoffed. "Family? Is this what family does to each other? I'm pretty sure he sent you crying to my house in the middle of the night—twice, now, I might add—and now you're crashing on my couch. Or is it not the way it looks?"

His smirk made her blood boil. She nodded at the door. "Excuse me, please."

"Fine. Hear him out." Charlie raised his hands and stepped aside. "But I'll be right inside if he tries anything."

Tamryn took a deep breath, opening the door as the engine cut off. She stepped outside, eyes downcast, shut the door behind her, then swallowed and looked up.

Her heart stuttered in her chest.

Jake climbed off his bike, flannel shirt unbuttoned over a bare chest and low-slung sweatpants, dark hair standing up and falling in all different directions... disheveled had never been so sexy. She inhaled a shaky breath, then stepped to the edge of the porch.

He looked good enough to eat, and she'd be wise to hightail it right back inside.

Jake's gaze held hers hard and steady as he strode toward her, slowly, tentatively. She stepped down to the third step, but stopped. He could meet her in the middle.

"What are you doing here?" she asked, her voice almost too loud in the serenity of early country morning.

His ice-blue eyes stared straight to her core. "Come home."

Her breath faltered. "Jake..."

"You don't belong here, with him. You belong with me." His lip curled as he looked past her to the house. "Does soldier boy even know how to take care of you?"

She exhaled a long sigh. Until Jake realized she wasn't looking for someone to take care of her, they'd continue this back and forth, never truly getting anywhere but right back where they started. He'd always be the white knight and she'd always be the damsel he had to save, protect, whatever. A relationship—of any nature—wouldn't work for them if he couldn't see past the little girl she once was.

Tamryn blinked long and hard, drawing in a deep breath. "I don't need to be taken care of, Jake." Her voice cracked, tears threatening, their presence always so close, so near to breaking free these days, so at the ready.

Jake shook his head. "My words aren't coming out right, TB. That's not what I mean."

"Then tell me what you mean."

"Can I come up there?"

A floorboard creaked just inside the door.

"Probably not a good idea. I don't want you to wake the guys."

Jake's jaw hardened, but he gave a curt nod. "Come down here, then, please?"

She squared her shoulders, a war battling inside her. She sucked in a breath as her heart won over her head, and she stepped the rest of the way down the stairs, closing the distance between them too quickly to change her mind. Close enough to smell him now, she inhaled his familiar, earthy scent. Her stomach fluttered around in her torso like a rum-soaked butterfly. She opened eyes she didn't remember closing, meeting a stare she didn't remember missing quite this much.

"Hey," he whispered.

"Hey."

"I miss you."

She smiled. "I miss you too, Jake."

"Then it's a deal? You'll come home?" He smiled, his right cheek dimpling.

"I wish it was that easy, but I don't think you get it. Still, after all this time, you don't get it. I'm not a little kid anymore. I'm not just someone's little sister. I don't need you, or Reed, or anyone else for that matter"—she shot a quick glance back at the house where Charlie probably listened at the window—"looking out for me or taking care of me. I'm a grown woman now. I can take care of myself. I have dreams, and goals, and I want you to..." She paused, really considering her words, what she truly wanted from Jake. "I need you to *see* me, Jake."

"I do. I do see you, TB."

She didn't correct him, didn't remind him—again—that she didn't go by TB anymore, that TB had died with Colby, with her youth, her innocence. With that wild and carefree version of herself she'd had a brief glimpse of last night.

That was the *before* version of herself. Before she lost her brother and the world lost a bit of its luster.

116

"If you truly saw me, Jake, we wouldn't be here." She took a step back, the hardest step she'd ever made.

He matched her step, then followed with another so they were just inches apart.

She looked up into mournful blue eyes.

"I see you, God, do I see you." He reached for her chin, cupping it gently and running his thumb over her lip, pulling it gently from her teeth. He licked his lips, leaned down, and brushed them against hers, once, twice, so softly that she wondered if this was all a dream. Her heart pounded in her chest, cheeks burning and legs tingling, threatening to go out on her.

"Please come home to me, TB."

"That's not my home." The home where he'd tuck her back into her bed and close the door to bang someone else next door either tomorrow or next week. She clenched her eyes shut, willing the tickle of tears away, then stepped out of his grasp. "I'm not sure it ever really was. I'm sorry, Jake." She turned before opening her eyes, then ran back up the steps and into the house.

"Oh, but this is!" Jake shouted after her.

Charlie stood just inside the door, but she didn't stop, didn't allow him to console her and feed his hope any further. She refused to allow him the satisfaction of seeing her in tears once more over stupid Jake and her stupid feelings for him. She didn't need any *I told you so* right now. She passed him and didn't stop until she was safely inside the bathroom, door closed and locked behind her.

She plopped to the floor, slid her fingers into her hair, gripping roots, forehead on palms, and cried for Jake Johnson again.

Jake couldn't move. He wanted to, oh how he wanted to, but his feet remained firmly in the dirt. He wanted to run after her, but didn't. Wanted to call her name, but couldn't find his voice. Wanted to bang down the door, but couldn't remember how.

He'd finally done it, finally gone after her, and she'd shot him down. He shook his head, or, maybe it had been shaking all along, and tried to rectify what he'd hoped—expected—would happen with what *actually* happened.

"She doesn't love you," he whispered, so softly the breeze took the words away. He was a right fool. His chest burned. Constricted, throbbing…he recognized the feeling. He'd felt this raw, consuming ache before. First with Colby, then with Pop. He knew heartbreak all too well, it was the familiarity and torment of an ex-lover that wouldn't release him.

The door to the old Mills' place creaked open, and Jake's heart sprang to life again. He looked up, hope blossoming in his heart—

That Charlie punk stepped outside, arms crossed over his bare chest.

Jake's hope plummeted with each of Charlie's footfalls as he made his way to the driveway, stopping a few feet from Jake.

"She doesn't want to be with you, Johnson. Take a hint."

Jake shook his head. "That's none of your business."

Charlie stood taller, dropping his hands to his side. "No? Sure seems like my business."

Jake smirked. If it was a competition this kid wanted, Jake would give it to him, and judging by the flowering of purple and yellow on his cheek and the dark spot beneath his eye, Jake was already ahead in the game. He stood taller, towering over Charlie, and wider than him by a good two inches on either side, easy. He tilted his head and narrowed his eyes. "Look, kid, I get that you had a thing for TB back in high school, but that's in the past. Time to move on."

The kid glanced back at the house, then met Jake's gaze once more, a smile pulling at his smug mouth. "Sound advice. You should take it."

Jake squinted, then glanced past Charlie to the house. "I'm not giving up on that girl."

"*My* girl."

"What?" Jake's muscles went rigid; his fingers twitched, so he clenched his fists as he brought his gaze back to Charlie's. Was it possible to strangle a person with their own dog tags?

Jake wanted to find out.

"Why do you think she's staying here, bro, the good food?" He chuckled. "Nah. We're back together. I've been tryin' for a couple weeks now, but after last night, well"—Charlie grinned—"I guess I should thank you."

Jake deflated, his shoulders falling with his hope, his heart. He shook his head, but the kid's words made sense, and, one by one, each painful piece of the puzzle clicked into place. The way TB said goodbye to him right after Charlie reappeared in her life. The way she'd rushed straight over here when she moved out of Jake's house. The fact that even now, when Jake asked her to come home, she refused, running back into *Charlie's* house instead of into Jake's arms.

Arms that ached to hold her even still.

Jake's eyebrows drew down over his eyes as he met the kid's gaze once more. *I waited too long.*

Charlie smiled, then winked. "Have a good day, man. I'm gonna hop back into bed, if you know what I mean."

Jake leaned forward, but caught himself, clenching his jaw and his fists.

Charlie raised an eyebrow and chuckled, then turned and strode inside, his shoulders shaking at Jake's expense.

Jake's blood flowed hot, like lava burning through his veins. With twitching fingers and a shattered heart, he climbed back onto his bike and rode away from the girl he loved, once and for all.

He'd never been anyone's joke, and the thought of TB and Charlie laughing at what a fool he'd just made of himself cut like a motherfucker.

Tearing into The Bar, Jake went straight for the whiskey, but not just any bottle. He strode behind the two rows of shelves where he kept his bar stock, slipping into the tiny office he rarely used. Beside the desk on a small, wall-mounted shelf sat a picture of him and Colby, sitting on the back of Jake's pickup, tailgate down, feet up, fishing poles in hand. Jake's arm around Colby's shoulder, the two of them almost looked like brothers.

Hell, they'd *felt* like brothers.

Jake reached beside the picture for the bottle of Tam o'Shanter, gripping the neck and wiping the layer of dust off with the hem of his flannel shirt. A high school graduation gift from the old man, Jake had eventually tucked the bottle away, saving it to celebrate Colby's safe return from Afghanistan.

He smirked. "Well, that's not going to happen, is it, friend?" Heart in his throat, Jake opened the bottle, inhaled a deep, whiff, hints of oak and spice tickling his senses. His eyelids drooped as his mouth watered, then he raised the bottle to the photograph. "Cheers, brother. Here's to really muckin' things up."

He brought the bottle to his lips and took a long pull, the amber liquid burning his throat in the best possible way, heating his chest as it descended. He closed his eyes, allowing the flavor to consume him, chocolatey, spicy, hints of ginger on the finish...

After taking a moment to give the aged whisky blend the respect it deserved, he raised the bottle to the sky, nodded once to his Pop, then once more to nineteen-year-old Colby in the photo, then Jake chugged, desperately in search of oblivion.

Chapter Nineteen

Apathy cradled Tamryn like an old afghan, steeped in years of use and worn to perfect softness; she wrapped herself in the sweet oblivion of no longer caring. A week had passed since Jake's early morning visit, and Tamryn had barely pulled herself out of bed. She'd likely be fired from the Dixie, and Charlie could only cover for her at Old Faithful's for so long. Not that he wanted to. He'd probably quit helping her soon, a fact that should have pulled her from her funk, but only made her desire to curl up into a ball that much stronger.

She retrieved her cell phone and turned it on, the first time she'd done so in days. A series of beeps and notifications bombarded the silence, and she considered turning it right back off.

And then it rang.

A familiar, custom ringtone, his number stared up at her from the screen.

Her fingers twitched, her hand aching to grab the phone. She desperately wanted to hear his voice, but she wasn't ready to talk to him. As she stared at the screen, debating, the call ended, solving her dilemma for her. She set it on her bedside table, then, with a sigh, she plopped back onto the pillow. Maybe she'd call him later to check in.

The familiar song filled the silence again.

She glanced at the cellphone. What if something had happened to Reed or Randy? She couldn't very well ignore Jake's calls forever, could she?

The sickening clench in her stomach answered the question for her and Tamryn plucked the cellular from the nightstand. She pressed the green button, brought her phone to her ear, and shook her head; she probably could have held off a little longer. "Jake. Why are you calling me?"

"I know you don't want to talk to me, but, well…"

Silence as she held her breath, ticking down the seconds of his hesitation.

"Thanksgiving is this week, see, and…well…"

Her heart swelled in her chest, even as she knew she had to decline. For her own sanity. "I can't, Jake. I'm…" she searched the small room for an excuse, a lightbulb idea, but nothing came to mind. "I'm…busy." Lies. She rolled her eyes; she'd have to do better than that.

"You have to come, TB." Jake's voice came through the phone strained, muffled by the hand he likely ran over his beard stubble. "You know it won't be Thanksgiving without you."

Tamryn closed her eyes and inhaled a deep breath through her nose. The holidays hadn't been the same these last couple years since Colby died, and frankly, the thought of spending them without even Jake loomed over her like a threatening storm cloud.

Tamryn shook her head as her mouth opened to utter the words she knew she'd instantly regret: "I'll be there." Against her better judgment, she'd spend Thanksgiving with the man she loved.

"Really?" Jake's voice clearer now and an octave higher than it had been, he cleared his throat and tried again. "I mean, great, cool, yeah, so…will you bring the usual?"

Tamryn smiled, shaking her head again. That excitement in his voice… What had she just agreed to?

Little sis coming home for the holidays, that's what. Nothing more.

"Yes, Jake, I'll bring my pull-apart bread."

"And the pies?"

"Without question."

"Okay, cool. It's a date. I mean, you know, I'll see you Thursday."

"Bye, Jake."

"Wait—"

She pulled the phone back to her ear and held her breath.

"Do you need a ride? I mean, I can come get you…"

She closed her eyes as she considered. On the one hand, she missed Jake so much she was tempted to say yes to anything he asked.

But on the other hand, having her own vehicle might be a good idea in case she needed to escape Jake's orbit with lightning speed. Charlie would let her borrow the truck, she was sure of it. "No, I think I can manage. But thank you for offering."

"Okay, kiddo. See you Thursday."

"Bye, Jake." As she pressed 'end' on the phone, her stomach battled between excited flutter and nauseated doom. Kiddo. Again. Could she really throw on a plastic smile and spend Thanksgiving with the one person she wanted more than anything on earth but couldn't have? "Well, you're going to have to now, stupid."

"Talking to yourself again?" Charlie chuckled as he filled the doorway.

Tamryn looked up, sliding her phone back onto the nightstand, guilt weaseling its way into her chest. "Hey, Charlie." She stood, turning to fold the blanket she'd been curled up with. "Yeah, I guess I was."

"Crazy people talk to themselves, you know it?" He grinned.

"Like attracts like, Charlie Morris." Tamryn winked, then stepped past him toward the hallway. "You need your room?"

"Yeah, just wanted to grab some clothes out of the closet. You don't have to leave or nothin'."

"It's okay. I should get some fresh air. I haven't been outside for…" She waved her hand in the air. "Days, I guess. Where you off to?"

"Me? Oh, just heading out to pick up Roc and Steve. We'll go shoot some skeet, then probably wind up at the bar. You workin' tonight?" He eyed her warily, probably expecting the same response he'd been getting—and passing along to her bosses—all week.

Tamryn took a deep breath, then smiled. "Yeah, I think I am." She paused at the door to her temporary bedroom. "Hey, thanks for everything this week, for covering for me and all."

"Sure thing." He glanced around nervously. "So, Tam, uh, before you go…"

She poked her head back into the room, her stomach knotting ever so slightly. "What's up?"

Charlie ran a hand through his messy brown hair. "Well, Thanksgiving is next week, you know, and I'm heading over to Pop and Suzanne's house with Roc. Probably stay for the four day weekend, maybe do a little muddin' while we're out there. You used to love muddin'"—he stopped rubbing his head and met her gaze, head slightly bowed—"I don't know…you wouldn't want to come along, would you?"

Tamryn inhaled a deep breath and smiled tight-lipped. "I'm sorry, Charlie, but I've made other plans. Thank you for the invite, though."

Charlie's shoulders straightened as his eyes narrowed. "With him?"

Tamryn shook her head gently, then nodded; better to just be honest. "Yes, Charlie. I'll be okay."

"I don't know why you still bother. He doesn't care about you." The slight snarl in his words forced Tamryn to turn around.

"Thanks, Charlie. That felt swell. Not that it's any of your business, but he obviously does care about me, since he called to make sure I'm coming home for Thanksgiving."

Charlie's eyebrows shot up. "Home?"

Tamryn shook her head. "You know what I mean."

"Yeah," Charlie scoffed. "I think I do. Enjoy your *Thanksgiving*."

Chapter Twenty

Four days of the silent treatment from Charlie was all Tamryn could take; it was time to find a place of her own. She'd left Jake, only to fall back into the same routine, once again allowing a man to think he had any damn say in her life.

Well, no more of that. After the holiday weekend, the house hunt would begin.

But first, gluttony.

She held the phone in her hands, her finger hovering over the *send* button. "Heaven help me, it's just a phone call!" She pressed send, then plopped onto the bed, eyes squeezed shut like that would save her from this phone call and this man and this entire day she was about to spend with him.

Jake answered after one ring, his voice breathless. "TB, what's up?"

"Hey, Jake, Happy Thanksgiving."

"Hey, yeah, you too. You're still coming, right?"

Tamryn smiled as she answered. "Yes, Jake. I just… any chance that offer still stands?"

"Yeah," Jake answered too quickly. "I'll give you a ride."

Tamryn tilted her head. Was that excitement in his voice? Her brain took her to a place where the meaning of *ride* meant something entirely different and heat rushed to her cheeks. Thank God Jake was on the phone and not standing in front of her.

He cleared his throat. "You still there, TB?"

She shook her head, waving her hand to push her dirty thoughts away. "Yes, I'm here. So, thanks. For the ride, I mean."

"No problem. I'll be there in, say..." He paused as he considered, and she glanced at the clock. "Thirty minutes?"

"Okay, sounds good. See you then."

"See you then."

She pressed *end* on the phone and flopped back onto the bed. "Lord, give me strength."

After she found herself a new place to live, she'd need to buy a car. Anything would do at this point; freedom was the only acceptable outcome. Relying on everyone else in her life was no longer an option.

Thirty minutes left her with no time to shower and get ready, so she'd have to do that at Jake's. Had he left any of her toiletries in her old bathroom? She rose from the bed—no time to waste—and gathered a long-sleeved maxi dress and a sweater in case there was a chill in the air tonight, then headed to the bathroom to grab the essentials in case Jake had cleaned out her bathroom in her absence. It was foolish to think he'd left remnants of her around his house.

She threw her toiletries into a cosmetic bag, then headed for the kitchen as the timer beeped; time to pack up the bread and get the pies finished up so they were ready to stick in the oven as soon as she got to Jake's.

Twenty minutes later, with her heart in her throat and her gut at her feet, Tamryn walked to the mailbox at the edge of the property. Jake would be there any minute and doubt gnawed at her mind with every passing second. Had she made a huge mistake in accepting his invitation?

Her phone buzzed in her purse and she jumped, so preoccupied that even the slightest sound had set her heart to racing. She pulled the cell out of her purse, grinning when a familiar New York area code appeared on the screen.

"Louise!" she squealed.

"Thelma!" Luce replied. "I'm coming home!"

Tamryn's grin widened, her best friend's words warming her from head to toe. "It's a Thanksgiving miracle!"

"It is!" Luce chuckled. "I'm at the airport now."

"La Guardia?"

"No, silly, *our* airport." She paused, letting her words sink in. "Surprise!"

Tamryn jumped up and down, nearly knocking over the insulated cooler with the pies. "When? Where? I mean, where are you spending Thanksgiving?"

"With you and your entourage of hot old men, duh. New York boys just aren't the same, Tam; it's a goddamn shame, let me tell you."

Bouncing on her toes, Tamryn watched for Jake, so excited to tell someone else that Luce was on her way. "I'm so excited, Luce. I've missed your face so much." Tamryn searched the horizon. "God, I have so much to tell you."

"Uh oh. What's wrong?"

Tamryn closed her eyes and blew out a raspberry of air. "So much. Too much to even get into right now. I'll tell you when you get here."

"Yeah, you will. Over too many of Reed's famous Thanksgiving cocktails, preferably."

"Deal."

"Is it Jake?"

Tamryn sighed. "Yes, it's…everything is so messed up." She paused as a motorcycle roared down the highway, closer and closer to the old Mills place. He wouldn't bring the motorcycle, would he? Tamryn's pulse sped. She'd been begging him to ride that thing for years. Would he really choose a day when she had so much to carry to finally grant her wish?

Her eyes widened as she considered climbing on behind him and being so close to him when she really should be staying far the hell away from him. She could swear she smelled the fresh scent of his skin, and he wasn't even within a mile of her yet. "Oh, God, Luce. I'm so screwed." She placed her hand on her forehead. She'd ditch the pies and the bread if it meant riding behind Jake.

This was bad, so bad. Dangerous, even. "I have to go. He's almost here."

"Wait, what? Who? Jake?" Luce moved the phone around, muffling her words when she called a taxi. "Damn you, Thelma, you tell me what's going on right now! Don't make me wait!"

The roar of the bike drew closer, and Jake turned the corner, rumbling down the old dirt road. A red bandana was tied around his face, and as he approached, he reached up to untie it.

"Tamryn!"

She shook her head, pressing the phone closer to her ear. "Sorry, Luce, I was"—she swallowed the hard lump in her throat—"distracted."

"No shit?" Luce barked a laugh. "I can't wait to hear this story."

"I'll see you at Jake's."

"Wait! Is he on his bike?" Luce screeched as Tamryn pressed *end*.

She stood there, struck dumb as Jake stopped his bike beside her. His white t-shirt was tight around his tanned arms, and his smile set her heart on fire.

Tamryn was so royally screwed.

"Hey," he said.

"Hey." The single word was breathless, giving too easily away the effect he had on her. Had he gotten even sexier since she'd seen him last? Was that possible?

He licked his lips and dropped his gaze to her mouth, sending heat rushing to Tamryn's core. It took all of her might, but she looked at her cooler and the bag of various other necessities at her feet. "Where will this fit?" She didn't look back up at him, for fear of melting into a puddle of lust at his feet.

"I've got that covered, kid." He stepped off the bike, standing too close to Tamryn. "Why won't you look at me?"

She dared a breath through her nose, craving the familiar scent of him, then looked up into too blue eyes. "I'm looking at you," she said, her voice thick.

"I'm looking at you, too."

Her chest rose and fell faster with each nervous breath, but she held his gaze, growing all too aware of how much she missed him and how badly she wanted him. He slowly assessed her, and warmth spread in her chest, down into her gut, then lower as his gaze trailed over her skin. He shook his head, then looked into her eyes again, and her breath caught in her throat.

Jake's lips twitched on a smirk. "I love when you bake."

She smiled. "I'm aware."

"No, little Baker, I love your food—that's a given—but I really love when you make it."

She raised an eyebrow, waiting for him to expand on that statement.

"It's the sexiest fucking thing to watch," he said, stepping closer. He raised his hand to her face. "When you let loose and think no one is watching, and you take over the kitchen…" He closed his eyes on a long blink, then opened them again, nearly knocking her over from the heat of his stare. "I can picture it now. The way your body stretches when you reach for the flour. The way you dance around the room…"

Tamryn swallowed hard, her breath becoming thicker as the lust in his words made her heart threaten to stop beating. Had he watched her cooking when she thought he was distracted with other things? How many times?

"You're completely free when you bake, and it's the sexiest fucking thing I've ever seen."

Her lips fell open on a soft gasp, his words rocking her to her core.

He glanced behind her, then met her gaze once more. "Is anyone home?"

She shook her head, pulling her bottom lip into her teeth.

Jake ran his thumb across her mouth, releasing her lip. "Let's go inside."

She nodded, her mouth open, and her breath speeding up with her pulse. She'd say yes to anything he asked right now.

Chapter Twenty-One

Jake's dick twitched, his pants tightening against his erection. He knew seeing TB would be different this time, knew he'd feel more strongly toward her than before, now that he realized he needed her so badly, but he had no idea just how raw his desire to fuck her would be.

It consumed him.

"I don't think we should…"

He slid his hand up behind her neck and her words trailed off. "You don't think we should what?" He ran his thumb back and forth over her earlobe and glanced toward the house once more, then back at her soft mouth, then down at her chest as it rose and fell quickly with each brush of his finger on his ear. He didn't know which part of her he wanted to nibble first. Maybe he'd start with her earlobe, pulling it into his mouth, then move on to those perfect lips—he'd like to suck that plump bottom lip until it was swollen and red, branded by his mouth—then work his way down to those pert little tits.

"I don't think we should go inside," she whispered.

Jake's thoughts screeched to a halt. Wait, what? She wanted him to take her right here? Outside? He looked around, the idea of fucking TB out in the open like this making his dick press painfully against the zipper of his pants.

She cleared her throat and he closed his eyes, blinking long and hard to clear his brain. *No, dipshit;* of course that wasn't what she was saying.

The car grew closer and Jake opened his eyes as realization replaced the lust in TB's gaze.

Jake's jaw tightened. "Don't even tell me it's that punk ex-boyfriend of yours."

She swallowed and nodded.

Jake released her, then stepped back to watch as Charlie pulled his truck up beside them.

He glanced between TB and Jake, then lower, to Jake's obvious erection. Charlie's face hardened. "Hope I'm not interrupting anything," he snarled.

Jake raised an eyebrow. "You are." He winked; challenging this kid was too damn easy.

Tamryn stepped forward and rose on her tiptoes to lean into the passenger side window. "Hey, Charlie, did you forget something?"

"Yeah, I just…I felt bad about how we left things, and, well, it's Thanksgiving, and I didn't want you mad at me."

Jake's focus dropped to TB's ass, heart-shaped and perfectly displayed through the thin fabric of her dress. He reached down and adjusted his cock, too tight in his jeans. *Shoulda worn sweats.*

"Seems like you're doing just fine, though." Charlie cleared his throat.

Jake raised his gaze, then lifted an eyebrow and grinned.

The kid's eyes narrowed into thin slits, then he waved toward TB and Jake. "Have a great fucking day, Tammy." He started to drive away and TB stumbled backward.

Jake caught her before she fell, his blood heating to fire in his veins. "I'm gonna kill that fucking kid." His muscles tensed, he watched Charlie pull up to the side of the barn. If he sprinted now, he could catch the kid's jaw as he stepped out of the truck.

Tamryn turned around to face him, still in his arms, her body pressed along the length of his. With the warmth between them, Jake's anger slowly faded back into the lust that coursed through his veins. "Don't worry about him, Jake. He's just mad. I deserve it."

Jake searched her gaze. "What? I don't want to hear you talk like that. He almost ran you over—"

"It's fine, Jake, really. Please let it go." She pushed out of his arms, then straightened her dress and apron, shaking her head. "I'm still wearing my apron." She reached behind her to untie it—

Jake grabbed her hand. "Leave it."

She raised her eyes to meet his, her lips quirked on one side. "What?"

"I said leave it." *I'm going to fuck you in nothing but that apron.* He didn't say the words out loud, but she must have felt the promise in his gaze; a flush of red spread across her tits. Jake grinned triumphantly. "Ready to go?"

She nodded, pulling her lips between her teeth and taking a deep breath, then reached for the stuff at her feet. Jake turned back to the bike, adjusted his cock one more time—*down, boy*—then began strapping the cooler to the bike.

The door to the house slammed, echoing through the open front of the property as that Charlie kid stormed inside, all butt hurt about TB. *Serves him right.* Where had he been when TB was going through so much after Colby? Not here. Not taking care of things—

"Where am I going to sit?"

Jake smiled as he turned around to face her. "You mean to tell me after all these years of nagging me for a ride on this thing, you never considered where you'd sit?" He imagined her straddling him and his dick swelled.

She shook her head, scanning the motorcycle.

Jake opened his backpack and pulled out a small square of a seat with suction cups attached to one side, and placed it behind his seat on the back fender, pressing down good and firm so it wouldn't budge when he drove her across town. "See? Gotcha covered, kiddo."

Tamryn's mouth fell open. "Seriously? I can't fit on that."

Jake leaned forward, making a show out of looking at her ass, then straightened and smiled. "I think you'll manage. It's not too far of a drive."

"What else do you have in that backpack, Jake, your truck? So I can actually fit somewhere?" She laughed, reaching for his backpack.

He pulled it away from her and reached for her arm instead, catching her by surprise. "Hop on, little Baker. Let's go home."

She met his gaze, her lips pulled into a frown. "That's not my home, Jake."

His jaw tightened. "I know. Sorry." He pushed the rush of disappointment away. He'd change her mind today, make sure she could see that his home was her home. He handed her the backpack, hoping to quickly change the subject. He already missed the lust in her gaze. "Put whatever else you need to bring in here. You'll have to wear it, though, since there won't be room between us for me to wear it."

Tamryn swallowed, the movement drawing Jake's gaze to her slender throat. He loved the way he could elicit visible reactions from her with just the simplest of words. She slid her arms through the straps and settled the backpack onto her back, then he helped her onto the bike. Strapping his extra helmet to her head, he focused on her mouth. So full, so delicate...how had he never noticed her mouth before? She ran her tongue across her bottom lip and Jake shook his head, a low groan making its way up his throat.

He held her gaze, long and hard, until her breathing picked up, then smiled and straddled the bike. He settled into the seat, the cooler strapped in between his legs, and TB's body so far back he couldn't even feel her. He frowned. "You'll have to get a little closer than that, TB."

She wiggled forward, still hesitant.

"Wrap your arms around me."

She did as she was told, lightly placing her arms around his torso.

"Tighter than that."

She tightened her grip, but still held back.

Jake smirked. *We'll see about that.* He started the Panhead, the familiar vibrations rumbling beneath him. After he strapped his helmet on, he steadied the bike with his feet planted firmly on the ground, then reached back and slid a hand beneath each of TB's thighs. She stiffened in response to his touch and he chuckled softly to himself, then gave a quick yank, pulling her closer to his body until she straddled him, her thighs pressed tightly around him. He couldn't be sure, but was that a whimper he heard escape from her lips?

With a wild grin on his face, one hand on TB's thigh, and a painful tightness in his groin, he pulled away from the old Mills' farm.

Chapter Twenty-Two

Tamryn's heart thundered loudly in her ears, almost eclipsing the roar of the bike.

Heat burned at her center, and she fought against the urge to press more firmly against Jake, or the seat, or anything that would offer her some relief. Her body buzzed with anticipation, lit from within, aching for the promise of what he was going to do to her when they reached his house. The need in his gaze had been undeniable, and Tamryn's body reacted to every look, every touch with a raging fire that consumed every inch of her small frame.

She needed Jake in every possible way, but today, right now, she needed him inside her. Only then would the ache in her core be quenched. Her mouth watered at the thought and she adjusted herself so she more fully straddled the bike, trying to alleviate—or intensify?—the need burning between her legs.

He squeezed her thigh, then reached back further until his fingers were almost to her ass, and she nestled closer to him. Her core throbbed, desire pulsing through her veins.

The deep rumble of the bike did nothing to cool her need for Jake, and the way his hand rubbed her thigh, squeezing her and massaging her flesh beneath her sundress, Tamryn was damn sure she'd never even make it to his house without combusting first. Maybe she could tell him to pull off somewhere, go find a dirt road and disappear together. Maybe she could straddle him while he raced down the highway, then fuck him right here on this bike for all to see.

A laugh escaped her lips as embarrassment flushed her cheeks. She'd never had thoughts that were quite so...vivid.

And delightful.

Jake pressed on the gas, and the sensation rocked her backward, so she tightened her arms around his waist. She pressed her chest against him, wishing their clothes were gone, so she could feel the soft skin of his back against her nipples. Her hands dipped down a little at the thought. He moaned, and she felt the vibration of sound against her chest, her nipples tightening in response.

"Fuck." Jake tilted his head back slightly as he sucked in a deep breath and his shoulders rose with the movement. "What are you doing to me?" he yelled over the roar of the bike and the rush of the wind. He released her thigh, reaching into his lap to adjust himself.

Something about the wind and the rumble of the motorcycle between her legs filled Tamryn with a feeling of freedom. She didn't care that the wind made her sundress flap on either side of her where it wasn't tucked beneath her ass, half of her cheeks probably exposed to anyone they passed. She didn't care that the two of them probably looked like a couple of dogs in heat. Her body vibrated with courage and desire, igniting her skin, her heart beating had in her chest. She'd never felt more alive. Caution to the wind, she held her breath and released her firm grip on her own hands, letting one drop to Jake's hand on his cock.

He wasted no time, sliding his hand over hers and pressing her palm firmly against his massive erection. He slid his hand back behind him and gripped her bare thigh as he moved against her hand.

She kneaded him through his jeans, reveling in the rock hard cock she wanted inside her as quickly as possible. She whimpered as heat flooded her center, wiggling up closer, trying to eliminate every centimeter of space between them.

With a grunt, Jake pulled the bike to the side of the road, kicking the stand down in one quick motion as he twisted his torso around to claim her mouth with his. She sucked in a breath as his tongue dove deep into her mouth, shooting electricity clear down into her toes. She moaned, the sensations almost too fucking good to handle as he massaged her tongue with his. He gripped her neck with one hand, then reached between them and cupped between her legs, massaging her center. She arched, pressing against his hand, the desire to dry fuck his palm nearly knocking her off the bike.

Panting, he pulled back, his lids heavy over his bright gaze. He stilled the motion of his hand against her panties. "Either you need to show some restraint, Tamryn Baker, or I'm going to fuck you silly right here on the side of the road."

The threat stole her breath and sent a shudder through her body all at once.

His eyes flicked back and forth between hers, and a languid smile pulled at his lips. "Right here it is, then—"

The deafening blare of a horn broke the moment, and she looked up as a minivan drove past them. *Oh my god.* She swallowed hard, eyes wide. *There could be kids in there!* She looked back at Jake.

His lips twitched as he fought a smile.

Tamryn shook her head. "You're trouble."

He shrugged. "Can't help it. You bring out the best in me." He moved his palm between Tamryn's legs and she gasped, thrown back into the strong desire to let Jake have her right here on the side of the highway. He held her gaze as he moved his hand, slowly, deliberately, testing her. His eyes begged the question, *'How far will you let me go?'*

Tamryn considered, swallowing hard as he drew more heat to her center with each slight movement of his hand.

"Let's go," she whispered, the words heavy in her mouth.

"Right here?" he asked, his smile devilish.

Tamryn rolled her eyes and pulled her dress down. "No, not right here."

Jake growled, dropping his gaze her lap. He shook his head. "It's a damn shame." He removed his hand, then met her gaze. "Behave."

Tamryn grinned, licking her lips. "Only until we get there."

Lust flashed in his eyes, and he gave a curt nod. "Deal." He turned back around and settled onto the bike again. She settled behind him and wrapped her arms higher up on his chest, then closed her eyes and prayed they'd be back at his place when she opened them again.

She waited to open them until he stopped the bike and cut the engine. Jake jumped off the bike and scooped her up into his arms, pressing his face into the crook of her neck and breathing deeply. He opened his mouth and sucked gently against her collar bone, then moved his way up to her ear, pulling her earlobe into his mouth as he stepped inside the house.

With one quick movement, he kicked the door closed behind them and lowered her feet to the ground.

Unable to keep from touching him any longer, Tamryn slid her hands beneath his shirt, dragging her fingertips across the ridges of his abs, then tugged his shirt up and over his head. She ran her hands over his shoulders, up into his hair, down his back, touching and feeling her way all over his chest, back, and shoulders, reveling in the softness of his skin, the taut muscles beneath that clenched and trembled against her palms.

Desire wound spindly fingers up into her chest, down lower into her groin, gripping relentlessly, pushing her toward what she knew was about to happen, what shouldn't—*couldn't*—happen, plummeting her toward him, toward passion, toward love, toward fire.

The fire that would surely burn her to a crisp.

Should she let it?

She shook her head. "We can't do this." Even as she muttered the words, she knew they were false. They could, and they absolutely would.

Jake's breaths came in and out in quick succession; his gaze dropped to her lips, pupils constricting as he focused on her mouth. He licked his bottom lip, slowly, torturously, and all she could think of was where he might put that tongue later. He tugged her harder against him, pressing his hips into hers and freeing a whimper from her mouth as his erection pressed hard against her center. "I disagree." He silenced any retort with a crushing kiss, and Tamryn's eyes slammed closed as he plunged his tongue into her mouth, the heated result of which flowed like fire through her veins.

There'd be nothing left of her after this was over, no way she'd recover, no way anyone would ever compare to Jake.

Desperate to be even closer to him, Tamryn slid her arms around his neck, then hauled herself up, circling his waist with her legs as she opened her mouth wider to welcome him. Resolve disappeared amid the stroke of his tongue and the warmth of his body against hers, his hands on her ass, his dick pressed between her legs.

The word *no* lost all meaning.

All she could think was *yes*.

Chapter Twenty-Three

Jake took a few steps toward the wall, then pushed TB up against it, his cock pressing almost painfully into the thin strip of lace between her legs. He'd nearly torn through that scrap of underwear back on the bike, and he had a strong desire to rip it off with his teeth now that they were back at the house. He slid his hands beneath her skirt, gripping the bare cheeks of her ass and groaned as he pressed harder against her. "Fucking hell, TB."

Leaning forward and bracing her against the wall with his torso, one hand still holding her ass, he moved his free hand between them to slide the thin fabric aside. Gripping her ass where it connected to her thighs, he braced himself, then kneeled before her, positioning his face just mere inches away from her exposed center.

"Jake," she said on a gasp.

He didn't wait for anything else, for any yes or no that might slip from her mouth. TB had a tendency to overthink things, and this wasn't something he'd allow her to talk herself out of. He needed her right now, more than he'd ever needed a woman, and the way she whispered his name, he knew she needed him just as badly.

He leaned forward and spread her lips with his tongue, pulling her thighs apart to open further around his head. Her hands flew into his hair, curling around the strands as he lapped at her wetness.

"Jake..." She moaned, then gasped. "Oh...God...don't...don't drop me," she panted.

"Never," he spoke against her skin.

Her legs tensed and relaxed on his shoulders, squeezing and releasing his head as he plunged his tongue inside her, suckling her clit and drinking her in like the life force she was. Inhaling the perfectly sweet scent of her, he moaned against her lips and she clenched her thighs around his head.

A few more strong licks and her thighs began to twitch, so he tilted his head back and looked up at her.

"Jake," she whined.

"What's wrong? Should I stop?"

She rolled her eyes back into place and looked down at him, lids heavy with want. She swallowed audibly; her ass flexed against his hands as she fought to keep her orgasm at bay as it surged toward her. "Yes."

Jake raised his eyebrows. "Yes? Stop?"

"Yes." She smiled a slow, fluid grin. "I want you inside me."

Jake's body burned with desire, TB's words setting his nerves into overdrive. "Soon."

He drove his tongue inside her, plunging deeply until she bucked against his face and her legs shook around his head. Wetness flooded his mouth, and he suckled her, his dick swelling with jealousy.

"Jake, oh my god..."

He settled her panties back over her center, then gently slid her down to the floor, careful not to hurt her in his haste to bury himself balls deep within her walls. Sitting back on his heels, he looked up at her.

"Undress for me."

Her chest heaved with each breath. She started to slide the apron off, but he shook his head. TB's eyes widened, then she nodded, and worked around the apron. She dropped her sundress to her ankles.

As she slowly stepped out of her panties, Jake stepped out of his jeans. Her gaze, smoldering, fell to his erection. She licked her lips absently and his dick rose in response. He sat on the chair in the entryway, then reached for her. "Come here," he whispered. Anticipation filled his veins with electricity, his body humming with the carnal need for her burning inside him.

She met his gaze and pushed off the wall, shakily at first, then more purposely as she regained some strength in her legs. She stood boldly before him, bringing that perfect pussy back to near mouth level. He lifted the apron and his mouth watered. A growl rumbled low in his throat. He focused on the wetness still glistening on her soft mound, battling between the need to taste her again and the desire to feel her slide down around him.

The latter won. With a groan, he pulled her to him, nipping at her belly, then wrapped one arm around her waist to lock her in place. He looked up into those beautiful gunmetal blue eyes. "Sit," he said, the sound a near growl in his throat.

She obeyed, wrapping her arms around his neck, then straddling him until the tip of his dick rested against the softness of her center. He pressed into her gently and she gasped, bringing her gaze to his. He leaned forward and kissed her, pressing his tongue into her mouth so she could experience how unbelievably good she tasted. His dick twitched again, anxious to dive deep into the promise of her perfect form.

She bit his lip, pulling it gently into her mouth. The sucking noise she made sent him right over the edge, and he pressed up and into her with one firm stroke, careful not to go too far too fast. She'd need a second to adjust, that much he knew.

She rocked her hips, easing down more fully onto him. She grimaced with the pain, and Jake froze, watching her face for any further signs he should stop. Maybe he was too much for her. She pressed further onto him, her eyes rolling back into her head. A smiled curled her lips and she tilted her head back, arching her body against him to fully take his length and size within her. Raw, animal sounds purred in her throat as she rocked and moved against him, her body the perfect size, tightly gripping him and dripping wetness all over the tops of his thighs as her body prepared her for more. More rocking, more thrusting, more of him.

Her movements grew faster, small breasts bouncing as she took control, guiding herself toward orgasm, her clit rubbing deliciously at the base of his dick.

He pounded deeper, harder, then tugged the apron down and closed his mouth over her breast as they rocked wildly together. He sucked as he thrust, teasing her nipple with his teeth, moaning against the soft flesh—

She froze.

Jake pulled back, searching her face for signs of pain. "What's wrong?"

She tilted her head forward to look at him, her eyes afire, lips parted on heavy breaths. "I'm going to come again."

Jake grinned. "Good."

"You didn't put on a condom."

"I know. I'm sorry. I just…I didn't think." All he could think about was being inside her.

Something dark flashed across TB's eyes, too fast for Jake to pinpoint. He squinted, but she leaned forward, tightening her arms around his neck as she brought her mouth to his once more and pressed down onto his dick.

End of conversation.

Words flew from his mind as he pushed deeper into her, harder, faster, throbbing as he thrust, gripping her small frame as she gripped him between her legs. She clawed at his hair, his shoulders, then tightened her fingers into his skin as she shook around him, clenching his cock with vicious strength as she came. He sucked one nipple hard into his mouth, teasing the tip with his tongue and teeth, then splayed his hands across her back to hold her to him, allowing her to milk every last ounce of her orgasm before he dared move even an inch.

Melting around him, her body relaxed as the final pulses of orgasm quaked through her.

Jake stood, holding her legs tightly around his waist as he walked to the wall and pressed her against it. With the added support of the wall, he thrust into her hard, rocking her head back with the motion as he held her hips, positioning her tightly to him as he flooded her with his release.

He pressed one hand against the wall as his body shook, pulsing and throbbing as every last drop left him. Weakened, he leaned his head against the wall, his mouth positioned in the crook of her neck as he caught his breath. He kissed her bare shoulder, then licked his lips, the salty tang of her sweat sending his heart pounding.

She tasted too damn good. He opened his mouth again to caress her shoulder with his lips and tongue, wanting to taste more of that salty sweetness, when his eyes focused on the tiny arrangement of freckles that shaped an abstract heart on her shoulder.

He froze.

Colby used to tease her about wearing her heart on her sleeve.

Colby. Her older brother.

Colby. His best friend.

What the fuck was he doing? He drew in a deep breath. Jake had sworn to take care of TB. How was *fucking her against the wall* supposed to keep her safe, protect her, look after her?

And he hadn't even put on a damn condom. What if he'd knocked her up?

Holy fucking hell, Jake was a world-class piece of shit.

Seconds, maybe moments passed by while Jake's mind spun, until his thighs burned enough to shake him from his thoughts.

He stood straighter, gently releasing TB's legs from his waist and helping her stand.

God, she was beautiful.

But off limits. So damn off limits that agony tore through his chest.

Jake grabbed his jeans and his t-shirt, staring at the ground by her feet as he quickly dressed, realization setting in like ice across his heart. Reed was right; Jake loved this girl. He'd loved her long before she'd walked out of his life, long before Colby's tour of duty, long before...

"Ah, hell." Jake bent to grab TB's dress. He'd loved her as long as he could remember, but none of that mattered. He'd promised Colby to look after her, not fuck her silly, and fucking her would lead to one sure thing: a broken heart. Hers or his or both, he wasn't sure, but someone would break if he let this go any further than what they'd just done. He'd fucked up, but he didn't have to fuck *her* up. He'd never had a real relationship in his life, and TB didn't deserve to be the Guinea pig in that experiment. He'd lose her and betray Colby in one swift motion, and that couldn't happen.

Holding her dress out to her, gaze still on the floor, he said, "You should get dressed. The guys will be here any minute."

"Jake?" Her voice wavered on the single syllable and his heart cracked clear down the middle. She knew. "Don't do this."

"I have to hit the shower." He walked away, avoiding her gaze, his chest squeezing the life out of his heart. He couldn't make this mistake again, couldn't betray Colby. He clenched his fists against the pain, tightened his jaw against the finality of it all.

TB wasn't his to claim, wasn't his to love. She was his to protect, and that was all.

Chapter Twenty-Four

Ice. It's what Tamryn saw in his eyes, what splashed through her veins, coursing streams throughout her heated, sated body, freezing her from the inside out, morphing the lava that flowed through her veins just moments ago into jagged shards of glass.

At the epicenter, her heart, a broken, shattered mess of rejection.

From burning hot to freezing cold, he'd flipped the switch as soon as he came, as if they hadn't just shared the best sex of their lives.

Stupid girl. This obviously wasn't the best sex of *his* life.

She gripped her dress to her stomach and watched as Jake disappeared into his room, shutting the door behind him without so much as a glance over his shoulder after just being inside her.

Tamryn's chest bloomed with ache, her knees weakening from the agony, but she stood taller, rose to her full height as regret slammed a vise around her destroyed heart.

She shook her head; shock kept the tears from falling.

He'd fucked her and left her. She was no better than some chick he'd picked up at The Bar. A quick lay he'd never have to deal with again.

A good old fashioned Jake Johnson fuck 'n chuck.

Her sharp bark of a laugh broke the silence, but Tamryn slammed her mouth shut and grabbed her bag from the entryway. She headed for her old bathroom and slammed the door as hard as she could.

Childish? Maybe. But she couldn't think of anything else to do or say, and he needed to know she was good and pissed.

She opened the door again, then slammed it shut a second time. A crack split the wood down one side of the door and Tamryn grinned triumphantly.

She turned on the shower faucet and stepped inside, gasping as the water cascaded onto her skin, freezing cold and still warmer than she felt, frozen to the core by the man she loved and now loathed.

Showered and dressed, jaw clenched tight, Tamryn placed the pies into the oven and arranged the pull-apart bread onto a platter, pausing to consider…Could she sabotage Jake's portion of bread, but not the others?

Working quickly around a kitchen she knew better than she knew its asshole owner, she eyed the clock, watching her time so she could slip out before anyone arrived. She prayed she'd catch Luce before leaving, but if not, she'd call her on her way back to Charlie's. The two of them sit beside the pond and drink their Thanksgiving dinner.

The front door pushed open and Tamryn froze. *Shit. Please be Luce.*

"Yo, anyone home? It's eatin' time! Soo wee!" Randy's voice preceded him, his boisterous laughter echoing through the old house.

Tamryn threw the plastic wrap away, mind spinning for a way to get out of this.

"Hey, good lookin'!" Randy entered the kitchen, buttoned-up dress shirt untucked on one side and a thirty-pack of beer in hand, one bottle already open and at his lips.

"Hey, Randy. Happy Thanksgiving." Tamryn smiled, and hoped he wouldn't notice it was forced.

He raised his beer in the air. "To you as well, Miss Baker. Glad to see your face around these parts again." He surveyed the kitchen, then inhaled deeply, a smile curving his lips as he brought his gaze back to Tamryn. "You made your famous stuffing."

"She sure did," Jake said, entering the kitchen, looking like he stepped out of some magazine article about how to avoid the wolf in sheep's clothing. Tamryn's heart fell to the floor as her stomach tightened with want and rage, an odd feeling that made her wonder if she'd vomit from the pressure cooking inside her.

"You know, for someone so tiny," Randy said as he glanced at her, "she sure can cook a mean Thanksgiving."

"I'm not tiny." Tamryn crossed her arms, glaring at Randy.

"Nah, she's the perfect size to ride on my shoulders, huh, TB?" Jake winked and she nearly fell over from shock.

Tamryn's face heated to about three-hundred degrees and her mouth fell open. The very *vivid* vision of straddling Jake's face just a short while earlier flooded her mind. She scoffed, nearly choking on air, eyes wide and mouth agape. What the hell? Was he seriously going to act like nothing had happened since then?

Jake turned to Randy, reaching for a beer. "Let's get these babies in the icebox out back. I think we should eat on that old picnic table. It's unseasonably warm today; we should take advantage of that."

He'd taken advantage of something today, hadn't he?

With barely a glance in her direction, he headed out the back door with Randy, all smiles, like nothing had happened. Like he hadn't just made love to her and left her, then mentioned it all casually in front of his friend like nothing was wrong.

Everything was wrong! She couldn't stay here, couldn't subject herself to his hot and cold.

Tamryn groaned and slammed her hand onto the butcher block, sending pins and needles through her palm. "Mother fu—"

"Careful, now, that's no way for a lady to speak." Reed entered the kitchen, eyes sparkling for his favorite holiday. "And, heck, Tam, you look too nice for cussin'."

Tamryn's cheeks warmed as she embraced Reed. "Thank you. I'm glad you're here." She debated telling him, quickly running through the whole story, but before she could find the nerve, the front door opened again and the distinct click of stiletto heels echoed through the house.

"Jake, honey, I'm home!" Gennie giggled.

Tamryn's eyes widened and her mouth tightened into a tight line. She met Reed's gaze and raised her eyebrows.

Reed leaned forward. "He swears they aren't sleeping together anymore."

"Does she know that?" Tamryn snapped.

"Hey guys! Happy Thanksgiving!" Gennie entered the room, all gorgeous and confident, her vibrant red hair cascading around her shoulders, perfectly pale skin crowning a corset that not only shrunk her waist but pushed her breasts up to near chin level.

Tamryn sighed, forcing a smile for Gennie. How was she supposed to compete with someone so...luscious?

"I just love Thanksgiving, don't you?" She kissed Tamryn's cheek. "Glad you're back, hon." *Not back.* Gennie moved on to plant a kiss on Reed's cheek as well. "You can eat and eat and it's totally acceptable." She placed a foil-covered dish on the counter, then turned to face them. "I hope you don't mind, but I brought my mama's famous sweet potato pie. It's to die for, believe you me."

Reed frowned, glancing quickly at Gennie. "Tamryn usually brings the pies."

"No, Reed, it's okay. Who doesn't want more pie?"

"Oh, honey, I didn't know. Jake didn't tell me...you know how he is." She winked, dismissing the thought with a flick of her wrist as she stepped onto the back porch.

Tamryn smiled as she gave a curt nod, her teeth clenched. Oh, she knew exactly how he was. What she didn't know was how the hell she'd last through this festive day with the knot she had in her chest and the pit still growing in her stomach.

"I need a drink."

"I'm one step ahead of you, buddy." Reed stepped past Tamryn to the bar in the living room. "One step ahead."

Luce stepped into the living room, sneaking up behind Reed, and Tamryn grinned as relief filled her chest. "What have I missed, old man?"

Reed jumped, then turned to face her. "Why if it isn't little Lucy Hammersley." He looked her up and down, settling his gaze on her jet black bob. "Only, not so little anymore, are ya?"

She embraced him, then stepped toward Tamryn. "You have no idea, Reed." She placed her hands on each of Tamryn's shoulders, then her smile fell. "Oh God, what's wrong?"

Tamryn shook her head, eyes welling up. "Not right now, okay?"

Luce's dark eyes flicked back and forth between Tamryn's, then she narrowed her gaze. "I'll kill him."

Reed stepped up beside her, a cocktail in each hand. "I have a feeling we're going to need these today."

Chapter Twenty-Five

If Gennie knew she wasn't still with Jake, she hid it well. Sitting beside him at the giant wood picnic table outside, she hung on his every word, as per usual, staring at him with those giant doe eyes…and who knows, she probably gave him a handy under the table while they ate. It was worse now that Gennie knew how Tamryn felt about Jake, even though she couldn't have known they'd had sex just a couple hours earlier. Every giggle or exaggerated bat of an eyelash cut Tamryn deeper than before.

Jake didn't seem to be feeding off of Gennie's attention, for whatever that was worth. He sure wouldn't say no to another round, though, not Mr. Can't Keep His Dick In His Pants. Tamryn glared at him across the table, still pissed that everyone sat down before her leaving only one available spot, smack dab across from Jake.

She'd barely eaten for the last forty minutes they'd been at the table.

But the martinis Reed made continued to flow and she was on her second. No, third. No…

She leaned over to Reed and placed her hand on his shoulder to steady herself, then brought her mouth close to his ear. "How many of these have I had?" She didn't think her words were slurred, but she ran her tongue over her teeth again and swallowed. "How many—"

"Reed," Jake barked. "How's your dad's old Chevy coming along, bro? Ready for a joyride yet?" His seemingly harmless question contradicted the hard glint in his eyes.

Reed tilted his head, leaned over to whisper to Tamryn, "Three," then wiped his mouth and set his napkin on the table. "You think Pop will let you near his Chevy after what you did to Bertha?"

"Shit, that old thing? We did that car a favor sending it off that way. Burials at sea are a big deal."

"My folks sure didn't think so." Reed's jaw clenched as he held Jake's gaze.

Gennie giggled beside Jake. "Now, this sounds like a story I need to hear! We don't live anywhere near the ocean." She sipped her glass of wine and side-eyed him over the rim.

Luce laughed sweetly—too sweetly and fake as hell to anyone who knew her well. "That is a *hilarious* story, but one for another day. I'm more interested in what you've been up to *lately*, Jake." She spat his name.

Tamryn's stomach curdled and she swallowed the lump of now-un-chewable meat. "Excuse me," she mumbled as she pushed out of her seat and fought to slowly walk to the kitchen without stumbling. Face burning and tears welling in her eyes, she paused just inside the doorway, unsure of her next move. Should she go to the bathroom, have a good cry, then return to the festivities?

Or bolt?

"I think she's had enough, Samuels."

Definitely bolt. Tamryn stepped further into the kitchen, searching for her keys. The screen door to the patio swung shut behind her.

"She's definitely had enough of something, Johnson," Reed snapped. "What exactly did you do to her today?"

"Yeah, *Johnson*. I haven't seen her this upset since..." Luce's words trailed off.

Tamryn's heart pinched; Luce had loved Colby like a brother.

"What's goin' on, y'all?" Gennie asked, finally cluing in to the tension that took up more of the Thanksgiving table than the actual meal.

The porch screen swung open as someone stepped inside behind her, and Tamryn turned around.

"What's wrong?" Reed asked. "What did he do to you?"

Tamryn wiped at her cheeks, shaking her head. "Nothing. Just checking on the pies."

He stepped toward her, frowning. "Now, Tamryn Baker, you're one of my oldest friends. And you're a terrible liar."

Tamryn laughed, her voice catching on the sound. "It's a Baker thing." She shrugged. "I'm okay, Reed, really. I just…I shouldn't have come here."

"Still lying. Try again."

"I need to go. Can you help me find my keys?" She turned her head and stumbled, righting herself against the butcher block island. Who stumbles while standing still? She grinned through the tears. She didn't even have a car, thus…no keys to be found. She laughed on a sob. "Maybe I'll call a cab."

"I'll take you home."

"Will you now?" Jake filled the doorway, muscles tight as he stared down his friend. "I brought her here. I'll be the one to drive her home." He glanced quickly at Tamryn then back at Reed. "I thought you said this wasn't a thing." He waved his hand between Reed and Tamryn, eyes narrowed.

Reed stood taller, mimicking Jake's stance. "We're not doing this again right now. She's not okay, and I'm not going to let her drive home."

Jake looked past Reed, eyes softening around the edges. "TB? You okay?"

Tamryn shook her head, eyes closing on a long blink. "I'm fine, Jake. Why wouldn't I be?" She waved her hand between her and Reed the way he just had. "This isn't a thing." Scowling, she motioned more wildly between herself and Jake. "And this sure isn't a fucking thing, so no need for concern there, *big brother*."

Jake tilted his head, eyes narrowing for the slightest of seconds, so Tamryn smiled sweetly.

"She's drunker than Cooter Brown." Jake glared at Reed. "But then you already know that, don't you, buddy?"

Reed stepped forward, squaring his shoulders. "I don't think alcohol is the problem, *buddy*; she was messed up when I got here. What did you do?"

"You two peacockin' again, boys?" Randy pushed the screen door open and stepped inside. "Always a damn pissin' contest with you two."

Luce and Gennie followed behind Randy. *Too many cooks in the kitchen.*

In slow, somewhat blurry motion, Tamryn watched as Randy bumped into Jake, sending him forward. Reed reacted to the sudden movement of Jake rushing toward him, swinging his fist in a backward arc, then clocking Jake across the jaw.

With the sharp *crack* of knuckles on skin, Jake's head whipped back. In a flash, he righted himself, cocked his arm back and swung at Reed, and in seconds the guys were a mess of limbs and blows on the floor. Randy and the girls tried to stop the chaos, but arms and legs swung out, knocking Gennie to the floor. A knife block teetered on the edge of the island, but Tamryn steadied it before it fell onto Gennie's head.

Tamryn watched the boys on the floor, then her brain kicked into gear; this was her time to escape without any questioning. She grabbed Reed's keys off the hook by the pantry, then slipped quietly from the kitchen as Gennie's shrieking filled the room and Randy jumped into the melee to stop his friends from killing one another.

Luce would surely notice her absence and follow her outside, but Tamryn hoped to be long gone before that happened. She scanned the dirt lot for Reed's truck, then jogged to it as quickly as she could. She had only moments before Luce came looking for her.

She climbed in, then slammed the key against the ignition, repeatedly bumping metal against metal. Leaning down, she held her hand as steady as she could, closed one eye to streamline her vision, and slid the key into the ignition. The engine rumbled to life and she screeched out of the lot, sending a cloud of dust up behind her as she tore out onto the highway.

She giggled as the truck tipped to one side, a tire in the air as she hit the road, a small apathetic part of her broken soul wishing for a crash. They were fighting over her well-being again, but had any of them noticed she'd disappeared? Jake didn't care about her unless he thought she was fucking someone else. Well, he could go fuck himself. .

She held the wheel as firmly as she could, one eye squeezed tightly shut. The road blurred before her, at times appearing as one straight road, then morphing into two. "Shit." She slammed her fist against the steering wheel, sending the truck into the opposite lane for a few long seconds. She shouldn't be driving.

What was she *thinking* getting behind the wheel in her condition?

She looked over her shoulder to make sure the road was clear and started to pull to the side, but the steering was different in Reed's truck than Charlie's, easier and quicker to respond, so the truck swerved quickly to the right, nearly plowing straight off the shoulder and into the field below. She yanked the wheel to the left, heart thudding in her ears and right leg trembling on the pedal, but she overcorrected, and the truck tipped onto two wheels, rocked a couple of times, skid toward the ravine running parallel to the road.

The sharp sound of metal screeching along asphalt was almost deafening. The angry moan of metal reforming under pressure screamed into the serene afternoon. Then the screech of something stretching and cracking as weight shifted unnaturally. The truck flipped onto its side, slamming Tamryn against the opposite door, then slid to a stop against a grassy bank. The whine of the engine idling in a car still running with no road to meet was only slightly louder than the unmistakable trickle of liquid hitting the ground. The scents of burning rubber and gasoline filled the air.

Pain radiated through Tamryn's skull, blackness closing in around her vision as something wet trickled into her eye. Crumpled up into a ball, she couldn't move her right arm, pinned beneath her body. The more she tried to move, the more pain surged within her, nerves firing on full blast even through the haze of too much alcohol. Neck tilted and twisted to the side against the ground, she allowed herself a quick moment of thanks that the window had been down and she hadn't crashed into glass.

The things you think of in times like this.

She stared at the blades of grass just inches away from her nose as her eyes lost focus.

The slow whir of spinning tires lulled her into the darkness waiting just behind her eyes.

Chapter Twenty-Six

Jake stood, pushing Reed away and searching the room. "Where's TB?" His heart jumped into his throat as the memory of keys scraping the counter floated to the surface of his mind. She'd left while they'd been rolling around like a couple of punks, and he only just registered the sound, the realization. "She's driving." Eyes wide, heart pounding, he met Reed's gaze. "What have we done?"

Pushing past him, Reed ran for the front of the house and rushed outside. Jake followed, panic seizing his chest, TB's girlfriend on his heels.

"What the fuck did you guys do to her?" Lucy asked, her gaze accusatory as she glared between Jake and Reed.

Reed ignored the question, scanning the parking lot. "Shit. She's in my truck."

Jake's heart froze in his chest as panic gripped him. "She can't have gotten far; come on." He pulled his keys from his pocket and hopped behind the wheel of his own truck as Reed jumped into the passenger seat. "Stay here in case she comes back," he hollered at Lucy.

The girl's eyes flared with anger. "She better come back!"

"Fuck!" Jake slammed his hand against the wheel and raced toward the highway, screeching to a stop at the edge. "Which way?"

Reed glanced in both directions, then back at Jake. "Charlie's?"

Jake shook his head in frustration, then hooked a right and left half of the rubber from his tires on the road outside The Bar.

Scanning the road from side to side, checking each parking lot they passed, Jake raced toward the west end of town. He couldn't think, could barely focus; fear gripped his chest with relentless force.

He couldn't lose her too.

"What did you do to her, Jake?"

Jake shot a glare at Reed, then softened. "What didn't I do?"

"I mean *today*."

"I know." He shook his head, shame warming his cheeks. "I fucked her, Reed."

Reed ran his hand over his face. "Then what? That alone couldn't have caused this."

Jake glanced at his friend, cringing from Reed's frown. "I gave her the ol' Jake Johnson fuck 'em and forget 'em."

Reed sucked in a breath. "No, you didn't. Not Tamryn."

"I promised Colby I'd take care of her." He ran a hand through his hair. "I can't touch her, Reed; she's Colby's kid sister. I can't touch her! I promised him!" Jake's knuckles whitened on the wheel.

"You promised to protect her, Jake, to look after her, keep her safe—"

"I know!"

"Don't you think protecting her heart counts as keeping her safe?"

Jake sucked in a breath. "I told you, I made a mistake! It won't happen ag—"

"Oh God."

Jake side-eyed Reed. "I know, man, I really fucked up."

Reed's wide eyes stopped Jake's words. He followed his friend's gaze to the side of the road, and his heart nearly jumped from his chest.

Wheels still spinning, Reed's old Ford lay on its side in the field.

Jake skidded to a stop, jumping out of the truck as it rolled a few more feet, the old truck slow to register it was in park. "Tamryn!" he ran to the truck, searching the surrounding area for TB. "Tamryn! Answer me!"

She moaned, muffled and distant, and he swung his head around, swiveling from side to side as he spun in a slow circle, searching for her. Fuck, if she was pinned beneath it...

"In here," Reed shouted, stepping up onto the bed of the truck and motioning toward the cab. "Call nine-one-one!"

Jake yanked his phone from his pocket and dialed as he ran to the truck and peered down into the driver's side window. The operator answered, but Jake didn't hear anything past the roar of blood in his ears. The phone fell from his grasp. TB lay in a heap against the passenger side door, her neck bent at an odd angle, blood trickling a map of red lines all over her face. Tears flooded his vision; he blinked frantically to bring her back into focus. "Her neck...it's..." A strangled sound left his lips and he squeezed his eyes shut.

A few feet away, Reed spoke into Jake's phone, the sounds nonsensical in Jake's ears.

"TB, I'm here. I'm here. Dammit, please don't leave me. I can't lose you too. Please hold on, help's coming. I'm here, TB, I'm here. I'm so sorry. I'm so sorry."

He muttered the words over and over, a whispered plea, waiting for help to arrive and staring at his heart outside of his own body, crumpled and broken inside Reed's totaled truck. "I'm so sorry. I'm so sorry."

I'm so sorry.

His arms ached to hold her, his heart ached to heal her.

And it was all his fault.

Chapter Twenty-Seven

A slight concussion, a broken pinky, severe whiplash, a Tibial shaft fracture in her left leg, and a few bruised ribs…She was lucky to be alive, they'd told him. Because of the booze. Both the cause of the accident and Tamryn's ultimate salvation, keeping her body loose during the critical few seconds of that crash.

Jake had never left her side. He rode with her to the hospital, held onto her unmoving hand as they wheeled her inside on the gurney, stood outside the door as they examined her, patched her up, ran tests, whispered assumptions and judgements about the twenty-two-year-old drunk driver who 'could have killed someone'.

He wanted to scream at them, wanted to punch something. This wasn't TB, wasn't the beautiful girl he knew. They didn't know who they were whispering about! She didn't just go around drinking and driving, carelessly taking her life—and the lives of others—into her own hands.

He wanted to scream at them, "I'm the reason she did this! I should go to jail!"

But he didn't. Because it wouldn't matter. It wouldn't fix the pain she felt—more pain he'd caused.

TB had drunk at least three martinis, which in her small frame was well over the legal limit, then gotten behind the wheel. She was lucky to be alive. No thanks to Jake.

If only he'd paid more attention to her broken heart instead of his own...

He paced her hospital room now, matching his steps to the slow beep of the monitors, reassuring himself with the steady tempo of the beats.

Reed appeared in the doorway, flowers in hand. "You been home yet?"

Jake clenched his jaw. "No. I'm not leaving her."

Reed sighed, then stepped inside the room. "I can't imagine she'll want to see you. I'm sorry, man, but..."

Jake gave a curt nod. "I know. Just...just give me a little more time. I can't leave her yet."

Reed smiled sadly, placed the flowers on the bedside table, then leaned over and kissed TB's temple. Jake's chest tightened, but he didn't say anything. He would never voice his jealousy again.

Reed straightened and met Jake's gaze, shaking his head as he stepped toward him. "There's nothing between us, Jake. She loves *you.*"

Jake searched Reed's gaze, his heart a thick lump, blocking his breath from his lungs. He shook his head, then cleared his throat. "She can't love me. I'm no good for her."

Reed frowned. "Not right now, you're not. She deserves better than what you're willing to give. So does Colby." He patted Jake on the shoulder as he passed. At the doorway he paused. "Luce is on her way."

Jake tensed. She'd given him nothing but scathing lectures since the accident.

"It's been three days. Go home, man."

Tears slipped down Jake's cheek. He'd let her down, let Colby down...

He stepped toward the bed and sat in the chair beside her. Taking TB's small hand in his, he leaned over and rested his forehead on her hand. "I really messed everything up, didn't I?" He kissed her hand, careful to avoid the IV. "But I love you, kiddo. I love you so much. I'm sorry it took me so long to figure it out...I'm...so sorry I broke your heart." He looked up at her peaceful face. "How many times?" He thought of all the women parade in front of her, brought into *their* home, the casual fucks, the nights with Gennie clawing at his back, TB right down the hall. A sob escaped his lips. "How long," he whispered, the words so muted he could barely hear them himself, "how long have you loved me?"

Jake stood, wiping the tears from his eyes. He licked his lips and swallowed hard, the gaping hole in his chest threatening to swallow him up. This next part would be the worst moment of his life, worse than his father's death, worse than losing Colby…

He'd rather die than he walked away from her, but it was time. He'd caused her nothing but pain.

"I'm no good for you, TB. Look what loving me has done to you." He glanced around the hospital room. "I have to honor my promise to Colby, honor my love for you. I have to keep you safe, and that includes your heart."

If that meant staying away, so be it.

The monitor beeped a few times in quicker succession. Jake's heart froze with his breath as he watched the lines spike, then slow again.

Jake leaned over her, brought his lips to her temple, just beneath the crown of bandages, and kissed her gently. "I think I've always loved you too," he whispered. "Goodbye."

Allowing himself one long second to take in her face one last time, really take it in, memorize the softness of her cheeks, the slight lift of the tip her nose, he stood, then turned around and left the hospital room—and his heart—behind.

Everyone he loved passed away. And now, he'd almost lost TB.

Never again.

Outside the hospital room, he pulled his phone from his jacket pocket, ignored the agony ripping through his chest, and dialed Reed.

He picked up on the first ring. "What's wrong? Is she okay?"

"She's the same. I'm leaving now. Luce isn't here yet. Come back so she's not alone when she wakes up."

A tear slid down Tamryn's cheek, but she kept her eyes closed. Her nose began to tickle as it ran, but she fought against the urge to swipe at her face, not wanting to alert Jake to the fact she was awake. Her heart left her body as Jake walked out the door. He'd always have her heart, in its entirety, but she had to let him go. He was right; look what a mess she'd made of things, all in the name of loving Jake Johnson. They were no good for one another, and as much as that realization destroyed her soul, it was the truth.

"Don't let her know I was here." Jake was outside her room now, his voice getting softer the further he walked away from her.

Her eyes flew open as she fought a sob, bringing her hand to her mouth and pressing hard against her lips as more tears fell.

"Just trust me. She can't know." Pause. "Exactly, man. I can at least give her that."

Tamryn's pulse thundered in her ears as she wrestled the need to call Jake back into the room. He loved her, and she loved him, and, dammit, why wasn't that enough? The beep from the monitor sped as her thoughts careened around in her brain, so she closed her eyes again and fought to breathe normally.

Minutes passed as, slowly, the chaos in her mind calmed, and her pulse returned to normal, the beeping slowing back to a rhythmic cadence.

The chair beside the bed creaked, and she opened her eyes.

Reed sat down, leaning forward, his elbows on his knees. He searched her gaze. "You know."

Tamryn shook her head.

"Lies." Reed scooted the chair closer and took her hand. "You heard him leave."

She bit her lip as tears pooled in her eyes, then nodded.

"Oh, Tamryn, I'm so sorry. He doesn't know what else to do." Reed squeezed her arm above the wrist. "It's Jake," he said with a shrug.

She'd managed to fall in love with the most emotionally ill-equipped man on earth, and simply loving him enough hadn't been…enough.

"I just thought I could love him enough for both of us."

Reed nodded. "I know."

"What now?"

"Give it time."

She snorted. "Haven't I?"

Reed's smile didn't reach his eyes as he shrugged. "I don't know what to tell you."

"I wrecked your truck."

Reed chuckled. "Yeah, well, that thing was a heap anyway. Now I have an excuse to get the old Ford into the shop and get that baby running again."

Tamryn's eyes blurred with more tears. "I'm so sorry, Reed, I don't know what I was thinking. I can't believe I did that. I'll pay for it."

"No, Tamryn. I'm not mad, and I refuse to take your money. Colby would kill us both if he knew we allowed you to leave like that. And I'm the one who poured the damn drinks."

"It's not your fault."

"Maybe not entirely, but I helped. And I owe you better than that."

Tamryn smiled, not sure what else to say. Fact was, Colby would have killed all three of them for this mess. He'd have been so disappointed in her.

Reed's gaze changed a bit, his eyebrows straightening as he watched her.

She tilted her head. "What is it?"

He pulled his bottom lip into his mouth, then sighed. "Well…"

Oh God. "Give it to me straight."

"You're going to have a DUI."

Tamryn's heart sank and she closed her eyes. "Shit." Shaking her head, tears streamed down her cheeks. "What have I done?"

"You could have died, Tam, could have killed someone. In the whole scheme of things, a DUI sucks, and it will be expensive, and you'll probably lose your license, but you're alive."

Tamryn barked a curt laugh. "Such as it is."

"No, don't talk like that. You have plenty of livin' to do, and you're lucky you survived that crash with only a few minor injuries."

She sighed, chewing on her bottom lip. A DUI. Embarrassment warmed her chest, her cheeks, regret and shame twisting icy fingers around her heart. She could have killed someone. A mom. A minivan full of kids…

"I don't know what we would have done without you, Tamryn Baker."

"You're about to find out." Luce stepped into the room, scowling. She glared at Reed. "I'm not exactly sure how or why, but I have a feeling you're as much as part of this as he is." She stepped to the side of the bed, squeezing between Reed and Tamryn.

"Don't be mad at Reed, Luce, it's not his fault."

She shot a glare back at Reed. "Bye."

Reed stood, then dipped his head and headed for the door. "I'll be in the cafeteria if you need me."

"We won't," Luce snapped.

Tamryn's tears fell, and she turned away from Luce and those all-knowing eyes of hers.

"You sure picked a shitty way to welcome me home, Thelma."

Tamryn laughed through the tears. "I'm sorry, Luce."

"Don't worry, you'll make it up to me. Right after you tell me everything."

Tamryn turned her face back to Luce, then scooted slowly into a sitting position, careful of her beaten body. "Everything?"

"Oh yeah, girl, *everything*."

She'd start at the beginning of the end, since starting at the very beginning was pointless—Luce had always known of her feelings for Jake. Tamryn swallowed the knot in her throat, then met Luce's gaze. "I slept with Reed."

Chapter Twenty-Eight

Each day without Jake passed by in a fog. Losing her driver's license was a pain in the ass; losing Jake Johnson was an insurmountable mountain she climbed every day. Waking up to face another circle around the sun without him made even the things she once loved pointless and drab.

Nearly three months since the crash, and Tamryn was nearly healed. The only visible sign of what had happened was a slight limp in her walk when the air was cold enough to seep into her bones. Recovering from bruised ribs wasn't an overnight thing, and even after all this time taking it easy and not overdoing it at either job, she still felt a twinge of pain when she moved the wrong way or sat up too quickly, a constant reminder of the mistakes she'd made that nearly cost her life.

In her heart, however, the damage was far greater. The invisible scars of losing Jake, of carrying the shame that comes with drunk driving, of knowing she'd let everyone down; those scars would take far longer than three months to heal.

Far longer. If healing was even a possibility. So far, she didn't think so.

Work had been good, even though she'd been taking fewer shifts and trying to "stay down" as Charlie frequently reminded her to do. But, regardless of taking it easy, Tamryn had finally saved enough money to get out of Charlie's house. He'd been hovering since the accident, always asking if she needed something, offering to drive her here and there, insisting on catering to her like she was bedridden, and smothering Tamryn to the point of suffocation.

If her heartache didn't kill her, Charlie's overprotectiveness just might.

She appreciated his concern, really she did, but the time had come to spread her wings once and for all. Her whole life, she'd lived under someone else's watchful eye, whether her parents, Colby and Jake, or now Charlie and Roc, she'd never truly set out on her own. Though she didn't plan on going very far—she had first and last month's rent set aside for the tiny apartment above Syd's coffee shop—she would be living alone for the first time in her twenty-two years.

The concept both thrilled and terrified her, but that was probably natural, and she tried to embrace the anticipation. Less than a week remained until the current tenant moved out, so she just had to get through each moment of doubt with a pep talk, and she'd be living on her own in no time.

Walking to the mailbox, she retrieved the stack of three days' worth of mail and flipped through its contents as she walked back to the house, stopping dead in her tracks when she recognized that old familiar scrawl.

She inhaled a shaky breath as she read her name in Jake's handwriting.

Tamryn slid her finger across the words as though she could feel the sender's hand as he wrote her name and address. She brought the envelope to her nose and inhaled deeply, then rolled her eyes, glancing around to make sure no one had witnessed the ridiculous action.

With a quick shake of her head, she flipped the envelope over, hands shaking as she slowly opened the flap, careful not to damage whatever lay inside. Hope warmed her chest, sending her heart to racing. Had he written the words she knew he felt for her, finally found them within himself and made the first step?

On bated breath, she unfolded the tri-fold paper.

A check fell to the floor.

Jake's familiar, sharp handwriting scrawled across the page, one singular line, perfectly centered. Her stomach sank.

"Now you can be free," she read aloud, her voice and heart cracking on the final word.

This was goodbye.

Tamryn blinked, releasing a quiet flood of tears, then bent to pick up the check, vision blurred.

When she was finally able to will the tears to subside long enough to read the amount on the check, she gasped, slapping her hand against her mouth.

Twenty-five thousand dollars.

She blinked, once, twice, her eyes obviously still blurred from the tears; she couldn't have read that correctly. She closed her eyes, counted to three, then opened them again and focused.

Twenty-five thousand dollars.

She counted the zeroes, just to be sure, but her mind hadn't tricked her.

Her thoughts raced, but one thing was clear: she couldn't keep this money, no matter the reason for it or where—*who*—it came from. Jake did not have this much money, so what had he done to get it?

One more thing was clearer still… this wasn't something she could just ignore and move on from. They'd have to talk.

She had to go see Jake. No matter how painful it had been to stay away from him all this time, seeing him would cut far deeper, but it was necessary and she'd have to find the courage to do so.

She folded the paper back around the check and slipped them both into the envelope, then stepped back inside and tucked the envelope into her purse. She retrieved her cell phone and dialed Reed's number.

"Hey, you," he answered after two rings.

"Hey, Reed, how are you?"

"Good, good, and you?"

"Um…" Tamryn chewed on a hangnail, settling into the couch. "I'm good, too, I guess. I mean…"

"Okay, what's up? I know that voice."

"Did you know about this check?"

Silence answered her on the other end of the line.

"Reed." She sighed. "You know I can't keep this. Where did he even get this kind of money?" She ran her hand over her forehead.

"The where isn't really important, Tam, he's not hurting for money. Never has been, but you wouldn't know it to look at him."

Tamryn slumped further down in the couch. "I had no idea," she whispered.

"Yeah, well, no one does. But that's not important. He didn't do anything unseemly to get it. That money is yours, and you're going to keep it. You know Jake's not going to let you give it back."

"Reed, I can't. It's too much."

"Look at it like it's all those paychecks he withheld from you, somewhat illegally."

"Somewhat?" She laughed. "That wouldn't even be half of this, Reed, and you know it."

"Eh, who's to say?" She could hear the smirk in his voice.

"I'm not keeping this."

"Okay. But don't say I didn't warn you. He's not going to just accept no for an answer and move on."

Tamryn sighed and closed her eyes, resting her head against the back of the couch. "Now I have to see him."

"Yep."

"Ugh."

"Yep." Reed chuckled softly.

"Something tells me you're enjoying my suffering, Reed Samuels."

"Oh, very much so, Tamryn Baker."

She sat up and looked at the clock on the DVR. "I'll need a ride."

"I'll be there in five."

"Make it twenty-five, and you've got a deal."

"Done."

She pressed *end* and stood, then walked toward the window to look outside, remembering the day Jake stood at those steps with his flannel open and waving in the breeze. "Damn you, Jake Johnson," she whispered on a sigh.

"Anything good in the mail today?"

She jumped and spun around to Charlie.

He raised an eyebrow. "Whoa, you all right?"

Tamryn shook her head. "Yeah, sorry, you startled me. I thought you were in bed."

"I was." He shrugged, then stepped toward her to retrieve the mail. "Bill. Bill. Bill. Junk. Junk." He tossed the stack on the coffee table with a grunt. "What're your plans for this evening? Workin'?" Charlie pulled the gallon of orange juice from the fridge and drank straight from the bottle.

"Charlie Morris!"

He grinned, then swiped the back of his wrist across his mouth. "Sorry, Ma." He winked and retrieved a cup from the cabinet.

Tamryn glanced at the clock once more, then headed for her room. "I have to get ready. I'm leaving for work soon."

"This early?" Charlie followed behind her. "Need a ride?"

She stopped at her doorway and turned around to meet his gaze. "No, thanks though. I have someone picking me up."

Charlie's smile faded into a thin line. "Him?"

Tamryn sighed. "No, Charlie, not him."

His eyes narrowed briefly before he turned around. "How are you getting home?" he asked as he headed back down the hall. "Need me to pick you up?"

Tamryn closed her eyes and shook her head. "I'll figure it out."

"Suit yourself."

Maybe she could move into that apartment above Syd's sooner rather than later.

WHISKEY BURNED

Chapter Twenty-Nine

The drive to The Bar was quiet, save for the random clunking and rattling the old Accord made as they hit bumps and potholes on the way from the Mills' place to the other side of town. Reed had purchased this car right after the accident, something to get him from A to B while he worked on fixing up his dad's old car.

What would she say when she saw Jake?

Would the sight of him reduce her to tears?

She swallowed the saliva that rushed to her mouth as her stomach churned. Seeing Jake would surely elicit a rush of feelings from her, both good and bad she was sure, but it had to be done. It was time for Tamryn to finally do what she'd been planning, time to stand on her own two feet. And that meant handling difficult things like an adult. Time to face the music.

Being near Jake after these three months apart would be far more difficult than anything she could remember in recent years. Staying out of his orbit was tough; stepping back into it would surely kill her.

"Breathe, Tamryn." Reed reached across the center divider and patted her leg. "Passing out won't do you any good."

Tamryn forced a smile and inhaled a deep breath.

"One more, just for fun."

She laughed uneasily, then did as she was told, closing her eyes and breathing in through her nose, out through her mouth. Reed was right: passing out would not be helpful. She imagined Jake catching her as she fainted, the perfect image of an old-time knight in shining armor stepping up quickly to save the princess in distress, the lens all rose-colored and ridiculous. That was what she'd actively fought him and Reed about—saving her, and here she was, imagining it—and not hating the idea. "Holy crap," she muttered.

"What is it?"

"I'm so screwed, Reed." She shook her head, then looked over at him. "I can't do this."

"Okay. Then let's head to the bank so you can cash that check."

Her stomach somersaulted. "Not happening."

Reed grinned and pressed on the gas. "Roger that."

His phone rang between them and they both looked down. Luce's face shone from the screen. Reed quickly grabbed the phone and pressed the button to send her to voicemail, but he hadn't been quick enough.

"Um, Reed?"

His cheeks flushed, and he focused on the road.

Tamryn tilted her head, staring at the side of his face. "Luce hates you."

"She did, yes."

Tamryn frowned. "What am I missing?"

Reed patted her knee. "Nothing, really. Don't pitch a fit." He side-eyed her. "We just talk from time to time."

Tamryn rolled her eyes. "Oh, God, she calls you to check in on me, doesn't she?"

Reed grinned. "Possibly."

They pulled into the parking lot out front of The Bar, the sinking feeling in Tamryn's gut intensifying until she thought she might actually get sick. "I need a barf bag."

Reed laughed, tossing his head back. "Stop it. It's just Jake." He pulled the car to a stop, then turned to her. "Look, Tamryn, you're in love with Jake. He's in love with you."

The words brought a tingling to the backs of her eyes, but she forced them open wider so she wouldn't cry.

"You know it. We know it. Hell, the whole damn town knows it." Reed tapped two fingers against his temple. "It's just that you chose the most emotionally-stunted guy on earth and then expected him to embrace it immediately."

Tamryn narrowed her eyes, a slight tilt to her lips. "Are you saying Jake's dense?"

Reed snorted a laugh. "Nah, you think?"

Tamryn inhaled a deep breath and nodded. She could do this. She could see Jake, give him his check back, and maybe, just maybe, they could take a step—however small—back toward being friends again.

Or, more than friends, but she didn't want to get her hopes up.

She smiled and gave a quick nod. "Okay. I can do this."

"Yes, you can."

Tamryn's smile faded slowly. "What do I say?"

Reed laughed. "What do you want to say?"

So much. Nothing. She didn't know. Too many things had gone unsaid between them, and look where that had gotten her. Drunk driving, broken bones, and an even more broken heart.

"I don't know." She shook her head. "I can't accept this check." She held up her purse.

"Fair enough. Lead with that."

"And then what?"

Reed raised his eyebrows. "You know, between the two of you...I swear." He shook his head. "Why don't you tell him the truth?"

"About what?"

"About everything, Tamryn. Everything."

Tamryn swallowed hard. "Everything?"

Reed nodded. "Everything." He squeezed her hand. "Start with how you feel. He has a right to hear it from you."

She nodded, though she couldn't bring herself to outright agree with Reed. Tell Jake how she felt? That was easier said than done, something she'd proven time and time again. But she could go in there and start with giving him the check back. Once she got a feel for how the conversation was going, she'd consider telling him how she felt. Hell, maybe he'd swoop her up into his arms and profess his feelings first. That would make this conversation a heck of a lot easier.

She gave a curt nod, more to herself than Reed. "Okay, let's do this."

"I'll be right here waiting for you."

Tamryn's eyes widened and her heart stuttered. "What? You're not coming in with me?" She looked around to see if any cars were in the parking lot. Maybe Gennie or Randy were inside. She couldn't be alone with Jake. No way. Not yet.

"This is between you and Jake. I'm staying out of it." He raised his hands in surrender. "Go on."

Tamryn stared at Reed for a good long minute, then shook her head. "You're a terrible person."

"Tell me how you really feel." He winked, then nodded toward The Bar. "Go on, git."

Tamryn stepped out of the car and shut the door gently. She scanned the area once more, the primal need to flee waking up with a roar inside her. Taking one last deep, soothing breath, she tamped down her escape mechanism and stood tall, squaring her shoulders as she approached the door.

"Lord, give me strength." She placed her palm against the door. "And for the love of all things holy, please don't let me pass out." She opened the door, stepped inside, inhaled the familiar whiskey and wood scent of the Johnson men, then waited impatiently while her eyes adjusted to the change in light.

He stood behind the bar with his back to her, shirt off and shoulders glistening with sweat.

Tamryn fought back a groan. *Kill me now*. She took another step inside the bar, even though every cell in her body told her to retreat.

Abort! Abort!

Seeing him was too much. Too much familiarity, too much longing, too much pain.

Jake looked up at the clock on the wall. "You're late, bro."

Chapter Thirty

"Hey, Jake."

Jake's body went rigid even as his pulse sped. He'd know that gentle voice anywhere. "TB," he whispered. He stared at his hands, covered in grease from wrenching on the old ice machine, then swiped them on his sweatpants, grabbed a wet rag, and turned around. Dressed for her shift at the *other* bar in town, in a black Old Faithful's collared shirt and jeans that hugged her perfect legs, Jake couldn't tear his eyes away from her. Either TB had grown in the last few months they'd been apart, or his abstinence was about to get the best of him. As she approached the bar, heat rushed south. He'd never slept with anyone right there on the dancefloor. How quickly could he get those jeans off of her—?

Instantly he regretted the thought. One look at TB and he was right back into lusting after his best friend's little sister. They had to repair what had broken between them; their friendship and lifelong bond was far more important than his suddenly relentless desire to fuck her till her toes curled.

He stifled a frustrated groan and stepped around the bar.

One step at a time, he walked toward her. One step at a time, they'd fix the broken pieces of their relationship.

One step at a time meant taking things slowly, not slamming her against the wall and making love to her like she deserved.

"Dammit," he growled.

TB stopped abruptly, eyes wide. "Sorry. I shouldn't have come."

"No." Jake froze, panicking. He raised his hands in the air. "Sorry, that wasn't…it's not what it sounded like." *Fuck.*

TB frowned. "It sounded like you just said *dammit* when you saw it was me."

"I did." He grinned, hoping the motion didn't look as pained as it felt. "Just not about you. I…I remembered something I forgot to do earlier. A…um…a phone call I have to make." He ran his hand through his hair. "Anyway, how are ya, kid?" Tossing the bar towel over his shoulder, he took another step toward her. Like a magnet, his body was drawn to her; approaching her slowly was hell. "You look good."

TB smiled nervously, her cheeks pinking just the slightest bit. She dropped her gaze and it was all he could do not to rush forward those last few feet and lift her chin.

"All healed?" he asked, hoping the change in subject would bring her gaze back to his.

She looked up at him and smiled. "Yeah, for the most part." Her smile faltered briefly; she was holding something back.

Jake frowned. "What's wrong? Are you not taking it easy? Bill won't let you take time off, or what?" He nodded toward the logo on her shirt. That asshole Bill was probably overworking her.

TB shook her head. "No, Jake, I've been taking it easy. Bill let me take off as much time as I needed. But it's been three months, and I can't afford to never work again, you know."

His jaw tightened. She could afford to not work if she was still here with him. He would have given her all the time she needed. He held her gaze, struggling to find the right way to say just that.

"Speaking of which," she said, looking away from him once more. She dug in her purse and pulled out an envelope. His envelope. "I came to return this."

"What?" He rocked back as if she'd pushed him. "Why? No. That's yours." He raised his hands, palms out.

TB finally looked at him again, then took a few steps toward him. "No, I can't accept this. It's too much."

"It's what I owe you." He took a step backward.

She matched his step, not allowing him to get away. "You know that's not true, Jake."

He scowled, searching her gaze for a chink in the surface, a weak point. He couldn't find anything, no way in. He shook his head.

"Jake, please. Don't make this hard. Take the check back; I can't accept it."

"No." He crossed his arms and her gaze dropped to his chest, a flash of something he recognized but didn't believe.

Lust.

He dropped his arms and stepped toward her. As he pulled the towel from his shoulder, her eyes watched every move. He stopped just on front of her.

She closed her eyes. "Take the check, Jake."

"No."

Her chest rose on a deep inhale. "Please, Jake. Don't make me beg."

His lips twitched. Oh, he could make her beg, all right. He reached up and gently grasped her jaw, his thumb on her lip. So much time had passed, and yet no time at all—the chemistry between them was still so palpable he could taste it.

"No, Jake." She stepped backward. "That's not what...that's not why I'm here." She extended the envelope toward him. "Take it."

"No. It's what I owe you."

TB groaned. "Stop, Jake, just stop. We both know this isn't what you owe me."

"Fine. I matched it." He raised his eyebrows in challenge.

"What?" TB tilted her head, her eyes narrowed.

Jake squared his shoulders. "I matched it. Every cent you made here, I matched."

She frowned and his heart pinched. This wasn't going well at all. "Why?"

"Because I promised I'd take care of you."

Her eyelids fluttered, but she didn't close her eyes. "There it is again."

"What?" Jake frowned.

"Your need to take care of me, like I'm your kid or some wounded fucking bird." She whipped the envelope at his chest. "I. Am. Not. Yours. To. Take. Care. Of. I'm not your cross to bear anymore."

Jake shook his head, his mind racing. How was this going so downhill so fast? "It's not, I mean, I want to make sure you're happy, make sure you have everything you need." He reached for her but she stepped back. Didn't she know how much he loved her? Couldn't she feel how perfectly their bodies were drawn to one another? The air between them sizzled with their magnetic pull.

"God, Jake, don't you get it? That's not what I want from you!" She spun on her heels and stomped toward the door.

"Wait!" His heart pounding frantically in his chest, he scrambled for the right words. "Wait, please." She paused, and he exhaled, then strode toward her. He stopped beside her and looked down at perfect blue eyes, angry but familiar, so familiar. "Wait," he whispered one more time.

"What, Jake?"

"Don't go."

"Why? Tell me why." She searched his gaze, her eyes softening from rage to...hurt. Why was she sad? Why was she always in pain when he was near? "Tell me why I should stay, Jake."

He placed his hand on her elbow. She flinched, but didn't pull her arm away. Now was the time, his moment. He could hear her say the words, get her to admit how she felt about him. Then he could be honest with her in turn and the two of them could move forward. Together.

"What is it you want from me, TB?"

She sighed, then pulled her arm out of his grasp. "For starters, it's *Tamryn*."

With that, she pushed out the front door, leaving him in the dust-filled glow of a disappearing and reappearing ray of sunlight as the door swung back and forth in her wake.

He inhaled a shaky breath, but didn't move, frozen in place, his heart on the floor where she stood just seconds ago. "What the fuck just happened?"

Chapter Thirty-One

For the next two days, Tamryn's broken heart was a relentless punch to the gut. If only she could put *that* in a box and tape it up tightly for safe keeping. She focused on packing and cleaning up Charlie's house so it would be nice when she moved out, but even pre-move busywork was no match for the constant reel of Jake playing on and on in her mind.

Jake on his bike, riding up to see her.

Jake tugging on her ponytail playfully.

Jake on the stage, singing beside her.

Jake in her arms, her body fitting so perfectly with his.

Jake standing there before her, finally asking her what she wanted from him. That was the worst memory of all, the one that ignited such fresh, searing pain within her soul. So what if he couldn't leave her childish nickname behind? Was it really that big of a deal? She'd always been TB to him...who cares? Had she really just pushed him away over a *name*?

Her heartache intensified, the pain relentlessly reminding her of how much she loved him, and how much she'd just given up because of something as petty as a fucking nickname.

"Ugh!" She threw a stuffed animal at the stack of boxes along the far wall of her room.

She'd never be over Jake Johnson, that much she was now sure of. This wasn't a passing crush, or a love that a girl could just move on from. Jake was the one, the perfect guy for her, and she'd lost him before she'd even had him. But he hadn't fought for her either, only let her walk away.

What a sad story indeed.

Once she was settled in at her new apartment, she'd figure out a way to make things work with Jake. He was emotionally unavailable and as ill-equipped as they came, but she knew without a doubt he was hers. She wouldn't give up on him.

As she surveyed her dozen or so boxes, she realized she'd left more than her heart at Jake's; could she really sum up her entire life in twelve measly boxes?

Jake plucked a few chords on his guitar, looking around the room. He missed the way her smile lit up the bar, the way she looked so free, so fucking sexy when she stood on that stage beside him. He missed the scent of muffins and cupcakes that would fill his whole house, sometimes as late as three o'clock in the morning, his little midnight baker. He missed the way she'd grown up before his eyes, somehow morphing from little kid to a woman who'd consumed his entire being.

The Bar wasn't the same without her.

Hell, *he* wasn't the same without TB.

Seeing her last week had solidified what he'd known and ignored all along; TB belonged here, with him, and his life wasn't whole without her. But after their most recent meeting, he felt even further away from her than before. He'd sent her that check, not to win her back—though his heart had secretly hoped for that—but to do the right thing. For her, for Colby. . And, truth be told, to know if she wanted him after the playing field was on level ground. Who knew his gesture would backfire so badly? Fixing things between them seemed more than impossible now. You can't just un-light the match after the inferno is raging. And that's what this was, a full-blown dumpster fire of his mistakes. Too many goddamn mistakes to count. His relationship with TB, his promise to Colby, his heart… everything had gone up in smoke, and he was dumbfounded as to how to fix the havoc he'd wreaked.

But oh, he would fix it. You bet your ass he'd fix it.

His heart wouldn't let him do otherwise.

"Tamryn's moving out of that Morris' kid's place today." Reed stepped onto the dance floor, approaching the stage.

"Good for her, man." Jake struggled to keep his smile at bay.

"Yeah, keep pretending that doesn't twirl your skirt, Johnson."

Jake looked up at his friend and grinned.

"That's what I thought." Reed clapped him on the shoulder. "Inventory is done and done."

Jake stood and set his guitar back in the case. "Well done, man. I think we beat last year's record. Ready to go pick up your new baby?"

"Hell yeah I am." Reed stepped around the bar, holding up his new license place like a trophy for all to see.

BERTHA2

Jake shook his head. "You're a real class act, honoring the first Bertha that way." He couldn't say the words without laughing.

"Bite me, Johnson." He stepped through the doorway and elbowed Jake as he passed. "You should have paid for this plate after what you did to Bertha."

"Why didn't you just dive down to the bottom of old Mills' Lake and get the plate off that heap of junk?"

Reed paused, then turned back to face Jake. "And disturb her final resting place?" Reed grinned, eyes wide. "I'm no grave robber."

The drive out to Lee County took over an hour, and the two rode in silence most of the way, Jake too focused on his mess of a life to offer much in the way of conversation. As they neared their destination, Reed cleared his throat.

Here it comes. Jake side-eyed Reed, bracing for the deluge of shit he was about to get. "What is it, bro? Get it off your chest."

"You know, buddy, just when I thought you couldn't fuck things up worse, you go on and fuck things up worse."

Jake shook his head. "You don't have to tell me; it's my shit show, remember? I'm quite aware of the mess I made."

"Are you?" Reed leaned forward in the seat. "Because from where I'm sitting, it's been a good three days and you've done nothing to clean up said mess."

"Trust me." Jake snorted. "If I knew how to clean this thing up with TB, I'd Mr. Clean the hell out of it. Every time I try to make things right, I fuck things up worse."

Reed sighed, shaking his head. "Do you love her?"

Jake glanced at him as he crossed over the county line. "You know I do."

"That's how you fix it."

Jake scoffed. "Oh? It's as easy as that?"

"It's as easy as that. Tell her."

"Right, bro, 'cause it's that easy."

Reed groaned in frustration. "Yeah, it's that easy. What the hell, man? It's Tamryn Baker we're talking about. Just tell her you love her and get on to making me an Uncle or whatever."

Jake laughed. "That's putting the cart before the horse a bit, don't you think?" Jake smiled, imagining TB pregnant, covered in flour and nothing but that tiny apron, making his house a home the way only she'd ever been able to do.

"Just tell her, man."

Jake considered the idea, but somehow, just telling her how he felt didn't seem like it would be enough, not after all the mistakes he'd made. He needed something big, a grand gesture. Something that would knock her socks off and make sure that she knew, deep down inside she *knew* he loved her and only her, and would never stop showing her just how much.

Gramps' Garage sat just on the outskirts of Lee City proper, the anchor store of a small L-shaped strip mall, and the best customs shop in the tristate area. Jake pulled the truck to the back where metal roll-up doors opened up onto a hot rod shop much larger than what the front exterior would lead you to believe. Three eighteen-foot bays made up the back of the building, and smack dab in the center was Reed's 57 Ford F-100 pickup. After years of rusting in the old Samuels' barn, she was shined up like a new pair of shoes, jack-o-lantern orange and waiting patiently for her owner.

Jake looked at his friend as he pulled up to the shop, a Cheshire cat grin pulling at Reed's cheeks. He shook his head. "You're like a damn teenager in a titty bar, you know it?" Jake whistled as he put the truck in park. "She's sure pretty, though, buddy."

The shop's owner—Reed's second cousin's friend's brother or something—Chris "Gramps" Ward waved and walked to meet them. His salt and pepper hair stood high like Elvis's, and tattoos lined both arms from knuckles to neck. "What do you think?" He asked as he slapped Reed's hand into a firm shake. "She everything you hoped she'd be?"

Reed nodded, grinning wildly as he approached his new girl. As he ran his hand slowly and delicately over the hood, Jake stepped away to give him some alone time with BERTHA2.

Jake roamed the sidewalk of the strip mall, passing various storefronts and shops as he took his time meandering. Reed would be a while, and Jake used this time alone to continue pondering. There had to be a way to win TB's heart.

Tearing him from his thoughts, his nose picked up the scent of sweet cinnamon and his eyes closed as he tilted his head back and inhaled. He paused, searching the parking lot for the source of the smell. A bakery sat on one endcap of the strip mall, a short line forming out the door.

A bakery.

The Bakery next to The Bar.

Jake's pulse quickened and his mouth watered, but he didn't have time to try the place out, regardless of how badly his stomach wanted to urge him forward, or how long it had been since he'd had a decent muffin. His thoughts whirled chaotically in his head, a tornado of ideas and questions spinning as he tried to make sense of the process, the idea.

He finally had a plan. *Her* plan. It had been there in front of his face all along, but he'd been too damn blind to see it.

Warmth spread through his chest as excitement filled him, spurring him forward. He turned on his heels and raced back to the shop, the idea forming into perfect alignment in his brain, a solid image of what needed to be done to show her just how sorry he was and how terribly much he needed her back in his life, his home.

He pushed through the front doors of the shop and raced past the receptionist. "Reed?" he shouted once inside the garage, a bit too loudly on this quiet Saturday morning. All the mechanics turned to him, their eyebrows raised. "Sorry. Sorry." He cringed, meeting Reed's gaze as he stepped out from behind a low divider wall.

"Everything all right, buddy?"

Jake grinned. "Everything is perfect."

Reed stepped toward him. "Yeah? Then where's the fire?"

"No fire. I need your help with something."

Reed's eyebrows rose and he smiled, nodding slowly as he realized what Jake needed from him. "If it involves cleaning up this mess you made, I'm in."

Jake smiled, his chest expanding with the anticipation. He nodded, the movement quick and bouncy like his heartbeat. He'd finally realized how to show TB how much she meant to him, and he'd make Colby proud in the process. When all was said and done, no matter how she felt about him, Jake was about to finally do right by her, and this realization set his soul afire.

Because doing right by TB had been the goal along, and this was his chance.

Chapter Thirty-Two

Charlie and Roc finished loading the last of the boxes into Charlie's pickup, then strapped them down and closed the tailgate. Tamryn stepped back into the house and took one last, quick look around. It wasn't like she couldn't return for any forgotten items—like she had much to leave behind—but something inside her really wanted this to be a clean break.

No loose ends, no lost items, no reason to come back.

She might only be moving a few miles away, but in her mind, she'd already begun imagining what life would be like in New York with Luce. She'd spend the next six months planning her move, then say goodbye to this town and her mistakes forever.

Eventually her nerves would subside. Who wouldn't be nervous about such a big move?

It was fear of the unknown, nothing more.

Or so she kept telling herself.

"Yo! You ready to go, Tammy?" Roc called from the truck.

"Yeah," she shouted. "Be right out!"

She quickly surveyed the home once more on her way to the living room, then shut the door behind her and locked it, careful not to slip the key into her pocket like she usually would. No spare keys to Charlie's house for her. Not anymore. He'd have to find a place to store a Hide-A-Key or find some other ex-girlfriend to hold it for him.

Roc climbed out of the passenger side so she could slide into the middle, then hopped in again behind her.

"Ready?" Charlie asked, starting the truck.

Tamryn nodded. "As I'll ever be."

Charlie frowned. "You know you don't have to do this, right? I mean, you can stay with Roc and me for as long as you want—"

She placed her hand on his on the steering wheel. "I know, Charlie. Thank you. But it's time. I have to do this, have to go be alone for a minute, you know? See what it's like?"

Charlie shrugged and focused on the road as he pulled out of the dirt road leading to the Mills' farm. "I know, Tamryn. I get it."

"We'll miss you cleaning up around here," Roc said with a laugh.

"Jesus, Roc, no wonder she's leaving."

Roc slid his arm around Tamryn's shoulders and gave her a squeeze. "Shit, Tammy, you know I'm kidding. It's the baking I'll really miss. Kidding!"

Tamryn smiled, resting her head against Roc's shoulders. "I know, I know. I'll miss you guys too. It's been nice kinda having the old gang back together like this."

"You're not kidding." Charlie placed his hand on her thigh, leaving it there a bit too long, solidifying Tamryn's need to break out on her own. Charlie still had feelings for her, feelings she'd never be able to reciprocate. Staying with him wasn't fair to either of them.

She pulled her purse up onto her lap so he'd move his hand, then pretended to look for something. "Oh, shoot, I almost forgot." She dangled the key in front of her. "You'll need this back."

"No, keep it. We might need it someday when dumbass over there locks himself out."

"Hey," Roc said. "Like I'm the dumbass who lost his truck keys for a whole week."

Charlie laughed. "Whatever, man." He glanced at Tamryn. "Keep it."

"I can't." Tamryn pictured a quote she'd just seen on Instagram: *No is a complete sentence.* She didn't need to offer up an explanation.

Charlie somehow seemed to understand the truth in her words. He extended his hand and she dropped the key into his palm. "Thank you, Charlie, for everything."

He smiled sadly, his eyes still on the road as he drove toward the center of town. "Don't mention it, Baker. I'll always be around if you need me."

Tamryn nodded, but hoped that wasn't true. She wanted Charlie to find someone new, someone who could love him the way he deserved, and Lord knows his next girlfriend wouldn't want him responding to

Tamryn's every beck and call. More importantly, though, Tamryn didn't want to need help from him or anyone else in the future.

They pulled to a stop just out front of Syd's coffee shop, the outdoor seating area nearly full with the afternoon rush of high schoolers.

"Yes," Roc whispered, his eyes wide. "High school chicks."

Tamryn elbowed him, but he jumped down from the truck and walked over to the patio.

"Right," Charlie said on a laugh, "like he could get with any of those chicks."

Tamryn laughed as she slid off the seat and stepped down from the truck.

"Charlie? Charlie Morris?"

Tamryn turned to the sound of the voice as a tall girl with long brown hair stepped past the gate to Syd's patio and joined them on the sidewalk. She looked familiar, but Tamryn couldn't put a name to the face.

"Elena?" Charlie nervously glanced at Tamryn, then back at the girl. "Hey, how are you?"

She stepped closer and wrapped him in a hug. "I'm so good! We just moved back!"

Tamryn narrowed her eyes, trying to remember who this girl was. He'd said Elena, but the name didn't ring any bells.

Charlie stepped back awkwardly, then motioned toward Tamryn. "You remember my, uh, my ex, Tammy, I mean, Tamryn?"

"Hi." Tamryn stepped forward and extended her hand. "Tamryn Baker." She tilted her head. "Elena, was it? It's nice to meet you."

Elena gripped her hand, shaking vigorously, a smile pulling at her lips. "You don't remember me. Of course you don't." She shook her head, laughing. "I was like, what, fourteen when you guys graduated? And definitely not on your radar." She glanced shyly at Charlie, then back at Tamryn. "I used to live down the street from Charlie, that two story house with the giant Virgin Mary statue in the front yard."

Tamryn's eyes widened. "Oh my gosh, I totally remember you!" What she remembered was an awkward little girl with choppy bangs and braces, not this gorgeous woman standing in front of her. "What... how old are you now?" Tamryn looked her up and down, unable to hide the shock. "I mean, sorry, you just...you look a lot different."

Elena blushed, then pushed her long hair back over one golden-brown shoulder. "Almost eighteen. I graduate in June." She glanced quickly at Charlie, then back at Tamryn, smiling shyly.

"Well," Tamryn said, glancing between Charlie and Elena, "welcome back."

"Thanks. It's good to be home." Elena smiled at Charlie, holding his gaze.

Hmm. Maybe this was the girl Tamryn had hoped for, the one who would give Charlie the kind of relationship he deserved. Tamryn took a few steps backward slowly, then turned and headed for the back of the truck just as Reed approached.

"Who's that?" he asked, nodding toward Charlie and Elena as he retrieved a couple boxes.

"That's Elena. Sanchez, I think, but I can't remember. She used to live by Charlie."

Reed raised his eyebrow, his hazel eyes sparkling as he peered over Tamryn's shoulder. "Oh yeah? Where's she live now?"

"Ha, Reed, not a chance."

"What, she's out of my league?"

Tamryn laughed. "Not hardly. But she's only seventeen."

"Ah, jailbait. Damn." Reed nudged Tamryn's arm on his way past, then headed for the stairs behind the coffee shop that led to her new place.

She grabbed a bag of clothes and the vacuum, turning to follow Reed as her phone rang. She set everything back in the truck bed, and retrieved her cell from her purse. "Hello?"

"Hey there, little Baker sister."

"Hey, Randy. How are you?"

"Fine as wine, fine as wine. So, hey, you got a minute?"

Tamryn leaned back against the truck. "Yeah, but I can't be long, or Reed will unload all of these boxes himself."

"Oh, shoot! Is that today?"

Tamryn rolled her eyes. "Sure is, Randy."

"Ah heck, I'll be over in twenty to help out. I'll bring the booze."

With a laugh, Tamryn said, "Cool. I'll buy the pizza."

"Sounds like you've got yourself a deal." Randy cleared his throat, then paused long enough to make Tamryn cautious. "So, I'm planning a surprise party, for, um, Reed's birthday."

She exhaled a sigh. "Oh yeah?" Tamryn looked up at the apartment. Reed danced around in front of the large window that overlooked the main street. She shook her head, pressing the phone back to her ear. "When?"

"Saturday, the fourteenth. 'Round seven or so? Can you make it?"

"Sure. Where?"

Randy cleared his throat again.

Tamryn closed her eyes. *Don't say it, don't say it.*

"Jake's place."

Chapter Thirty-Three

As Bert—the one taxi driver in town—inched his old minivan closer and closer to her destination, Tamryn's stomach twisted in knots, her pulse racing. She couldn't believe she was about to walk into a place so full of painful memories. Memories she'd fought hard to move away from during the past three months, and even more so in these past few days. Memories that still felt raw and exposed, urging her to focus on her big move.

Was she running from her problems? Probably. But Tamryn couldn't focus on that when she was so busy actively ignoring the little voice inside her that begged her to reconsider.

This place was home, memories, mistakes, and all. Could she really walk away?

"Almost to Jake's place," Bert announced, as if Tamryn hadn't grown up in this town and knew exactly where they were.

She sighed. Even if she didn't know by the landscape, she could swear she felt each inch of distance between them slip away as she grew nearer to Jake.

Bert pulled up to the front of The Bar, and Tamryn's stomach tightened further, the knot twisting past discomfort to the point of pain.

God, what was she doing here? This was another huge mistake in a long line of many.

Reed, she reminded herself. His birthday was the only thing that would bring her back to Jake's bar, so she held tightly to that small fact. This was for Reed. She could suffer for an hour or two if it meant being a part of Reed's birthday celebration. He'd always been there for her, always gone above and beyond. Showing up for his party was the least she could do to repay him for years of love and friendship. Hell, who knew when she'd be here for another one once she left for New York?

Bert looked back at her in the rearview, eyebrows raised. "All set?"

She'd been sitting idle too long. Tamryn bit her lip and stared out the window. Draped with drop cloths and tarps, the empty storefront beside The Bar resembled a construction site. Tamryn shook her head, dropping her gaze to her lap. He must've sold it or leased the space out to give her that check, selling her dream to give her freedom she hadn't even taken. If her heart could break further, it would have with that realization. But there weren't any pieces left big enough to break, even if Jake had moved on without her, he had sold her dream space without even knowing about her dreams.

She looked around the dirt lot, surprised to see that Bert's van was the only vehicle parked there. Maybe she'd gotten the date wrong. Maybe she'd come too early. Maybe she'd been instructed to go in through the back and she'd forgotten. Would she ruin the surprise?

What had Randy said? The conversation was a blur in her mind, the only clear point—the only thing she'd *thought* about since the phone call—was the fact that she had to come back here. Back to the place where she'd loved and lost *everything*.

She shouldn't be here. Her heart pounded harder in her chest, lungs tight. She had to leave. She couldn't see Jake. It was still too soon, too raw. She hadn't quite gotten over him, wondered if she ever would; seeing him would be too painful.

I can't do this.

"What were you thinking?" She ran her hand over her face.

"You okay, Miss Baker?" Bert asked, turning around in his seat.

"No, I'm sorry. I shouldn't be here. Please take me home. Quickly." Tamryn wiped her sweaty palms on her black jeans.

"You sure?"

"Yes. Please, Bert."

Bert frowned, but he shrugged and threw the car into reverse. "Whatever you say."

The taxi van lurched to a halt, tossing Tamryn against the front seat since she'd unbuckled when they arrived. "Ow, what the…?"

Bert slapped the steering wheel and rolled down the window. "What the hell, Randy? I could have killed you, boy!"

Tamryn looked behind the cab. Randy grinned, shaking his head, then held up his finger and thumb, showing how close they'd come to hitting him. "Sorry 'bout that, Bert. Couldn't let ya leave with our girl here."

Bert shook his head. "Miss Baker has changed her mind. Go on and step aside so we can get on our way."

Randy met Tamryn's gaze through the back window and shook his head. "Afraid I can't do that."

"Randy!" Tamryn handed Bert a twenty and opened the door. "I'm sorry about this, Bert. I'll get a ride home from here."

"I'm just a phone call away if you change your mind again."

Tamryn nodded and stepped out of the cab. "Thank you." She rounded on Randy as she slid the door closed. "Who does that?"

"What, runs people over?" He laughed. "Shit, kid, I was just about to ask ol' Bert the same thing." He leaned forward conspiratorially, bringing his thumb and forefinger to his mouth. "He been hittin' the old Devil's lettuce again?"

She shook her head, crossing her arms across her chest. "You could have been hurt."

"You were trying to leave. Can't have that."

Tamryn narrowed her gaze. "Where is everyone?"

"They parked behind the bar," he whispered. "Come on. Reed will be here any minute. We don't want to ruin the surprise."

She inhaled a deep breath, squared her shoulders, and fought back the urge to cry, the urge to run, and the urge to scream.

She could handle this. She could handle Jake.

Randy placed his hand on her back and led her to the door, then opened it and stepped aside. "Go on in, then."

Tamryn side-eyed Randy, then peered inside the darkened bar. Her pulse sped as she scanned the blackness. What if Jake brought a date?

Oh God. Her stomach churned at the thought. She couldn't do this.

"Go on. Ain't no one gonna bite you." Randy patted her back, nudging her forward.

She stepped inside, and the doors closed behind her, but she barely registered the sound as the room was suddenly aglow with muted amber light.

Her breath caught in her throat. Tiny, twinkling lights decorated the bar, strung up from one corner to the other, draping, then coming to a point above the dancefloor, the soft glow of white lights the only illumination in the room. Jake and Randy had really gone above and beyond for their friend, and Tamryn couldn't help but be impressed.

She brought her hand to her mouth, searching the dimly lit room for the other party guests.

Jake stepped out from the shadows. "Surprise."

Chapter Thirty-Four

Tamryn gasped, turning toward the sound of his voice, heart plummeting to the floorboards. He'd ditched his usual t-shirt and worn-in denim or sweats, for black jeans and a dark gray button-up that did nothing to conceal the hard lines of his frame. Sleeves rolled up, his forearms exposed, she studied the familiar hands of this hard-working man she loved.

"You look…" Jake shook his head, then licked his lips, his gaze slowly caressing her from head to toe. "I've missed you."

Her eyebrows bunched, words escaping her. Where was everyone else? Where was Reed?

The slow rhythm of Johnny Lee filled the room, the jukebox springing to life on its own. She glanced over at the machine on the wall, then back to Jake. She shouldn't have come here.

Jake took a step forward.

She *really* shouldn't have come here. Tamryn shook her head, heart thudding in her ears.

Another step forward.

God, she loved him.

His normally unruly hair was brushed and styled, and Tamryn's fingers itched to mess it up, to grasp it and hold his head to hers, his lips to her mouth.

She met his gaze and sucked in a breath. She'd missed those blue eyes, the intensity they could hold, the unspoken words they whispered.

She swallowed hard, then ran her tongue over her teeth to clear the thickness from her mouth. "Where's Reed?" She shook her head, confused. "What about his party?" Even as she asked the question, it felt wrong.

Jake grinned. "Silly girl. Reed's birthday isn't until June."

Tamryn shook her head. Had she been so preoccupied that she'd completely forgotten Reed's actual birthday? "I don't understand. What if I'd remembered that?"

Shaking his head, Jake laughed. "I blame myself for not giving Randy explicit directions on how to get you to come here." Johnny Lee sang on in the background, and Jake took another cautious step forward, his smile fading back into a more serious expression. "I've always loved this song. It's not just because Johnny Lee is the finest singer this side of the nineteen-fifties"—he winked—"or that Bud's my hero; it's more than that. It's the poetry of it. The ache of never finding love, never knowing its *right there*. If only I'd get out of my own way."

He stopped, leaving a foot between them, and his cologne wrapped around her like a summer's breeze, pulling her, lulling her into the warmth of him. She inhaled deeply, her heart fluttering in her chest, and pulled her bottom lip between her teeth.

"This is our song. But you knew that." Jake reached up, placing his fingers beneath her chin, his thumb resting just below her mouth. He gently pulled her lip free of her teeth, then ran his thumb over her lip. "You were never singing for them, you were singing for me."

Tamryn swallowed hard. "*With* you."

"And it's not because we sang this song together more times than I can count." He shook his head, smiling sadly. "I'm that guy in the song. I'm the idiot who was always looking for love in all the wrong places."

A tear slid from her eye. Tamryn licked her lips and his gaze fell to her mouth, causing her stomach to tighten.

He met her gaze once more. "But it was right here all along, wasn't it?"

She fought the smile that threatened to break free, tried to ignore the growing puddles in her eyes.

"Ah hell. I'm no good at this." He dropped his hand, but she reached out and caught it, sliding her fingers around his. "You're not supposed to cry."

"You're doing fine, Jake."

He smiled, averting his gaze, then rubbed his free hand over his hair, messing it up as she'd wanted to. *Perfect.* He brought his gaze back to hers and smiled. "Come with me? I have something to show you."

"Where are we going?"

"You'll see." He moved his hand so his fingers could twine with hers, then gave her hand a squeeze. "I'm sorry, but I know I'm no good with words." He searched her gaze, inhaling a visibly deep breath. "I hope you can hear what I'm about to show you." He gave a curt nod, then tugged her forward, leading her back outside into the night. "Close your eyes."

Tamryn narrowed her eyes and tilted her head as she looked up at him.

"Just do it, TB."

He led her next door and stopped in front of the empty building. The space that was once almost hers, but was now under construction for someone else, for someone else's dream.

But now, standing in front of it, Jake's hand very lightly resting on her lower back, hope surged within her and she *knew.*

Anticipation began a dizzying dance in her chest.

She finally closed her eyes.

"I really fucked up."

Tamryn smiled.

"I'm sorry, TB. I...I just never realized. Or, I guess I never *let* myself realize. I was so hung up on taking care of you, of honoring my promise to Colby. *Shit.*"

She didn't open her eyes, but she imagined him frantically rubbing the top of his head, messing his dark hair further, a nervous habit he'd had as long as she could remember. Tamryn focused on her breathing, waiting for what he'd say next, biting the inside of her bottom lip to keep from grinning.

"Damn, TB, I can't do this with your eyes closed. Please look at me."

She opened her eyes, met his bright gaze, and sucked in a breath.

Eyes crinkled around the edges, his smile lines appearing far deeper than she remembered, his eyebrows bunched together, he chewed on his bottom lip. She'd never seen him nervous. Jake didn't do nervous. Jake was the embodiment of confidence and composure. He searched her gaze, then sighed, and she fought the urge to wrap her arms around him and save him from the torment of trying to find the words to say how he felt.

No, he owed her this much. An explanation, an apology, and maybe something more.

His heart would be a good start, but she didn't want to hold out for that. Hoping for her love to be returned was what had gotten them into this mess in the first place.

But the way he frantically searched her gaze…

He ran his hand through his hair, and Tamryn reached up to grab it without thinking. His fingers squeezed around hers, and he brought her hand to his chest. "I really screwed things up." He shook his head, mouth opening and closing as he searched for his next words.

Tamryn held her breath.

"You're the best thing that ever happened to me. I've been a real shit."

She smiled, just barely, but didn't say anything for fear of halting his apology.

"I didn't realize it then, and it took me a good long while, I admit, but you've always been the one for me. Everyone knew it. You knew it." He paused, glancing up at the sky. "Colby knew it."

Tamryn drew in a shaky breath, eyes tickling as tears formed again, but still, she dared not speak.

"Ah, hell, I don't want to make you cry." He dropped her hand, then ran his hands down his face. "This isn't going how I planned at all."

"Jake." She reached up, sliding her hands into his and pulling them away from his beautiful face. "Keep going."

He met her gaze, then smiled, revealing that perfect, single dimple. "I love you, TB. I've never loved anyone but you."

"You broke my heart, Jake." She inhaled a shallow breath as he pressed closer.

"I know, TB, and I'll spend forever showing you just how sorry I am, if you'll let me. I want to be the man you deserve, the man…the man your brother wanted me to be. I want to be…hell, TB, I just want *you*. All of you, some of you, whatever you're willing to give. I know I fucked up, and I know I don't deserve your forgiveness, but I'll do whatever it takes. I'm yours, Tamryn Lynn Baker, without a doubt, completely yours."

"Kiss her already!"

Tamryn jumped at the sound of Luce's voice behind her. She quickly glanced over her shoulders but couldn't see anything in the shadows cloaking the building. "What's going on, Jake?" She squinted up at him, her lips twitching on a grin.

"You'll see."

She pressed up on her toes. "You should probably do what she says."

Jake flashed a bright smile, then brought his lips to hers in a flash, wrapping his arms around her and crushing her against his hard chest, threatening to knock the breath from her lungs. She opened up to him, and he plunged his tongue inside her mouth, gliding along the length of her tongue with a need so wild she felt the ache all the way in her toes.

He slid his arms tighter around her waist, lifting her off the ground, his tongue doing magical things to hers, sending shivers throughout her body, down each limb until every inch of her buzzed with lustful excitement. She wrapped her arms around his neck and held on tight as they shared a kiss that finally said in unison, *I'm yours.*

When he pulled his lips away and set her feet back on the ground, her legs were so weak she gripped his forearms for balance.

"Ready?"

"For what," she breathed.

"Your surprise."

"That wasn't it?" She bit her lip, dropping her gaze to his mouth and loving the way she could still feel the pressure of his tongue against hers.

Jake grinned, then whistled. "What, that kiss? Please." He dipped in and gently tugged her bottom lip in between his for a brief second. "That kiss was only the beginning, little Baker, I plan on kissing you until you can't catch your breath, every damn day for the rest of your life." He paused, searching your gaze. "If that's okay with you, of course."

Tamryn's response came in the form of half laugh, half snort, then she blushed, embarrassed by such a ridiculous noise. Couldn't he just kiss her until she couldn't breathe right now? What surprise could be better than Jake finally admitting he loved her?

Jake's eyes sparkled as he watched her internal debate. He winked, then turned her in his arms to face the storefront beside The Bar.

Reed and Randy emerged from the shadows, slipping out to the porch through drop cloth curtains hanging over the door.

Tamryn watched them step to either side of the doorway. "Where's Lu—?"

"Shhh," Jake whispered, his lips so close to her ear that her skin vibrated beneath his hush and her chest warmed. She leaned back into him, and he wrapped his arms around her small frame, holding her tight against his chest. Damn, that felt good.

"Finally," Luce whispered as she stepped up beside Reed. "I'd about given up on you two." She and Reed grabbed onto a rope that dangled from the roof. Randy did the same on the other side, and together, the three of them stepped backward, away from the building, pulling the drop cloths with them.

Tamryn gasped and she brought her hand to her mouth.

Neon so bright it was blinding. The Bakery.

Right next to The Bar.

His and Hers. She laughed on a sob, a sound so awful she figured it made her recent laugh-snort almost adorable. She turned in his arms, shaking her head because words eluded her. There was too much joy, too much relief, too much love to speak.

Jake's eyes glistened. "You like it?"

She nodded, swallowing the thickness of emotion in her throat.

"You love it?" A lone tear escaped his eye. Just one, but enough.

She pushed up on her toes, and grasped his face. "I love it." She paused, searching his gaze. "I love *you*, Jake."

Jake's grin spread wide across his face. "I love you, too."

His lips closed over hers in a crushing kiss as he lifted her up into the air, holding her pressed firmly against his body.

Right where she belonged.

Chapter Thirty-Five

"All right, all right," Reed said. "I don't want to break up this love fest, but let's get this show on the road!"

Randy whooped, and Jake pulled back, looking down into hungry blue eyes. He groaned low in his throat; he'd put that thirst in those baby blues, and he was beyond ready to quench it. He needed to be alone with her.

"You promised to steal my breath." TB smiled and Jake's groin tightened in response to the soft huskiness of her voice.

"Oh, I will. Right before I make you scream my name so loud the earth quakes in response."

She sucked in a breath, her pale chest rising visibly.

"Mmm," he moaned, dipping in for another kiss. He looked over her shoulder at The Bakery. "Guys, I think I need some time alone with Tamryn."

"Right after the Five Cent Tour, Johnson. We had a deal."

"A deal?" TB asked.

"Mhm. If they helped me with this, they could be here for the big reveal." Jake looked back into Tamryn's eyes. "I'm not sure I can wait to be alone with you, though."

"I know the feeling." She ran her hands over his chest and Jake shook his head.

"Come on, guys"—Randy burped—"It ain't like you two haven't already done it."

"Randy," Luce chided.

Jake closed his eyes. *Fucking Randy.*

"You told them?"

He dared a peek to see her expression. "Maybe? You mad?"

She shook her head and smiled. "Nah. A lady never tells, but you are no lady."

Jake rolled his eyes. "Come on. They'll never leave us alone if I renege on my promise." He released her and slid his hand into hers. "All right, on with the surprise. But after this, you all should know I'm going to need her to myself for at least three-to-five days."

"Days?" TB squeaked, her eyebrows flying up.

Jake paused, considering. He let go of her hand to slide his palm over her perfect ass, then watched the blood rush to her cheeks, her chest. He shook his head. He'd need at least a few *weeks* to properly apologize to this woman the way she deserved. "Ready for the Five Cent Tour, Miss Baker?"

She bit her lip, then looked ahead at The Bakery, her smile spreading from ear to ear. Sliding her hand back into his, she started forward. "Come on," she urged, the excitement in her voice bringing his focus back to the gift he was about to give her, his grand gesture.

"So," he began, bracing for her wrath. "About that twenty-five grand I owe you…"

TB stopped dead in her tracks and looked back at him. "I told you no, Jake."

"Here we go," Randy mumbled.

Luce shushed him.

"Just give me a chance to explain." He walked with her to the wooden porch, then up the three steps, stopping in front of the door. The lights were off, so she couldn't see anything, but he couldn't help but smile as she peered into the darkness, hoping for a glimpse. "Were you one of those kids who opened presents before Christmas, then rewrapped them so no one would know?"

Tamryn looked back up at him, her smile sheepish. "No. Maybe."

"Listen." He took both of her hands in his. "I've been saving every dollar you've made, every cent, and matching it. It wasn't something I decided to do after I thought I'd lost you, TB, it's something I've done since Day One."

"Okay," she said, tentatively.

"There was also an account on the side, something that Colby had started, that the rest of us would contribute to when we had a little extra—"

Tamryn looked past him to Reed and Randy. "What? Seriously? Why would you guys do that?" She shook her head, disbelief all over her face.

"Colby was our best friend." Randy shrugged.

"We love you, kid." Reed chuckled. "What can we say; we're all suckers for the Bakers."

Tamryn frowned. "I don't want you guys thinking you need to take care of me. I'm not a kid."

"God, Thelma, they get it."

Tamryn shot her friend a glare, and Jake sighed, then bent at the knees enough to bring his eyes level with hers. "No one thinks you're a kid, Tamryn. We want to take care of you because we love you. You're one of us."

She dropped her gaze. "I just don't want you guys to look at me like a little sister for the rest of my life."

"Hey," Jake said, reaching for her chin to tilt it back up. "Trust me," he whispered for only her to hear, "the things I'm going to do to you are completely illegal in all fifty states—"

"Christ on a cracker," Luce shrieked. "TMI."

"—*if* we were siblings." Jake smiled, holding TB's gaze. "I'll spend my life showing you just how much you are not my sister."

Tamryn's eyes widened on a flash of something hungry and heat flooded her cheeks with the palest of pink.

Jake's dick swelled in his pants. "You gotta stop looking at me like that in front of our friends, though, baby."

"Okay, okay." Reed stepped up beside them. "Long story short, Tam, Jake took that money and put it into this." He waved his arm toward The Bakery doors, now open, and Randy flipped the interior lights on.

Tamryn gasped, pulling her hands from Jake's to place them over her chest. Jake watched her eyes as she scanned the interior, the walls a soft pink on the top half and what Reed said was called gingham decorating the bottom. Jake had done his best to finish what TB started, not changing anything and working off of what she'd told Reed about her dreams for the space beside his bar. By the awestruck expression on her face, he might have succeeded.

"Well," he said, suddenly back to feeling hesitant and a bit uneasy. What if he'd failed? "Go inside. It's yours."

She turned to him and reached out, grabbing his forearms. She shook her head, disbelief and tears in her eyes. "Thank you."

Jake shook his head and pulled her close, pressing his lips to her ear. "Thank you, TB. For loving me at my most unlovable." She shook in his arms, so he pulled back to peer into glistening eyes. "Why are you crying? Is it wrong?" Panic gripped his chest.

"No, you big idiot, it's perfect. You're perfect. I can't believe this is happening."

Jake grinned, warmth spreading across his chest. "Go on, then, go inside."

She held his gaze for a long few seconds, then nodded, her grin stretching clear to her ears it seemed, then she turned and nearly ran her friend over in her haste to get inside. The two girls linked arms and raced inside the new bakery. Randy followed behind them, but Jake stayed on the porch watching TB touch each table and chair, running her fingers over each appliance, pressing the fabric of the curtains between her fingers. She laid the top half of her body over the counter beside the register, practically hugging the glass display case. She and Lucy laughed and talked a mile a minute, dodging from one side of the store, then back again, and touching every inch of the new digs.

"You did a good thing here, man." Reed stepped up beside Jake, nudging him with his arm. "Gave her everything she ever wanted."

Jake turned to Reed. "She gave me everything I ever wanted."

Reed smiled, watching TB as Jake had been. "Probably more than you deserve."

Jake looked over as his friend's smile faded. "Don't break her heart," he said as he met Jake's gaze, straight-faced.

Jake placed his hand on Reed's shoulder and gave it a squeeze. "Never again, old friend. Never again." He left Reed on the porch and stepped inside, stopping just behind TB where she gazed up at the large canvas on the wall. This was his favorite part of the surprise, but his pulse sped in spite of how much he loved the photograph. What if she hated it? What if it caused her too much pain?

Without even looking, she reached back for him and grabbed his hand. "Where did you find this?"

Jake's heart sank; she hated it. "I'm sorry, I…"

She spun around and met his gaze, her eyes wet with tears. "Sorry? It's perfect, Jake. I can't even…" She turned back around, looking back up at the black and white photo of her and Colby baking together in their parents' kitchen. Jake thought they were probably about nine and four, but he couldn't be sure. He'd found the picture just after high school, when looking through old family photo albums with Colby. Something about it had spoken to him, something about it had made him slip it into his pocket that day and hold onto the snapshot all this time. Maybe he'd loved her even then.

Tamryn brought his hand to her lips and laid a soft kiss on his knuckles. "Thank you."

Jake swallowed, the action difficult with the thickness in his throat.

After a few minutes, she finally turned to him again, her eyes a little less damp, but her smile no less radiant. "Have I told you that I love you today?"

Jake grinned, leaning forward to brush his lips against hers, wanting so badly to taste her again. "You have."

"Good. 'Cause I do."

"I love you too." He pulled her close, then bent to nuzzle his nose against her throat. "Now, what's this I hear about you getting your own place?" He looked up into her eyes.

Her smile widened. "I moved into the little apartment above Syd's."

"So I've heard. Are you happy?"

She nodded. "I am now."

"Good." He ducked in to kiss her, groaning deep in his throat when her tongue darted out across his lips.

"Want to see it?"

Jake grinned, pulling back to look at her once more. "I showed you mine, now you show me yours?"

Tamryn's lids grew heavy, provoking tightness in Jake's pants. "Hopefully in more ways than one."

He nearly choked from her boldness. "Maybe we should just go to my place." He glanced toward the back of the shop. "It's so much closer."

"Maybe you two could just do it right here on the floor and make us all really uncomfortable," Lucy said as she passed them. "Oh wait, too late." She grabbed Reed and Randy by the arms and hauled them to the door. "Come on, boys, let's get knackered." The three of them exited the bakery, the door swooshing closed behind them.

Tamryn looked up at Jake. "You called her?"

"She's your best friend, right?"

Tamryn nodded.

"You just opened your own business, seems like a good time for friends to come around, no?" He squeezed her to him, and her gaze drew heavy.

"Want to lock the door?" She trailed her fingertips up his bicep, then over his shoulder.

Jake's eyes widened. "Right now?"

She nodded slowly, her gaze heavy. "Right now."

Chapter Thirty-Six

Jake wasted no time stepping away from her to lock the door of The Bakery, then turned around, and she was gone. He quickly scanned the small space for her, and her shirt flew out from behind the glass display shelves.

He grinned as heated excitement rushed through his veins. He slowly strode to the counter, unbuttoning his shirt as he approached. He dropped the shirt behind him as he stepped behind the counter and paused. She was naked from head to toe, save for the pink and green apron he'd purchased for her. He shook his head. "Just as I suspected." He unfastened his belt and started on his pants. "You look good enough to eat."

Something wicked flashed across her eyes and Jake's dick hardened, springing from his pants as he unzipped them.

TB stepped toward him. "Welcome to The Bakery," she whispered, trailing a hand up one arm, across his shoulders as she stepped behind him, then down the other arm as she stepped in front of him once more. She winked, her cheeks flushing, then she dropped her gaze to his erection and kneeled before him. "It would be our pleasure to serve you."

Jake tossed his head back on a moan as she took him in her mouth, then looked back down at her, not wanting to miss a single second of the way her mouth slid up and down his length. She took him in slowly, all the way until he thought for sure she'd choke, then slid back and looked up at him as she twirled her tongue around his tip. Her lips glistened, and the urge to grab her head was too strong to fight. He slid his hands into her hair on either side of her head and gently guided her back and forth along his cock. Each time she pulled back, she sucked the tip or ran her tongue over it until Jake's belly tightened, then she'd open wide for him and slide back down to the base.

The mouth of an angel, and fucking it was nothing short of heavenly.

She wrapped her hand around his cock, moving back and forth with the motion of her mouth, and Jake closed his eyes, tilting his head back. She moaned, and the sound vibrated throughout his body.

He pulled her head away and looked down into those hungry blue eyes, mustering all his strength not to finish in her mouth. "Careful," he whispered, the word heavy with lust. "Do that again and I won't be able to hold back."

One eyebrow rose briefly, then a devilish grin pulled at her perfect lips. She took him back into her mouth, gripped his shaft with her hand, then moaned. Jake's dick throbbed, and he gripped her hair, thrusting with every motion of her head. She cupped his balls with her free hand and Jake couldn't take anymore.

"Fuck," he groaned, gripping her hair and holding her head still as he thrust one more time, then held her still and filled her mouth, his legs trembling with the release. She pressed her hand around the base of his cock, milking him until every drop had been spent.

With her eyes locked on his, she swallowed, then leaned back on her heels. She licked her lips and smiled. "Was it good for you?"

Jake laughed, his shoulders shaking as he leaned to help her to her feet. "It was fucking *fantastic* for me." He wiped her hair back from her eyes, then grinned. "But we're only getting started."

Tamryn's belly tightened in response to the fire in his eyes. He picked her up, then placed her on top of the display case. "We'll have to give this place a good cleaning when I'm done with you." Heat rushed to her cheeks and chest, but he continued. "I have a feeling it's going to get very dirty in here." He pulled his bottom lip into his teeth as he looked her over. "Not that I mind fucking you on every surface I can find, but the customers might."

Tamryn glanced behind her at the door. If anyone walked by, they'd surely see her on display like this, even with the lights off. The counter area was still lit up by the hallway light, and a soft glow illuminated the front windows from the parking lot lights. She looked back at Jake, and all fear was lost to the heat of his gaze.

He looked between her legs, then past her to the front of the store. "Someone might see us." He licked his lips, then leaned forward, bringing his face closer to her center. "Tell me to stop." He brushed his lips against her belly, then gently dragged his teeth a bit lower.

Desire rushed south, tightening her core and sending a flood of wetness between her legs. She opened them further to give Jake a better view.

Jake cocked an eyebrow and looked up at her. "A little daring, tonight, aren't we?" He grabbed the sides of each thigh and pulled her closer to the edge of the display case, opening her legs around his head. "I like this side of you."

So do I.

He leaned forward, bringing his mouth to her center. "I like this side of you too." He teased her with a quick lick, then wrapped his arms around her lower back, pulling her all the way to the edge. Kneeling between her legs, he closed his mouth over her and ran his tongue up and down.

Tamryn sighed and opened her legs wide, placing her ankles on his shoulders, then leaned back on her hands. He gripped her ass, massaging her with his hands as his mouth massaged her clit. Reaching up with one hand, he splayed his palm over her breast and teased her nipple with his thumb. She arched further, and he slid his tongue inside her, plunging hard and fast.

"Oh, Jake," she said, sucking in a breath as he sucked on her clit.

"Mmm, he said against her, sending vibrations deep into her body. She opened her eyes and met his gaze. "Serves you right." He spoke the words against her skin, and she nearly came from the vibrations.

Reaching out, she grabbed his head, gripping his hair. She pressed herself back into his mouth and he moved against her, hungrily lapping at her wetness.

"Jake…"

"Hmm?"

"I need you."

He stood quickly, then grabbed her hips and turned her body so she could lie back along the length of the display case, pulling her ass to the edge. He ran his hand up her body, gripping her breast, massaging it as he leaned forward once more and closed his mouth over her. She opened her legs wider, gripped his hair, and moved her hips with each motion of his mouth, bucking wildly against his face while his tongue plunged in and out of her center.

Lights lit up the room as a car pulled into the parking lot, parking bin front og the bar. Tamryn froze. If they held perfectly still, maybe no one would notice them.

Jake released her breast, then tiptoed his fingers down her stomach, her skin dancing with each touch. She inhaled a shaky breath.

The lights shut off. A car door closed.

Jake pushed his fingers inside of her, then curled them up into her g-spot, massaging her inner wall. She let out a loud gasp, then gripped the display case on either side.

"Let them see us," he whispered.

Tamryn wanted to argue, but words had no meaning as her body reacted to the nimble way he moved his hand inside her, pressing against her while simultaneously sucking on her clit, pulling it into his mouth and teasing her with his tongue. Jake knew his way around a woman's body, and the feeling of his mouth on her was intoxicating.

I could do this all night.

As if reading her mind and daring to challenge her, Jake placed his other hand on her lower belly, pressing down against his fingers inside of her and intensifying the pressure to the point of boiling. Tamryn gasped, arching toward him, her body tightening around his hand as he thrust his fingers in and out.

"Oh, God," she moaned, grinding harder against him.

"That's it, baby, come for me."

With the words still barely freed from his lips, Tamryn's body shuddered, and she came in a frenzied quake, her body tightening and releasing as an orgasm ripped through her. He coaxed every last bit of orgasm out of her, his fingers moving slowly, gently, as she slowly came back down to earth, her body buzzing with satisfaction.

Tamryn opened her eyes just as he took his fingers into his mouth and tasted her. She blushed, looking away.

"Uh-uh," he said, shaking his head as he pulled her chin back to face him. "You don't get to be shy now." He reached into his jeans pocket and grabbed a condom, then watched her watch him as he slid it on. Her stomach tightened again at the sight of his hand on his cock. Jake reached for her hand and slowly helped her sit up, then stepped between her legs and slid his arms behind her back. "Hop on." He flashed a wicked grin, and Tamryn's heart fluttered in her chest.

"I'm not sure I can go again so soon," she whispered, doubting the words even as she said them. With his hard cock so close to her center, anticipation made her mouth water.

Jake shook his head. "Ye of little faith." He ducked down, pulling her nipple into his mouth. With one long, hard suck, Tamryn's back arched and her toes curled.

She gasped and squeezed his shoulders, pressing herself against his mouth.

When he released her, he teased the nipple gently with his tongue, then looked up. "You were saying?"

She laughed, then wrapped her legs around his waist. "Don't listen to me. I obviously don't know what I'm talking about."

He gripped her ass and lifted her off the display counter, then pressed his dick against her center. She gasped, and he closed his mouth over hers, the sweet saltiness of herself still fresh on his lips. With his tongue in her mouth, and her breasts pressed against his chest, Tamryn slid herself onto Jake's dick, tilting her head back as he filled her.

"Mmm," he moaned into her neck. "You're fucking amazing." He suckled her throat, sliding his tongue up her neck until he could pull her earlobe into his mouth.

She clenched around him, arching in such a way that her clit pressed against the base of his shaft. "You're not too bad yourself." She gripped his shoulders firmly, tightened her legs around his waist, then started to guide herself up and down his shaft.

Chapter Thirty-Seven

Jake's knock made Tamryn jump up from the couch and race for the door, but she paused and began to count to ten so he wouldn't think she'd just been sitting there, desperate for him to arrive. Which she had been. She stopped at five and opened the door. Who was she kidding? He knew she was desperate for him. They'd displayed just how desperate they were for one another for nearly seven hours last night, until she finally had to tap out so she could haul Luce into a cab and get her drunk ass back to Tamryn's apartment.

That had been early this morning, and after sleeping it off, Luce was currently on her way back to The Bar, where Tamryn and Jake would meet up with her and the boys for dinner.

Well, as soon as they could manage, anyway. Which, judging by the way Jake's hungry gaze set fire to her skin as he raked it up and down her body, she didn't see them leaving her tiny apartment anytime soon.

Or, ever.

"While you've been standing there talking to yourself," Jake said, tapping his head, "I've already fucked you five different, very colorful ways. Care to invite me in?"

Tamryn's belly tightened and she nodded, a grin splitting her face as she sucked in a shaky breath. "Did you run here?"

He nodded. His shirt clung to his chest, damp from sweat, and her favorite running pants hung down low on his hips. Hips she wanted to feel pressing against hers.

"So, this is your new place, huh?" Jake stepped over the threshold, and she breathed him in as he passed, unable to form words with all the desire buzzing in her veins. "Are we alone?"

Tamryn nodded, the motion lost to the back of his head. She closed the door behind her and he whipped around.

"Fucking finally," he growled as he wrapped his arms around her waist, crushing his lips against hers. When he pulled back, his lids were heavy, his eyes hungry. "I need you," he whispered, his voice rough with need.

Tamryn's breath caught in her throat. "I'm right here." She inhaled a few breaths, trying to steady herself, then pulled away from him, fighting for some semblance of self-control. "Ready for the Five Cent Tour?"

Jake's eyes narrowed as he held her gaze. "Maybe after I've fucked you silly."

Heat rushed south and Tamryn gasped, but with one quick movement he bent to slide an arm behind her knees and picked her up, cradling her against his chest. With his mouth so close to hers, she shivered with anticipation.

Jake smirked, his eyes twinkling. "Mmm, I don't think I'm the only one who likes that idea just a little too much."

Tamryn swallowed, then shook her head. Her mouth dropped open on a sigh.

His gaze fell to her lips. "Ready to lose your breath?"

Holy. Shit. Yes. Very much yes. She nodded, words running through her brain but somehow stopping before they reached her mouth.

"Bedroom?"

She raised a hand, pointing to the back of the small apartment.

Briskly, he made his way down the hall, never taking his gaze from her lips. She licked them out of habit, and his eyes rolled back in his head. "Naked. You. Now."

She giggled at his inability to form complete sentences, but the giggle died in her throat when he laid her on the bed, then slid on top of her.

"What's so funny, Miss Baker?" He pulled her hands up, pressing them into the pillows on either side of her head, and twining his fingers through hers. The weight of his body pressed down into her, but it wasn't enough. She needed him. Now.

Tamryn wiggled beneath Jake, spreading her legs out, then wrapped them around him, squeezing until she pushed up into his erection.

Half moan, half growl, the sound that slipped from Jake's mouth was pure heaven, and she pressed up into him again to tease a few more noises from his perfect lips. He nibbled her bottom lip, then slid one hand down her arm, the other still restrained beside her head, and slid his fingers up beneath her shirt. She arched into his hand when it molded around her breast, her sounds of pleasure and need now mingling with his.

"God, Tamryn, you're…" he pulled back to look into her eyes. "You're amazing. I want to…" He searched her gaze as his words trailed off.

"Please."

He nibbled her jaw line. "Please what?"

She closed her eyes and arched as he trailed his lips down her throat, her collar bone, her chest. "Please." His lips closed over her nipple, and she gasped as she pressed more firmly into his mouth. "Oh, God, *please*, Jake."

He licked a circle around the pert nipple tip. "Please what?"

"Fuck me five different ways."

His mouth still on her breast, he met her gaze, lids heavy. With one long, hard suck, he shot a current of lust straight down into her groin and she bucked in response. "I thought you'd never ask."

Tamryn closed her eyes as waves of pleasure radiated through her.

"Open your eyes."

She did as she was told, and he rewarded her by sitting up and removing his shirt. She reached for him, trailing her fingers down the hard planes of his abs. He watched the movement of her fingers, eyes wild with hunger, then began to unbutton his fly and back up off the bed.

Tamryn licked her lips, fighting back a giggle as excitement bubbled up in her chest.

When his pants hit the floor, giggling was the last thing on her mind. She sucked in a shaky breath as he climbed up the length of her, rested on his hands and knees, positioning himself above her just high enough that she had an unobstructed view of his hard length between them. Her body ached, heated, her legs trembling in response to his size, his closeness. She'd explode if he wasn't inside of her soon.

Jake gave a low whistle. "It looks like I'm bare-assed, and you're still dressed. Didn't I tell you to get naked?"

Tamryn smirked. "What are you going to do about it, Jake?"

Jake's lips twisted into a wicked grin, then he crushed her mouth with his, invading her with his tongue in long, hard strokes. She wrapped herself around him, the hard sharpness of his cock pressing into her in such a way that loosed a whimper from her lips.

He pulled back, eyes wild, and began the slow, painful task of undressing her. First, her tank-top. Slowly, he slid one spaghetti strap down her arm, then then the other, then he slowly slid the fabric down over her breasts, exposing them little by little. Tamryn practically vibrated with excitement. "Jake," she moaned.

"Patience, TB." He grimaced. "Sorry, I mean *Tamryn*. That's going to take some time, you know? Old habits."

Tamryn smiled. "Fuck it. Call me TB." *Call me any damn thing you want.*

Jake grinned, his eyes blazing brighter. "I love the way your mouth looks when you say that."

She stilled. "What? TB?"

He shook his head. "No. *Fuck*."

The way he said the word resonated deep within her, sending a thundering vibration down low in her belly. "Fuck," she whispered.

He groaned, moving with a sudden desperate haste to take off her jeans. She smiled as she watched him realize she'd forgotten a certain piece of clothing.

Jake growled, meeting her gaze. "No panties."

She smiled. "Whoops."

He hastily tugged her jeans down, then leaned forward to kiss the soft spot below her belly button. "Say it again, baby."

For Jake, she'd say nothing but that one word for the rest of her life. Especially if it made his eyes flare brighter like that. "Fuck me, Jake."

"Ah hell, Baker. Anything you want." He leaned over her, circling one nipple with his tongue, then the other, until both stood at rigid attention once more. Smiling, he slid lower, bringing his mouth level with her center, his breath teasing the sensitive skin there.

Tamryn's eyes fluttered closed when he placed his hands on her inner thighs, fingertips so close to sliding inside her but not damn close enough. He slid his palms down the length of her legs, sending shivers up her spine as her skin broke into goose bumps. He kissed the ball of each foot in turn, then sucked on her toe. Her eyes sprang open as pleasure surged within her, tightening her lower belly. "What...I didn't think I'd like that," she gasped. *What the hell?* No one had sucked on her toes before. It was...weird.

And good. *Holy shit, so damn good.*

He pulled her toe back into his mouth and sucked again, electricity shooting in a straight line from toe to groin. She wiggled from the pleasure building inside her.

He tickled her left foot.

Tamryn's eyes popped open, and she jerked her leg from his grasp.

Jake grinned. "Just making sure you're still with me."

"Oh, I'm with you," she murmured in a voice so throaty she almost didn't recognize it as her own. She cleared her throat. "I hate being tickled."

"I know." He laid her foot back on the bed, then stood, straightening to get a better view of her body. The heat of his gaze warmed her like a blanket as he caressed her with his eyes, drinking her in. He smiled when he finally met her gaze again, then slowly made his way back up the bed. "You hate being tickled. You hate when people save their gum for later—"

Tamryn opened her mouth to speak, but he held up one hand.

"Especially if they save it on their dinner plate."

Tamryn grimaced. *Ugh.*

"You hate meatloaf and canned tuna. Meatballs. Romantic comedies. 80's hair bands. Chinese food. You hate the sound of cardboard opening, especially frozen dinners."

She cringed, fighting a shudder; even thinking about that sound hurt her brain.

"You love the smell of freshly baked bread. You love jumping in puddles."

Smiling, Tamryn reached up, running her fingertips across his face, through his hair, as he continued reciting all the little things he knew about her.

"You love the scent of my cologne."

Tamryn tilted her head. "What?" Her cheeks heated.

Jake flashed a wicked grin. "You always sniff me."

Eyes wide, she scoffed. "Do not."

He leaned forward, bringing his throat an inch from her nose. She tried to fight the desire to breathe him in, but it was fruitless. She inhaled, closing her eyes as the most familiar smell in the world tickled her senses and warmed her from head to toe.

"See?"

She pulled him closer, closer, until her lips met the skin of his neck. She kissed him, mouth slightly open, then nibbled. "I do love the smell of you."

"Like I said."

"But it's not just your cologne. I love the way you smell even when you've been running."

Jake licked his lips. "That's the pheromones." He winked.

"Amen to that. I love those pheromones."

He leaned forward and kissed her quickly.

"You forgot something else I love."

He looked up at the wooden headboard behind her, eyebrows slightly bunched. "Oh, puppies. You're a hopeless puppy lover."

"True. But more than puppies."

"More than puppies?"

"Mhm." She lifted her head to pull his earlobe into her mouth. "Much more than puppies."

He groaned softly as she played with his ear. "What could it be?"

"Not what. *Who*," she teased.

Jake smiled, then brought his lips to hers once more, suckling her bottom lip and sending jolts down into her toes. "I love you, too," he whispered against her mouth.

She smiled, running her thumb across his lips when he pushed up once more to look at her.

"I'm going to make good on my promise now." He held her gaze.

Tamryn's pulse sped as he lowered himself over her. "Five different ways?"

"Oh, at least," he growled. "Until you lose your breath." Gently, he brought his tip to her center, teasing her with slow, deliberate movements. He guided his cock through her wetness until her body, so hungry for him, began to follow his every move, her hips rising to meet him with every stroke. He held her gaze as he slid inside, easing in gently, patiently allowing her body to stretch around him. She ached for him to proceed, her body burning, every point of connection a source of pleasure that begged to be pushed to the limit.

"Jake," she moaned, pressing against him, greedily taking as much of his length as she possibly could.

"What is it baby?"

"I need you."

Jake groaned. "I'm yours."

"*Now*, Jake."

With a guttural roar, he pounded into her, no longer holding back, no longer taking things slow, no longer worried about being careful with her. She'd asked for it and he was going to give it to her, and Tamryn nearly squealed with delight as he increased the speed of his thrusts. Each primal sound that escaped his lips brought her closer to the edge, each sound eliciting in her a reaction so raw, so uninhibited, she surprised even herself.

He gripped the headboard with one hand as the other slammed against her hip, holding her to him as his thrusts grew even more intense, filling her to the point of pain. Perfect fucking pain that her body needed, wanted, had to have more of.

"Oh, God, Jake!"

Something snapped behind her head, and she met his gaze. He paused for a brief second, glanced above her head, then looked back down at her, smiling sheepishly.

She could buy another headboard, but she couldn't wait a second longer for release. She slammed her hands against his chest and pressed her nails into his skin as she squeezed his cock inside her.

His mouth dropped open on another moan, then he looked down at her with hungry eyes, bringing both hands to her hips as he thrust harder and faster until both of them came together, gripping tightly to one another as if the world actually did tremble beneath them.

Tamryn awoke the feather-soft touch of Jake trailing his fingertips from her shoulder to her waist to her breast, circling around her nipple before making his way back up to her shoulder and starting the journey again. She smiled as his touch sent a message throughout her body: *More.* More Jake. More making love. *More, more, more.*

She rolled over onto her other side to face him.

"You fell asleep smiling."

Tamryn felt a familiar heat rush to her cheeks. "I'm still smiling."

"Good. I plan to make that "just fucked silly" smile of yours a regular thing around here." Jake winked, then leaned in and pressed a soft kiss to her lips. "And I don't know if you noticed"—he paused, pulling her earlobe between his teeth—"but we only crossed one of the list. Four more to go."

Tamryn's belly tightened in response to his words, the earlier promise of fucking her five different, colorful ways a very real possibility. She'd never leave her apartment again, if this was what days with Jake would entail.

Luce would understand.

Jake pulled back to meet her gaze, his expression slightly more serious. "I love you, kid. You know that, right?"

Tamryn nodded.

"You're safe with me. I'll never break your heart."

She placed her hand on his cheek, rubbing her thumb back and forth. "I know."

And she did know. Somehow, throughout all the bullshit they'd been through, she knew he'd never break her heart again. Tamryn smiled, her eyes gently closed, her body still sated and full, *deliciously* spent, yet quickly beginning to long for round two.

And three and four and five.

"But, TB?"

She met his dark gaze, surprised by his wicked grin. The flash of hunger in his eyes caused her breath to catch.

He quickly glanced above her head, then met her gaze, a devilish glint in his eyes. "I can't say the same for your headboard."

The End

The Flawed Heroes will return soon. Stay tuned!

Acknowledgements:

As usual, my thanks must first go out to *Tamara Mataya*: Without you, I would have given up long ago. You're the best CP, cheerleader, and ass-kicker a girl could ask for, and I love you so hard. You'll _always_ have a place at my table.

For my amazing cover artist, *Michelle Johnson*: you've got mad skills, lady! Thank you for always knowing exactly what I want, even when my thoughts are a jumbled up mess. Each book cover is better than the last, and I am so thankful for your artistic talent.

For my *friends and family*, both in and out of the writing community: I will be forever grateful for your unwavering love and support. *Mama*, thank you for always being eager to read my words…even when they're naughty.

Last but not least, my thanks go to *Jon*, my husband and rock: your hard work and drive has allowed me to continue pursuing this dream of mine. I promise to repay you with trips to Bass Pro Shops and custom pool cues when I'm rich and famous.

About the Author:

Jessalyn Jameson writes sexy, troubled love stories that break the rules and sit just outside the romance box. Jameson's couples mess up, break up, make up…and fight their way to their HEA. Nothing worth having comes easily—why should a happy ending be any different?

When she's not writing, you can usually find Jessalyn with a drink in hand and a far-off look in her eyes, always dreaming up her next chaotic couple.

@JessalynJameson
www.jessalynjameson.com

Made in the USA
Columbia, SC
20 June 2021